This was [illegible] [illegible]
Story they [illegible]
Love by the time they
got to London the
A fools. Just

CANDLELIGHT REGENCY SPECIAL

Great + 10

Candlelight Regencies

THE
INNOCENT
HEART

Nina Pykare

A CANDLELIGHT REGENCY SPECIAL

Published by
Dell Publishing Co., Inc.
1 Dag Hammarskjold Plaza
New York, New York 10017

Dell ® TM 681510, Dell Publishing Co., Inc.

ISBN: 0-440-14475-2

Printed in the United States of America

First printing—March 1981

CHAPTER ONE

The late August sun was hot on the fields and orchards of the Shropshire countryside. Everything looked peaceful and serene at the country house of Mr. Obadiah Burnstead—everything on the *outside*.

Inside, things were in an uproar. Serving maids scurried from the drawing room as muffled roars of rage issued from its depths. The aged butler attempted to maintain his dignity in front of the footmen, but all of them felt ill at ease. Mr. Burnstead's moments of rage were not met with equanimity by his household.

Jeannie Burnstead, making her way down the front stairs to her uncle Obadiah's drawing room, wondered vaguely what scrape her twin, Jeremy, had fallen into this time. Whenever Uncle Obadiah summoned her and Aunt Desdemona to the drawing room in this fashion, it was because one of Jeremy's letters had arrived. "Begging letters," Uncle Obadiah called them, and Jeannie could not disagree with this. In his several years in London, Jeremy had never managed to live within his allowance, and sometimes he lived outside it so drastically that he needed Uncle Obadiah's help to avoid debtors' prison.

At the foot of the stairs Jeannie turned right and almost collided with her aunt, who came scurrying from the kitchen wing. "Really, Jeannie, I do wish Jeremy would get his affairs in order," Aunt Desdemona said. Affectionately named Aunt Dizzy by the twins, she was a tall woman with deep-set mournful eyes. Now she sighed dramatically.

"I know, Aunt. I do, too." Jeannie took her aunt's fluttering hands in her own and tried to calm her. "But there is really very little we can do." She sighed, too. "Perhaps, as Jeremy grows older, he will learn." She hoped that this time it was simply a new horse, or even a new lightskirt, and not a large gambling debt. Jeremy seemed to be following in his father's footsteps. All the years until their father's death had not sufficed to teach *him* that gaming would never replenish his already weakened resources.

Aunt Dizzy did not seem particularly comforted. She sighed again more deeply as the two of them entered the drawing room. Though both women wore plain dark gowns, they presented quite a contrast: Aunt Desdemona's gaunt, tragic look and the blond youthful freshness that even Jeannie's drab clothing could not quite hide.

"You realize why I have called you here," Uncle Obadiah thundered from beside the fireplace. He turned to face them, his pot belly giving his body a strangely unbalanced look. It strained at his striped buff waistcoat in a way that threatened its buttons. His face, as he regarded them, grew redder and redder, and his belly seemed to swell with indignation.

Jeannie nodded along with her aunt as she settled in a chair. She did not care to be present when Uncle Obadiah was thrown into one of these rages, but she always tried to obey his wishes. It was one of the few ways to show her gratitude for his kindness in letting her retreat here after Lord Atwood had left her for that scheming heiress. Of course, it was foolish of her to blame the heiress. Atwood was a grown man. If his partiality for her had been as real as he made out, no heiress would have lured him away.

Jeannie brought her attention back to Uncle Obadiah. "The boy has gone too far this time," he bellowed. "Too far. He will have to handle his own debts. Let him marry Lady Flighton as I suggested. Her estate should keep him in funds."

"But Mr. Burnstead, my dear." Aunt Dizzy's voice quivered and a single, unshed tear hung on her eyelash. "The boy cannot marry someone he does not love."

"Hogwash and poppycock," roared Uncle Obadiah in a tone that shook the bisque shepherdess on the mantel. "You have noddled your head with all those birdbrained romances. How many times have I told you? Life is not like that."

The tear slipped from Aunt Dizzy's eyelash and made its way down her wrinkled cheek, where it was soon joined by others. "I'm sure it's an awful thing when a woman's only solace in life is begrudged her," said she in a voice that broke several times.

"And it's not as though my romances cost you a thing," she continued with an aggrieved sniffle. "I use my pin money for them. And I rarely order a new gown. You know that, Mr. Burnstead. You know that well!"

One of the buttons on Uncle Obadiah's waistcoat gave under the strain and went careening across the room. "Now, now, Desdemona," he replied in a voice that was reduced to half a bellow, "no need to go into a tizzy. You know that I'd never deprive you of your books. You read all of them you want to. But you don't understand about Jeremy, that's all. The boy's been gaming too much. Shot his allowance for the quarter, and plenty more, I'll wager. What I say

7

is—let the young buck stew in his own juices. I've warned him. Again and again I've warned him. He's got to be stopped before he grows into another Edward. And Lady Margaret's the one to do it. If he's in bad enough to the moneylender, he'll have to accept her. You know her father and I have been wanting their marriage these many years. Mark my word, she'll keep him in line."

Of that Jeannie had no doubt. Once, three or four years ago, Lady Margaret's father had brought her on a visit. When Aunt Dizzy made the two girls acquainted, Lady Margaret looked down her crooked nose and smiled derisively. In the whole three-day visit Lady Margaret had not made one nice remark to Jeannie.

Jeremy hadn't liked her either. "She's stupid, Jeannie, just stupid," he had said privately. "I detest the way she bats her eyelashes at me and simpers. And that cursed fan of hers. So help me, if she taps me playfully with it one more time, I'll break it and throw it in her ugly face."

Yes, there was no doubt in Jeannie's mind that Jeremy would hate being leg-shackled to such a woman. She couldn't blame him. What if Uncle Obadiah had forced *her* to marry someone she despised?

Since that dreadful moment at Lady Cholmondoley's ball when Atwood had told her that his parents had withdrawn their consent to the alliance, she had had no desire to consider matrimony again. The pain of Atwood's desertion had been deep, for she had formed quite a partiality for the fair, attractive young man. Added to that pain had been the agony of facing down the knowing looks of the dowager mamas and sweet young misses who had gloated over her misfortune. To avoid them she had retired to the country.

"There's nothing else for the boy to do," Uncle Obadiah was saying. "He must be made to see that."

Aunt Dizzy's tears were flowing copiously by this time, but to no avail. Uncle Obadiah was determined to ignore them.

"There must be some other way," cried Aunt Dizzy between sobs. "Give the poor boy one more chance."

"No!" The word issued from Uncle Obadiah's mouth like a thunderbolt, and Aunt Dizzy quivered as though she'd been struck. Then she set her thin lips firmly together in the pained expression of a martyr.

"You must understand, Desdemona; there is no other way."

Still wearing an aggrieved expression, Aunt Dizzy rose and stretched out a trembling hand for Jeannie's support. "Very well, Mr. Burnstead. I shall say no more." Leaning heavily on Jeannie's arm, she moved from the room.

"Jeannie, Jeannie, we must think of something. We simply cannot allow Jeremy to enter a loveless union like this," she said as soon as they reached the hall.

"But, Aunt, what can we do?" Jeannie helped her aunt up the stairs to her room. "Besides, Uncle Obadiah is very upset."

"He will calm down," said her aunt. "He always does. And then he remembers when he was young." She turned to her niece. "It's just that he's very worried. He doesn't want your brother to go the way your father did. Such excesses!" Aunt Dizzy lifted her eyes heavenward in mute testimony to the extent of those overindulgences.

"I know, Aunt. Papa gamed far too much. I remember our poor mama begging him not to go to White's. But it was an illness with him. He could not help it."

Aunt Dizzy wiped at her eyes with her lace handkerchief. "Yes, my dear, I know. Your mama was in dire straits many times. But they are at rest now. I have tried my best to be a mother to you."

"You have, Aunt, you really have. No one could have been better to us," said Jeannie as she opened the door to her aunt's room.

"Well, never having had any little ones of my own," Aunt Dizzy sniffled again, "and with you coming to me half-grown as you did, I'm sure I've made some mistakes." She sighed heavily. "Like that young man—Atwood. I thought he was ideal for you. He seemed so charming. And how dreadfully that business ended. He left you—and practically at the altar. And now this trouble with Jeremy."

"Now, Aunt," Jeannie tried to soothe her, "it wasn't your fault—what happened with Lord Atwood. He was just—not trustworthy. In any case you know most men marry for money these days."

"Oh, Jeannie! What is the world coming to?" Aunt Dizzy groaned. "Is there no more romance? No more love? First Lord Atwood and now Jeremy." Her tears threatened to come again.

"Now, Aunt. You know things are not always as they appear in books."

"But Jeremy! And Lady Margaret!" Aunt Dizzy sank into a chair and fluttered her hands helplessly.

"Yes, I know." Jeannie found herself a seat. "We have to think. There must be something we can do."

"Yes, that's it. Think." Aunt Dizzy furrowed her forehead deeply and pressed a hand to it.

"It's money that Jeremy needs," said Jeannie. "If he

could pay his debts, he wouldn't need to marry Lady Margaret."

"That's true, quite true," cried Aunt Dizzy. "But where can we get some money? My pin money is all spent."

"I have mine," said Jeannie. Since Atwood's desertion she had not bothered much with feminine niceties. "But I'm sure that it wouldn't be enough."

Aunt Dizzy sighed and absently fingered her opal necklace. "Money. Where can we get money?"

"That's it, Aunt! That's it."

"What's *it?*" her aunt asked in bewilderment.

"Jewels! I have my mama's jewels! The ones she kept back for me."

"But, Jeannie." Her aunt was plainly upset. "You can't give away your jewels. They're part of your dowry."

"Nonsense, Aunt. I've told you I'm not going to marry. And perhaps because of my sacrifice Jeremy will stop gaming. We cannot let him marry Lady Margaret. It would be sheer misery for him."

"Yes, of course. The boy cannot abide her, and she hasn't grown any sweeter through the years. Ahhhh! But your mama's jewels are here, and Jeremy is in London."

"Perhaps we can send them," Jeannie suggested.

"No, no. Mr. Burnstead would be sure to discover it. We cannot send a trusted servant off without his knowledge."

Jeannie nodded. If Uncle Obadiah found out what they were up to, he would put his foot down hard; but let them once accomplish their purpose, and Aunt Dizzy would be able to calm him down.

"Then I shall have to go myself." She said it firmly, but felt some concern.

"Jeannie! To London! I mean, you were so positive

about staying in the country. I'm sure I quite understood. The *ton* behaved just dreadfully."

"But, Aunt," explained Jeannie patiently, "I shan't have to go about in society. I'll just take the jewels to Jeremy and come back to Shropshire again." Nothing, she thought bitterly, would persuade her to stay in that terrible city.

"Of course, of course. You must excuse me, my dear. This dreadful business has quite unsettled my brains." Aunt Dizzy pressed a trembling hand to her forehead. "I will send Villers along. We'll tell Mr. Burnstead that—that—" She paused helplessly.

"That I am going to visit my old friend Catherine Amesley. Surely he will approve of that. You know he has been after me to return to London, to be seen again in society."

"You must understand, my dear. Your uncle Obadiah is thinking of your own good. He cannot conceive of a young woman not wanting to marry. I've told him that your heartache will heal, that the right man will come along for you. But poor Mr. Burnstead is so impatient!"

"Yes, Aunt, I know." Jeannie did not try to explain to her Aunt that she no longer felt heartache. That feeling had faded after some months. What she felt for Lord Atwood now was contempt. He had deceived her—young and naive as she had been—but she would not be deceived again. She would not trust another man. The rosy world of romance that Aunt Dizzy's books painted existed only in their pages. In the real world, exposing oneself to love brought only pain, not ecstasy. She did not intend to suffer that again.

"But now we must plan. I will leave tomorrow. We must pack a few things to make our ruse succeed. We can say I plan to buy more clothes in London. Yes, that's it." She rose and began to pace the floor.

"How very exciting," cried Aunt Dizzy. "It's just like an adventure in one of the novels."

"Now, Aunt!" Sometimes Jeannie felt that she was the parent. "You must not have such ideas. This is nothing like that. It's really a very simple scheme with no adventure involved—just a tiresome journey to London and another one back again."

"Still," said the unconquerable romantic, "you might meet some personable young man while you're in the city."

"Perhaps, Aunt. Perhaps." Again Jeannie felt it useless to try to talk her aunt out of her fanciful dreaming. "But come now. Why don't you lie upon your bed for a while and rest? I'll attend to my packing."

CHAPTER TWO

The next afternoon found Jeannie on the road to London. The closed carriage was one of Uncle's most comfortable, and Villers his oldest and most trusted groom. She felt perfectly safe in his care. She did feel some concern at deceiving Uncle Obadiah as they had. The poor man had seemed so extremely happy at her decision to return to the city. "Now, that's more like it," he had declared with a great smile. "You're sure to snare a man there, pretty young thing like you."

Jeannie sighed as she tried to settle herself comfortably on the brown velvet squabs. Lord Atwood had also spoken of her beauty in glowing, beautiful words, but his admiration had not proved sufficient to keep him at her side. She sighed again and mentally reviewed her appearance. She supposed her blond hair, green eyes, and slender figure were attractive enough, but she would not use them to lure a man.

The squabs were uncomfortable, and Jeannie moved again. It would be a long and tiresome ride, but it had to be done. All her life she had retrieved Jeremy from the suds. Perhaps it was because she was the oldest twin, having been born first. At any rate, Jeremy thought up the mischief, and she got him out of it. She smiled briefly, recalling the times he tied her petticoat to the top of the house or put fishing worms in Cook's pockets. Those had been fun days before they'd grown up.

But then they had gone to London—and everything had changed for the worse. At first the city had been fun. Her coming out and Lord Atwood's attentions had made her feel happy. Life among the *ton* had been exciting. What with the rounds of theater, opera, routs, and balls, she had hardly had time to realize that she and Jeremy were growing apart.

Then had come the horrible night when Lord Atwood said, "My parents have forbidden the match. You know they control my funds. I'm sorry, my dear." She had not believed he was sorry then and she did not believe it later when his engagement to the heiress was announced. Shamed by his defection and the talk about it, she had retired to Shropshire, and Jeremy had stayed on in the city—on the town, they called it. She did not like the set her twin moved among; they were too much like Papa's friends. But Jeremy, like Papa, had never been one to listen to advice, especially if it came from a woman.

Jeannie settled herself in the corner and prepared to nap. Last night she had had trouble sleeping. Her mind had gone racing madly, seeking some fallacy in their plan, questioning whether Jeremy would ever really leave his wild ways. Perhaps they were only postponing the inevitable. But always she came back to the same fact—whatever Jeremy did later, she must help him now, as she had always helped him in the past.

She might as well do something with her life, she thought bitterly. Aunt Dizzy believed that she would marry someday, but Jeannie did not. She did not particularly enjoy life in the country, where her main amusements were needlepoint and the reading aloud of Aunt Dizzy's French novels. Sometimes those novels

16

made Jeannie want to scream and stamp her feet, because they were so full of impossibly beautiful scenes of romance and love. But she did not scream. She continued to lead her life of placid boredom. Surely it was better than putting herself in a position of vulnerability again by trusting a man.

She closed her eyes. Enough thinking. Villers would stop at a good inn. Until then she would rest.

Some time later the carriage came to a halt with a jolt that sent Jeannie flying to the floor. Dazedly she straightened her bonnet and pulled herself up onto the seat. She peered out the window. While she had slept the sun had moved downward in its course and was now hovering slightly above the horizon. Villers's anxious face appeared at the window. "Are you all right, Miss Burnstead?"

"Yes, Villers, I am fine. But what has happened to the carriage?"

"We've lost a wheel, miss. It's a bad un, I'm afraid."

"Were the horses hurt?"

"No, miss. Fortunately we wasn't going so fast. They got stirred up a bit, but that's all."

"All right, Villers, I'll get out and wait."

Villers's aged face was creased with a frown as he helped her down. "It's gonna take a piece of work, miss. And it's getting on to dusk."

"Just do the best you can, Villers. That's all anyone can ask."

"Yes, miss. I'll do that, I will."

Jeannie picked her way off the road, which seemed in particularly poor condition here, and looked for a grassy place where she might sit without dirtying the gray pelisse that matched her gown. It was not a new pelisse, having been purchased for her season in London two years before, but it was still presentable, indeed, far nicer than most of the things she wore these days. She looked around. She certainly did not intend to buy any new clothes while she was in the city. In the sort of life she had chosen, clothing from London played no part at all.

She managed to find a grassy bank and settled there. She wished she had thought to conceal her mama's jewels somewhere about her person instead of merely putting them in her reticule. There were not many highwaymen about these parts now, but still this was a rather lonely stretch of woods. She shivered slightly; now she was being ridiculous. Too much reading in Aunt Dizzy's novels, that was her trouble. She began to think about her coming meeting with Jeremy. How pleased he would be to get out of this marriage with Lady Margaret. She pictured the look of relief on his face when he heard the good news.

The sun was sinking fast below the horizon and Villers and the coachman were still toiling with the wheel when Jeannie heard the sound of a carriage approaching. She looked down the road, but because of the sun it was impossible to see if the carriage bore a crest. Jeannie grasped her reticule and tried to look composed.

The carriage clattered to a stop. "Ho, some trouble here, I see," called a masculine voice. Jeannie sighed in relief. Obviously this man was an aristocrat and no danger to her jewels. In any case, she told herself, highwaymen did not travel about in coaches.

She rose from the bank, brushed off her pelisse, straightened her bonnet, and moved toward the carriage where the stranger was consulting with Villers about the condition of the wheel. He turned as she approached, and she found herself looking into a pair of dark eyes set in a dark, handsome face. His well-fitted coat and inexpressibles spoke eloquently of a good tailor and the arrogant tilt of the curly-brimmed beaver on his tumbled curls indicated a man well pleased with himself. Another London rake, she thought with resignation.

"Why, hello there. Allow me to introduce myself. I am Henry, Viscount Trenton, at your service." His smile was assured and cheerful.

"That's most kind of you, sir," she replied coolly, "but I don't believe we require assistance. My groom will take care of the needed repairs." She met his eyes coldly. The days when she would respond to an attractive man were over.

His smile faded, and his face grew more formal. "This is a bad stretch of road, Miss—"

She didn't want to answer, but his expression told her he would persist until he had her name. "Burnstead, milord."

"As I was saying, Miss Burnstead, this is a bad stretch of road, a popular place for highwaymen."

In spite of herself, Jeannie shivered.

"Now, it doesn't appear to me that this job will be finished before nightfall. Therefore, I propose to carry you to the next inn in my carriage. There you may wait in comfort until such time as your carriage is finished and comes for you."

Jeannie hesitated. The man made sense. It was not pleasant waiting here, and as far as her reputation went, there was little cause to worry about it anyway.

Then, from his waiting carriage, came another male voice. "I say, Trenton, how long are we going to tarry here? My wife gets all-fired angry when I'm late."

Jeannie had already stiffened at the sound of the familiar voice. Lord Atwood! She did not need Trenton's, "Easy, Atwood, I'll be along directly," to recognize the voice of the man who had deceived her.

19

She shook her head. "No thank you, milord. I am quite comfortable here."

He scowled and his heavy black eyebrows met in the center of his forehead. "You are being foolish. I am not puffing the bad reputation of this place."

"He ain't, miss, an' that's the truth," piped Villers from his place at the wheel.

"Come along now. I can't keep my friend Atwood from his beloved wife much longer." His tone made it clear that the wife was anything but beloved. For some reason that did not please Jeannie as it might have some women. Atwood had deceived still another woman; Jeannie could feel only compassion for her.

"Lord Atwood's dealings with his wife are of no concern to me," she replied, and was startled to hear the venom in her reply.

Trenton looked at her sharply. "Of course. *That* Miss Burnstead. You and Atwood were once affianced."

Jeannie drew herself up proudly. "Fortunately for me the match was called off."

"Yes. I can understand your not caring for his company, but I'm afraid you'll have to bear it for a little while. His country seat's only a few miles on."

Jeannie shook her head. "No thank you. I prefer to wait."

"Miss Burnstead!" Trenton was obviously becoming annoyed. "You are being foolish. I cannot leave you in this condition."

"I assure you, milord, I am perfectly safe here." She did not quite believe that, but at the moment the thought of facing a highwayman was preferable to facing Atwood.

The Viscount's face changed suddenly. "Afraid of him, huh?"

"I am not!" Jeannie's retort came angrily, her green eyes sparking.

"Then come along and prove it." Trenton regarded her quizzically, and his lips curved in a half smile.

"Please, miss." Villers looked up from the wheel. "You'd best listen to his lordship. He's right about this here piece a woods. And it'll be something rare if we get this carriage going right afore morning."

Jeannie hesitated only a moment longer. She certainly did not want to spend the night in the woods! That was too risky. Her jewels must go to Jeremy, not to some highwayman.

"All right," she said, stiffly accepting the arm his lordship extended to her. "But do not expect me to be civil to that—that creature."

"You may give him the cut direct," said Trenton briskly. "If only you'll come along."

"I say, Trenton," complained Atwood as his lordship came through the open door, "my wife will have my skin. Look out for your charmers in London, on your own time—"

As Jeannie settled into her seat, the light from the carriage lamp revealed her features. "Jeannie! Jeannie Burnstead! Whatever are you doing on this godforsaken piece of road?"

"I am traveling," said Jeannie stiffly. She forced herself to look him full in the face. Lord Atwood was still fair and attractive, but now she detected a weakness in the set of his chin, a certain sharp slyness around his eyes, and an overelegant foppishness about his dress. She felt surprised that she could once have thought she loved this man.

"That's the thing to do," said Atwood sadly. "Going to London, I suppose. I say, I'll be in town myself in a few weeks. Give me your direction, and I'll look you up. We'll have some fun." He made a face. "My marriage was a dreadful mistake. Horrible woman, my wife. You've no idea how I've missed you."

Jeannie heard his words in stunned silence. Did he really think that she would consent to see him now? He had not wanted her as a wife, yet he thought she would accept him as a protector! "I will not be receiving visitors while I'm in London," she said crisply. "And the sort of—alliance—you suggest is quite out of the question."

Lord Atwood did not seem particularly disturbed. "Now, now, my dear, I know your feathers were ruffled, but I'll make it up to you. A nice little establishment with a maid and some pretty new gowns. Perhaps even a carriage, though not upholstered in blue satin as this one is." He cast Trenton a look. "We'll get along famously, my pet."

Jeannie simply stared at him. "You are incredible," she said finally.

"Yes, my dear, I know. But come, your direction?"

Finding herself temporarily at a loss for words, Jeannie was surprised to hear Trenton intervene. "I think you have mistaken your target here, Atwood," he said. "The lady is telling you plainly that she is not for sale."

"Please, Trenton, do not speak so grossly." Lord Atwood made another face. "Perhaps you do not know that an affection exists between this lady and myself."

"An affection!" Indignation made Jeannie fairly quiver. "I must have had bats in my attic to form any partiality for you. You left me to the scorn and derision of the *ton* and now, now you want to capitalize on your desertion and subject me to a more complete degradation!"

Atwood heard this with nonchalance, then turned to Trenton. "I believe you are right, old boy. The lady is quite up in the boughs. Shame, too; she's a pretty little thing."

Jeannie, fighting an anger that made her long to hit Atwood with her reticule, began silently counting to herself. She was surprised to hear Trenton answer in a tone of contempt. "It appears to me that the lady has ample cause for her outrage. How fortunate for you that she had no one to reprimand you more severely for the dishonor you did her name."

Atwood looked startled at this attack from another gentleman, but managed to regain his old nonchalance. "Really, my friend, I think you are getting a little out of bounds. A bit of muslin is hardly worth a man's falling out with his friends. As I recall, you have kept more than one establishment in your time. Doesn't this very carriage have blue satin upholstery—because of a certain Harriette Wilson, London's leading demi-rep? An old rakeshame like you hasn't much room to talk."

"You are right about the carriage," said Trenton calmly. "And the establishments. I certainly make no claim to celibacy. But you are mistaken on two other counts. First, a bit of muslin and a young lady are two very dissimilar creatures, to be treated quite differently. And second, you and I are not friends. Acquaintances, perhaps, but not friends."

These remarks left Atwood speechless and for some minutes the three sat in silence. They were still sitting so when the carriage pulled up before an impressive country house—the family seat of Atwood's wife, Jeannie thought. She preferred not to take much notice of what was outside the coach and replied to Atwood's *au revoir*, with a stiff nod. There was no sign of the wrathful wife, but Jeannie's last glimpse of Atwood, trudging up the front steps, seemed to indicate that he little relished his homecoming.

The carriage pulled away and, to Jeannie's surprise, Trenton broke into laughter. "I have never seen such a fool," he said finally. "He certainly lives in her pocket, though from necessity and not choice." He turned to face Jeannie. "You are well out of a match with the likes of him."

Though she had heard him admit to being a rakeshame, Jeannie found herself warming to the Viscount. After all, he had taken her part, and it was no secret that practically every lord in London kept an incognita. Jeannie nodded. "I see that now. You were quite severe with him. I did not think there were any lords about these days who made such distinctions between a lady and a bit of muslin."

The Viscount smiled and Jeannie noted absently that he was quite a handsome man. "There are few of us left," he observed dryly. "But then, there are few real ladies left in the *ton*. Fashion has turned them all to bits of muslin."

"I'm afraid I do not understand."

"You have not been to the city for several years?"

"That's correct, milord. Not since—"

He nodded. "The French fashions are taking London by storm, and they are quite revealing—almost *dishabille*. In fact," he grinned at her wickedly, "even the most respectable ladies now damp their petticoats."

"Damp their petticoats! Whatever for?"

He chuckled at Jeannie's obvious bewilderment. "You reveal your innocence again. To show their figures."

"Oh!"

They rode some moments in silence while Jeannie attempted to digest this information. Then, glancing up at the Viscount, she was surprised to see him frowning. "Something is troubling you, milord?" she asked without thinking.

His frown deepened. "I have a problem, one I don't know how to resolve."

"Sometimes," suggested Jeannie, "it helps to talk." After all, he had been very kind to her.

He smiled. "You seem wise for one so young."

"I am twenty years old," she replied. "And you forget, milord. I have known my share of pain. I cannot feel, though, that I am very wise."

He sighed deeply. "My problem is a severe one, I warn you. I have reached the advanced age of six and thirty and have not yet married. My family, particularly my mother, is continually after me. It is my duty to produce an heir. The next in line, you see, is a bumbling weakling, far worse than Atwood. Though I have told my family repeatedly that I haven't yet formed a partiality that would lead to marriage, this fails to satisfy them. If I have formed no partiality in all these years they say, then it's unlikely that I shall. For the sake of the family, I should marry a certain woman whose lands abut mine."

"No doubt they think it very sensible," said Jeannie. "Six and thirty *is* old."

The Viscount chuckled. "Tact is not one of your outstanding characteristics."

Jeannie flushed scarlet. "Oh, I did not mean it in that way. It's just that if you've found no one—"

He nodded. "Yes, but they fail to consider that the woman in question is a perfect block with a tongue like a double-edged sword. When I resumed my old haunts, as I should be sure to do leg-shackled to such a harridan, my establishment would become a living hell. And what kind of life would the offspring of such a venomous union lead?"

Jeannie nodded in commiseration. "You have a problem indeed."

He eyed her strangely. "Enough of me for the moment. Divert my mind by telling me what you were doing traveling alone."

It did not occur to Jeannie to lie to this man who had been kind to her. "My brother is in debt," she said simply. "My uncle insists that he marry an heiress—another double-edged sword, and hatchet-faced to boot. I am taking my mama's jewels to him so that he may pay his debts and escape this disastrous marriage."

Trenton nodded. "And then?"

"And then I shall return to Shropshire. I have no desire to be part of the *ton*. I have experienced quite enough of their derision."

"They hurt you badly." It was a statement of fact, not a question.

"It is never pleasant to be left—practically at the altar," Jeannie said dryly.

The Viscount nodded. "Quite true. On the other hand, considering what has transpired today, you may wish to think yourself more fortunate at being left than at being taken."

Jeannie was forced to agree. "I fear you are right, milord."

"Why don't you stay in London awhile, move about in society a bit? You are still young and attractive."

Jeannie shook her head. "I don't believe I shall ever be able to trust a man again, nor my own feelings about one." She smiled wryly. "When I see what manner of a man I once thought worthy of my affections—" She shuddered. "It gives one pause. Who is to say that I should not make such a mistake again?"

He smiled at her gently. "You are older now and wiser. You would know better."

Jeannie shook her head. "Love is such an intangible entity. Who is to say how long it would endure." She shuddered again. "To think that I might have been doomed to a lifetime with that man. Better to live alone than to contemplate such an alliance."

"You are painting the picture with too many dark strokes," he said cheerfully. "Even I, who am no strong advocate of the institution, recognize that marriage can be good. I have steadfastly refused to marry because I could find no one I loved, but on closer reflection I believe the issue now to be one of respect. I could fulfill my duty to my family with a woman that I respect, failing to find one I could love. Yes, respect is the heart of the matter."

Jeannie considered this thoughtfully. "I do not intend to go about in society again," she said finally, "but I believe there is a great deal of truth in your remarks. Should I happen upon a suitable man whom I can respect, I may perhaps consider marriage again."

The Viscount smiled. "Wouldn't you be more likely to happen upon such a candidate if you were about in the world?"

"Don't press your point too far, milord," Jeannie said. "I have conceded this much. But there is no man living worth the derision and scorn I suffered after Atwood's desertion of me."

"Perhaps the ladies of the *ton* were jealous of your beauty," suggested the Viscount with a smile.

Jeannie laughed again. "I am passable, milord, perhaps even moderately attractive to some eyes, but beautiful I shall never be. Nor shall I ever have a dowry to equal that of the woman who now suffers as Atwood's wife."

"Perhaps that, too, is fortunate. Should you have more substance, you would never be sure if the offer were for your person or your pocket. Having little, you can at least be assured of some devotion on the gentleman's part."

"You are quite cheering, milord," said Jeannie with a small smile. "You almost make me believe that my life is not over."

"Of course it is not over. I wager you'll be married off in less than a year."

Trenton's tone allowed for no contradiction, so Jeannie merely smiled again. She would be leaving his lordship soon, and it was not at all likely she would see him again. Why bother to disagree? She would soon be back in Shropshire, in her quiet days of reading and sewing. That was the life she had chosen. She was not about to change her mind concerning it, no matter how sound the Viscount's reasoning.

CHAPTER THREE

By the time they reached the inn, Jeannie was feeling quite tired. "You look rather peaked," observed Trenton as the carriage came to a halt.

Jeannie sighed. "I am tired. Seeing Atwood was difficult for me, and I am worried about my brother."

He nodded. "Yes, I can understand that. Here, let me escort you in and see that you are properly taken care of. I know the landlady here."

"That is most kind of you, milord. You have already done far more than is called for." Jeannie prepared to alight.

"Nonsense." His lordship frowned. "I have done nothing that any gentleman might not do in similar circumstances." He raised a hand to silence her protest. "There is little use in talking. I intend to see that you are properly cared for."

Jeannie conceded. "This is most kind of you. I cannot thank you enough."

He smiled before he climbed down to assist her in descending, and she found herself pleased to have his help. Once dismounted, she leaned gratefully upon the arm that he offered. "This trip would have ended quite differently without your help," she said. Suddenly she found herself looking up into his eyes and saw that he was beaming down upon her. His gloved hand closed warmly over the fingers that were tucked

29

through his arm, and Jeannie felt a little catch in her breath. She told herself sternly that it was just because she had been away so long from the company of men. Viscount Trenton was merely being kind.

They were proceeding up the path to the inn, Jeannie thankful for his supporting arm, when they were brought to a sudden and abrupt halt by a loud exclamation. "Jeannie Burnstead! Upon my word! And with the Viscount Trenton!"

Jeannie felt scarlet flood her cheeks. She had quite forgotten the impropriety of a young woman traveling alone with a man like Trenton. "Lady L-lilington," she stammered. "It's not what you think. That is, we aren't—"

"Of course, of course," replied the dowager belle who peered at them from a face made almost ridiculous by the application of nearly a dozen of the beauty marks which had been in vogue in the previous century. The rest of Lady Lilington's attire was similarly antiquated, but she was apparently unaware of it. She preened and fluttered at Trenton as though she had seen twenty years rather than the fifty-some that her features so obviously attested to.

"Miss Burnstead's coach suffered a mishap some distance down the road," said Trenton smoothly. "I happened along and since it was growing dark I prevailed upon her to let me bring her to the inn."

"Yes, yes," said Lady Lilington, her aged eyes taking note of Jeannie's flushed countenance and coming to rest on the arm that was still linked through the Viscount's. "Jeannie, my dear, really. Does your aunt know about this?"

"Lady Lilington, please. I'm on my way to London. I'm going—" She paused suddenly, aware that she couldn't mention Jeremy's trouble because the news would then reach Uncle Obadiah. She gazed helplessly at Trenton.

"Miss Burnstead is fatigued," he said evenly. "I'm sure you'll excuse us while I secure her a room."

"Yes, yes, of course." The powder on Lady Lilington's face cracked in several places as she smiled, and it was clear to Jeannie that the elderly dowager did not believe a word of Trenton's smoothly given explanation.

Her knees seemed to weaken as Trenton led her on up the walk, still smiling pleasantly. "Your face has gone white," he whispered. "Go ahead, pretend to be ill."

It required no effort to do just that. All Jeannie could think of was the failure of their plan to help Jeremy.

"Mrs. Perry," said Trenton to the buxom landlady who appeared at the inn's door. "Miss Burnstead has had an accident. She needs a room to rest in."

"Of course, yer lordship. The poor lady looks took bad, she does. You bring her right this way."

Jeannie did not have to feign weakness, and she continued to lean heavily upon Trenton's arm as they followed the landlady up the stairs. "This is the best room, yer lordship. She'll be comfortable here, all right."

"Thank you, Mrs. Perry. I'll take care of everything now."

As the landlady bustled back down the stairs, Trenton thrust Jeannie rather unceremoniously into a chair. "Stay there till I come back," he ordered curtly and then he was gone, striding out the door and down the stairs with a determined look on his face.

Jeannie stared into space. Everything had happened

so fast that she could hardly collect her thoughts. If only Lady Letitia Lilington hadn't seen them. Anyone else might have been persuaded of the truth, but not Aunt Dizzy's bosom-bow, who read every new French romance from cover to cover and still lived in the last century.

She pressed her fingers to her temples. Whatever had put Trenton's back up like that? She tried to think what she could have done to turn him into such a surly creature. Surely he didn't blame her for their being noticed like that. Certainly the charming, gentle man he had been in the carriage had vanished. Of course, she should have known. He was a man, and men could not be trusted. Their characters shifted like the shadows from a fire. For a little while she had forgotten, lulled by Trenton's charm into thinking that he was different. She would not forget again.

The door opened to admit him. "Well," he said, "you've really done it up brown."

"I?" Jeannie was irate. He had no call to bristle at her like this. "It wasn't my idea to come to this inn. *You* were the one who insisted that I would be safer here. *Safer!*" she cried distractedly.

Trenton turned on her. "How was I to know that London's greatest gossip would happen upon us—and in such an incriminating circumstance?"

Jeannie felt her anger rising. This whole miserable business was getting completely out of hand. He had no right to talk to her this way.

"And you," he continued angrily, pacing the floor. "Of course, you had to say exactly the wrong thing."

Jeannie got to her feet. "You are being stupid. I—I know Lady Letitia's mind. She and Aunt Dizzy are bosom-bows. They live on French romances. I knew immediately what she would think."

He paused in his pacing to mutter, "If only I had spoken first."

"Milord!" Jeannie placed herself squarely in his lordship's path and confronted him. "You are not listening to me! Even all your charm, which I admit is considerable, would not persuade Lady Letitia out of the opinion that this is a romantic meeting between us."

He scowled down at her. "I have been known to charm worse dowager dragons than that."

"Indeed!" Jeannie's green eyes sparked at him. "And where do dowager dragons figure in the scheme of things? Are they young ladies or bits of muslin—or somewhere in between?"

"They are somewhere in between," he said crisply. "And there is no need to be so touchy. You behaved like a child caught out in mischief, babbling out, 'It's not what you think,' like that." He shook his head. "Just like a child in trouble."

"I am not a child," said Jeannie, stamping her foot angrily.

"Then do not behave like one." He turned and began his pacing again. "There must be some way out of this. Think, Trenton, think."

"It's really very simple," said Jeannie. "You go on to London by yourself, and I shall wait for my carriage and then be on my way."

"And what about Lady Letitia's tattle, which by now will be over half the county?"

Jeannie sighed. "I have been talked about already, and, as I do not intend to go about in society again, the talk will not bother me."

"But your chance to marry will be ruined."

Jeannie shrugged. "I do not intend to marry anyway. I told you that."

"Then what about *my* reputation?"

Jeannie stared at him in surprise. "But you're a man, an avowed rakeshame, as Atwood said. Such talk means little to you. What of Harriette Wilson? And your establishments?"

He scowled again. "You mistake me, Miss Burnstead. I have kept myself quite aware of the distinction between young ladies and bits of muslin, and I have never been intimately involved with a young woman such as yourself. Besides that, this is a deuced poor time for tales of my amours to be bandied about. I've already got my family on my back. How will this look to them?"

He took two more turns about the small room, his brows bristling, and then, suddenly, inexplicably, his face cleared and he broke into laughter.

Jeannie looked at him in amazement. Whatever was the matter with the man? Surely his wits hadn't been dislodged.

"That's it!" he cried suddenly. "That's the perfect solution. Why didn't I think of it before?"

Jeannie frowned. "Whatever are you talking about?" she demanded crossly.

"About our imminent marriage, my love."

"Our *what!* Your wits *have* been damaged."

"Indeed not," said Trenton, approaching her more closely. "This is the ideal solution."

Jeannie shook her head. "You are mad. You must be. What of your talk of love—and respect?"

Trenton reached out to hold her shoulders. "You are the first woman I've met in a long time for whom I have respect. Listen to me carefully. We could be eloping. Lady Letitia's babblings would mean little then. Or, better yet, you can have run away to me."

"You *must* be mad," said Jeannie, feeling as though

the bottom had fallen out of her stomach. "I cannot marry you."

His lordship did not seem to take offense. "Pray reconsider," he said cheerfully. "Your name is already—shall we say—tarnished."

"I do not care about my name," snapped Jeannie angrily.

"Indeed. I should have thought from your previous remarks that you cared a good bit." One of his dark eyebrows rose quizzically.

How irritating the man was, Jeannie thought. She was sorry she had let down her defenses during their brief ride. "The whole idea is mad," she said again. "It's true my name has been compromised, but that should not force you into an unwanted marriage. What about your desire to marry for love?"

"I have decided that respect is the most important ingredient," he replied. "Aside from your stupidity in this one instance, which may be pardoned, you are not a bad chit. You have a reasonable understanding, you have an attractive person, and I think you could produce healthy children." He grinned devilishly. "You are cursed with only one impecunious relative rather than a score. All in all, you are a tolerable young woman. We could make as good a marriage as most."

Jeannie shook her head. "It makes no sense."

"*Au contraire,*" said his lordship, "it makes perfect sense."

"You have told me what *you* stand to gain," she said. "What about me?"

Her mind raced, trying to comprehend this outlandish proposal.

"First, we shall travel posthaste to London and assist your brother. We can get there more quickly in my carriage. Second, you acquire a husband, a necessity for a young woman these days, and you do it without any of the mistrust you spoke of. Since there is no love between us, there need be no jealousy. This is a purely rational arrangement. I might also add that I am thought to be quite a catch." Now that he had the problem solved, he allowed himself some humor. "I am rich, handsome, titled—"

"And rather high in the instep," she commented dryly.

His lordship was not perturbed. "I might point out to you that among the *ton* I am considered a far better catch than Atwood ever was. All those dowager mamas and nose-in-the-air misses who gave you so much trouble before would be positively green with envy. Even Atwood might be given cause to think—if he is capable of such an action."

"This is madness," Jeannie repeated, but her tone indicated that she was weakening. They would get to Jeremy sooner, and with his lordship's help his debts should be easily settled; also it would be wise for her to marry someone she could respect—Uncle Obadiah's patience could not be presumed to last forever—and she had to admit that it would be pleasant to be envied by those women who had once treated her with derision, to be able to hold her head high once more.

"All these are quite adequate reasons for you to accept me," he said with a smile. "I, on the other hand, am willing to be shackled to a not very rich, sometimes babbling, child."

"I am *not* a child," cried Jeannie angrily. "Will you never learn that?"

"I shall indeed," he replied cheerfully and drew her into his arms. It was done so quickly that she had no notion of what was coming and so was unprepared to resist him. His lips on hers were soft and tender, gentle and persuasive, threatening to conquer her in a

36

way Atwood's never had. Jeannie felt the long male leanness of him against her body, and her heart pounded painfully in her throat. She forced herself to remain still.

"Milord!" she cried as he released her.

"What is it, my pet?" he said with an impish smile. "I was merely sealing our alliance. I should not wish you to buy a pig in a poke."

Jeannie colored up. "I did not accept you. You had no right."

The Viscount's eyes sparkled. "No woman has ever complained of my kisses before."

Jeannie bristled up immediately. "You are an extremely exasperating man. I wonder that any mama should want you for her daughter."

His lordship smiled darkly. "Ah, my dear, you forget. For those mamas, title and fortune suffice. I could be ugly as sin and with a disposition to match, and they'd still be after me. Now, with the incognitas it's another story. A good one can pick and choose her man."

"And the color of her carriage lining?"

The Viscount nodded. "Quite true. Little Harry is the best. But you've no call to fly up in the boughs. She and I parted company some months ago."

"I see." This, thought Jeannie, was incredible. She was acting as though what he did mattered to her.

"Now," said the Viscount briskly, "I suggest that we return to my carriage and the fresh horses I ordered. Mrs. Perry is packing a light repast. If we travel all night, we may reach London before Lady Letitia. Then we can circulate the romantic story of how you ran off to me. It will help me to convince my relatives if we make this a love match."

"But how can we convince them when there is no love between us?"

"I assure you," replied his lordship with that wicked grin, "I can play the love-smitten swain to perfection."

"Having already done it many times," retorted Jeannie, feeling exceedingly waspish.

His lordship looked startled. "Of course. The pretty young things seemed to prefer the little charade rather than coming to a straightforward business arrangement. But don't fear. I shall live in your pocket."

"Until you return to your former haunts." She eyed him as one might view a distasteful insect.

His lordship's dark eyes glittered. "Your memory is far too sharp for your own good. When I resume my old employments and companions, I shall do so discreetly. Many a man falls out of love as quickly as he falls in it. No one will have cause to bother you about it."

Jeannie frowned. Even though she didn't believe the nonsense in Aunt Dizzy's novels about love, she did believe that it was something worthwhile. However, it was quite probably rare, and it was certainly not going to appear in her life.

"You are quiet," observed his lordship. "Do you disapprove of my plans for our future?"

"It appears that I have little choice in the matter," Jeannie replied stiffly. "You have already made it quite clear that you have all the power. And I need to go help my brother."

She suddenly found her hand held by his strong brown one. The touch of his fingers on her own gave her an odd, comforting feeling. "Don't be angry with me, little one," he said in a strangely gentle tone. "I'm sure we'll deal splendidly together. Just give us a little time."

Jeannie found a sudden lump in her throat. It would not do to become a waterworks. Though she had not really said yes to the Viscount's proposal, it seemed like the best thing to do. She was dreadfully tired of life in Shropshire and this way at least she would have a husband and family to fill her life. She sighed heavily. "Very well then, I'll do it. Oh! Wait! My clothes! I have no clothes!"

He smiled gaily as he tucked her arm through his. "Capital, my love. You were so eager to get to me that you ran off without any clothes. That makes our match all the more romantic."

Jeannie shook her head. "You are hopeless, milord, simply hopeless. I wonder that I should accept this foolhardy plan of yours." But she allowed him to lead her out the door and down the stairs to the carriage. As she climbed in, she had to stifle a sudden giggle. It had just occurred to her that Aunt Dizzy would be in her glory at last. Not only would Jeannie have achieved a husband—but an elopement! Nothing this romantically wonderful had ever before entered Aunt Dizzy's prosaic life.

CHAPTER FOUR

The rest of the journey to London was a blur to Jeannie. Later she would recall waking occasionally to find his lordship's supporting arm around her. "Go back to sleep, little one," he said, and she did so gratefully, too exhausted to protest his use of such a nickname.

Her first look at the great house on St. James's Square that was to be her home was a blurred and hazy one. She had struggled out of the carriage and was leaning against it, waiting to follow his lordship through the iron gate, and up the steps to the door, when he turned suddenly and scooped her up in his arms.

"I can walk," she protested feebly.

"Of course you can," he said briskly. "I simply choose to carry you. It's far more romantic. Now be still."

She was too tired for further argument, Jeannie told herself, and besides, it was foolish to waste her strength on small disagreements. Something told her there would be far bigger issues between them.

"Budner," said his lordship, addressing the butler, "send a footman posthaste to Lady Helena. Say that I need her presence immediately." He chuckled. "Tell her that I have brought home my bride-to-be and I need her to serve as chaperone."

"Yes, milord. At once, milord."

Then the Viscount was carrying her up a wide, curving staircase. She heard the scurrying of feet. "Which room does your lordship wish?" asked a feminine voice.

"Whichever will take the least preparation, Pearson. I am sorry to arrive like this so unexpectedly, but the fewer people who know about an elopement the better."

"An elopement, milord!"

"Yes, Pearson. I have finally fallen to Cupid's arrow."

"But, milord! An elopement!"

"The young lady has a romantic heart," said the Viscount with a thoroughly convincing chuckle. How well the man could lie, thought Jeannie. That did not set well for the future. "And so to make it more romantic she ran off to me. But I have persuaded her that we had best call the banns and proceed in proper order."

"Ahhh! That was wise, sir. The lady's good name—"

"Right you are, Pearson. That is why I hastened home. Budner has sent for Lady Helena, who will no doubt arrive shortly in a terrible dither. You'd best prepare another room. Lady Helena will be staying with us until the wedding."

"Ah, milord. You've a mind for every detail, you have. Here, methinks the Green Room's probably best. 'Twas just aired a few days ago."

"Put Lady Helena next door then," said his lordship as he entered the room.

Jeannie had heard the whole of this conversation, but it seemed to be taking place at a distance. Much closer and more disconcerting was the realization that being carried in his lordship's arms was a rather pleasurable experience. Under her ear she heard the steady beating of his heart.

Trenton laid her gently on the bed. "Here you are, little one. Pearson will put you to bed."

She frowned; she did not like that nickname. There was something almost degrading about it. It was for a sweet young thing in love, not for a business arrangement like theirs.

"Get a good night's sleep," his lordship continued, "and we'll talk to Lady Helena in the morning." Before straightening, he touched her forehead lightly with his lips. He was certainly a good actor, thought Jeannie.

"Good night, milord," she murmured, and then he was gone, striding from the room as though he had just risen from a good night's rest. Jeannie, now more awake, turned her attention to the housekeeper.

"Whatever possessed you to go running about in this way?" Pearson shook her gray head as she came to help Jeannie off with her pelisse and gown. "You could have come to harm like that."

"I can take care of myself," Jeannie declared. Pearson looked somewhat startled, and Jeannie realized that she would have to be careful of what she said. She owed it to Trenton to back up his story. "I thought it would be fun," she explained with a small smile. "Life in the country is exceedingly dull." That was the truth, at least.

Pearson shook her head at such foolishness, but there was a sparkle in her eyes that seemed to belie her stern expression. "Well, life'll not be dull now, you can be sure of that. Not with his lordship as husband. But then, you'll be knowing even better than me what a great catch you've made."

Jeannie could only nod at this information. Pearson seemed to think that his lordship was quite a man. Even more important, she seemed to like him as a person. That boded well for their future; servants

43

usually knew a great deal about their master's character.

"Didn't you bring *any* clothes?" asked Pearson suddenly.

Jeannie shook her head. "That would have spoiled the fun."

Pearson grimaced. "You young folks! You've got no sense." She grinned. "But then, you did get his lordship, and the ladies have been after him these many years." Pearson's eyes narrowed shrewdly. "Going to be some of 'em as aren't going to like this. Imagine, his lordship losing his heart to a mere slip of a girl."

"I—" Jeannie stopped. Perhaps it would be best to let Pearson and the rest think of her as a young chit. That way she would have more freedom. "I believe I'll be able to deal with that."

Pearson nodded again. "Oh, they'll not dare cut you when his lordship's nigh. And I daresay Lady Helena will bring them in line."

Jeannie almost asked who this Lady Helena was, but suddenly realized that to do so would be impolitic. Her questions would have to wait until she had a chance to ask Trenton—alone.

"If you'll just wait a minute, I'll go along and fetch you back a nightdress." Pearson cast a look downward at her own ample figure and chuckled. "It'll be on the large side, no doubt, but you'll rest better in a proper nightdress."

"Thank you, Pearson." Jeannie found a sudden lump in her throat. "You're very kind to me."

"Humph? And what else should I be? His lordship's found someone to love after all these years. That'll make us all happy." With a smile, Pearson bustled out.

Jeannie felt a small pang at their deception, but she

reconciled herself with the thought that she would make the Viscount a good wife, far better than the awful woman his family had wanted him to marry. They would at least respect each other.

When Pearson returned some moments later, Jeannie had risen and taken a walk around the room. It was a room her mama would have liked—decorated in pale green with exquisite taste.

Pearson set a pitcher of warm water on the table and stood aside for Jeannie to wash. It was her first real wash since she'd left Shropshire, and it felt wonderful to be clean.

Pearson had just dropped the nightdress over Jeannie's head and she was struggling through its voluminous folds, when there came a brisk knock on the door. Before Jeannie, whose head had just emerged, could say anything, the door opened and his lordship entered. "I see that you've done a good job, Pearson," declared the Viscount. "Now you'd best get Lady Helena's room ready. And expect a rush of tradesmen for the rest of the week, particularly tomorrow. Miss Burnstead will need some clothes and it will be easier to have them come here."

"Yes, milord." Pearson sent Jeannie a warm smile and hastily exited, closing the door behind her.

"You have made a friend," observed his lordship, "thus confirming my opinion of you."

"I'm sorry she has cause to think me such a ninnyhammer," replied Jeannie, "but I had to explain about running away."

"And how did you do that?" inquired his lordship, taking a step closer.

Only then did Jeannie think about the nightdress. It was quite large and certainly showed far less of her than her gown had. Yet she felt suddenly undefended and exposed. "I—I told her I thought the whole

45

thing was exciting—romantic." She shook her head. "I feel foolish."

His lordship came still closer. He seemed to tower over her in a way she had never noticed before. Inside the heavy gown her knees began to tremble.

"There is no need to worry about Pearson's idea of you," declared his lordship. "She is already on your side." His glance slid over the room. "I came back because I remembered your mama's jewels. In the country, your guardians may have thought nothing of leaving them in your custody, but in the city we do not leave such valuables lying about."

Jeannie found herself staring up into his face as he talked. It was a darkly handsome face and its very lines spoke of authority and power. How many incognitas, she wondered, had set out to make a business arrangement with him and lost their hearts in the process? How many young heiresses had desired to make a connection with his lordship, not because of title or fortune but because his dark good looks had a strange effect on their fluttering hearts?

Jeannie grew aware of her own thudding heart. "There, over there, in my reticule," she said, gesturing toward the bed and banishing her addlepated thoughts. As Trenton swung around, her eyes shifted to the play of his shoulder muscles under his well-fitted coat. How strong and powerful he looked. The young ladies would certainly envy her.

He turned again to face her, the reticule in his hand. "Come here."

He was standing beside the bed, and behind him Jeannie could see where Pearson had turned down the covers. Her heart leaped up in her throat. Surely he wouldn't—not right here—not when he'd sent for Lady Helena. But she had had few dealings with men of his stamp, and had no way of knowing what he might do.

"Come here," he repeated, his eyes glittering darkly in the candlelight.

Somewhere in Jeannie a little voice cried out to beware, but somewhere else another part of her cried out to obey him. She took a hesitant step forward and stopped, torn by indecision.

She saw his brows draw together in a fierce frown as he tossed the reticule into a chair. "You are not making much of a beginning as a dutiful wife," he said darkly.

"I have not yet promised to obey," she replied sharply over the thudding of her heart.

His lordship took a step toward her. "And will you mean it when you do promise?" he asked, his brows still drawn together.

"I shall be as good a wife as—" Suddenly some demon inside her took control. "As good a wife as you deserve," she cried, and then stood aghast at her own temerity. They had made a business arrangement, and she certainly intended to live up to it. There was no point in baiting him like this.

For a moment his lordship seemed nonplussed, and then he shrugged cynically. "I believe you had better revise your thinking on that score. I do not intend to have my friends laughing at me behind my back."

"But it's perfectly acceptable for the ladies to snicker behind *mine*," declared Jeannie, wondering why she was driven to antagonize him so.

"You are being foolish," declared Trenton. "Any woman in this city would be excessively grateful to have me for a husband."

"You forget, milord, that I am not any woman," de-

47

clared Jeannie hotly. The man was an arrogant beast, almost as bad as Atwood in his conceit. She would not be able to stand living with him if she did not speak up now. "I assure you, milord," she continued, "I will not get in the way of your—amusements. But neither will I promise to love my cage."

Trenton advanced until only inches separated them. Trembling, Jeannie held her ground. He was only a man; she would not allow him to frighten her.

"You are an exasperating creature," declared the Viscount, his dark eyes probing hers.

"May I remind your lordship that this marriage was your idea? *I* merely wanted to get to London to help my brother." Defiantly she faced him, thankful that the long nightdress hid the trembling of her limbs.

His lordship sighed. "I have explained the entire situation to you. I still believe you are getting a good bargain."

Jeannie stiffened. "Please do not bother again to tell me what a good catch you are. It makes you so insufferably high in the instep. I daresay there must be more than one woman in London who would refuse you."

For long moments his eyes held hers. Jeannie stared back at him proudly. He needn't think she was going to be easily handled.

"You are very young," said Trenton finally. "Very young and very naive. After all, you are only a child."

"I am not a child! I'm a grown woman, and you know it!" The words burst from her in a wave of anger.

The glitter in his eyes told her too late that she had fallen into his trap. Unconsciously she took a step backward, but he was too quick for her, and his hands on her shoulders drew her to him.

Jeannie was both annoyed and frightened. The fact that they were to be married didn't matter to her at that moment. She felt that her dignity was being assailed. To what purpose were these kisses in any case? She would certainly fulfill her duties as a wife and mother, but feelings for him—those were out of the question.

His lips caressed hers, gently, tenderly, persuasively. Deep within her, Jeannie felt the faint stirring of an undefined emotion. She pushed it down into the depths from where it had sprung. No feelings were to be allowed in this marriage. Feelings left too much room for pain, and Jeannie had had enough of that for a lifetime.

When Trenton released her, she regarded him coldly. "I think, milord, that you forget yourself."

He did not seem put out by her coldness. "How so, little one?"

"First, this false display of affection between us is unnecessary when there is no audience."

His eyes sparkled. "I am merely practicing. I might add that you *need* practice. Had an audience been present, our whole plan would have been shot. You must be more pliable in my arms. Sweet and warm. Didn't Atwood kiss you?"

Jeannie felt the blood flood her cheeks as she glared at him. "You exceed the bounds, milord. What passed between Atwood and myself is no concern of yours."

He shrugged. "I merely thought that perhaps you were more responsive to him."

Jeannie's hands formed two small fists. "You forget, milord. I felt some partiality for him. With you and I, it is quite different. We are strangers, and our arrangement is not based on affection."

Trenton's face darkened. "No, it is not. On the other hand, I've no wish to be bedded with an icicle."

49

"Milord!" Jeannie's hands flew up to cover her scarlet face. "I—I shall fulfill my duties," she murmured through her fingers.

"Of course." His voice was so cold that she dropped her hands in surprise. He was scowling at her fiercely. "I must beg your pardon," he said stiffly. "It appears that I have forgotten the difference between young ladies and—other women. We seemed to be getting along quite well, and I presumed too much." He stared at her thoughtfully. "I do not desire to have a house full of discord. And I must have heirs. So long as you understand that, I suppose we shall deal together well enough."

"Yes, milord." Jeannie forced herself to face him. "I, too, want a peaceful existence."

"Good. Good night, little one." He turned toward the door.

"Milord?" She paused, uncertain. "I—I wish you would not call me that."

He raised a quizzical eyebrow. "What?"

"L-little one. I don't like it."

The flicker of a smile appeared on his lordship's dark face. "I don't know why not." He looked down on her. "You *are* little."

Jeannie shook her head. "It—it makes me feel like a child."

His eyes sparkled at her. "You are that, too."

"Milord! I am twenty years old!"

Trenton smiled. "And I am six and thirty." He shook his head. "Sorry, my pet. I like the name, and reserve the right to use it."

"But, milord—" Jeannie's protest was cut short as Trenton scooped her up in his arms.

"Hush," he commanded, dropping a light kiss on her forehead. "Do not remind me now that you are a woman." He grinned at her devilishly as his arms pulled her closer to his striped waistcoat. "I am not accustomed to dealing with young ladies, you remember. Atwood was right about one thing, my dear. I am a rakeshame. There's no denying it."

He strode across the room and deposited her on the bed. "You will see, little one. We'll learn to deal together, you and I. And sooner or later you will recognize the truth. I *am* an exceptional man." With a sardonic grin, he turned and made for the door. "Good night, Jeannie. Sleep well."

He shut the door softly behind him, and Jeannie reached down absently to pull up the covers. Arrogant, toplofty, excessively high in the instep—that was Trenton. She frowned as she turned on her side and settled down to sleep. Perhaps this marriage was a mistake. And yet—what alternatives did she have? At least here in the city she would have something with which to employ her time, something more than needlework and terrible French novels. With a sigh Jeannie fell asleep.

CHAPTER FIVE

When Jeannie opened her eyes the next morning, it took her a few moments to realize where she was. She looked at the green brocade curtains on the bed, wondering momentarily what had happened to her bright yellow ones. Then the realization hit her. This was not her sunny bedroom in Shropshire; this was London!

She threw back the covers and thrust aside the curtains. The room was full of sunshine. Gathering the voluminous nightdress around her, she rose from the bed. It was a lovely room, she told herself, admiring the delicate pastel scrolls that decorated the ceiling, and the plaster oval frames built into the wall—frames that housed a series of the most delicate landscapes. The whole room, from its marble-manteled fireplace to the delicate lyre-back chairs, spoke of excellent taste.

Jeannie moved to look out the window and saw that it faced on a back courtyard, now filled with a profusion of late summer flowers. The day was a beautiful one, the sun bright in the blue sky. Wrapping her arms around herself, Jeannie leaned out to sniff the air. Her trip had certainly turned out differently than she had expected. Jeremy would be so—

Sudden consternation hit her. How many hours had

she been in London already, and she hadn't even thought to send him word.

She began to search for her clothes but could find nothing. For a moment she stood angrily in the middle of the room. What did Trenton think he was doing? Then common sense took over. It was extremely unlikely that his lordship had had anything to do with the disappearance of her clothes. Most likely Pearson had removed them. The long day she had spent in them had left them in rather poor condition.

Jeannie rang the bell, and minutes later a cheerful housekeeper appeared, carrying a tray with a small pot of chocolate. "Good morning, miss," said Pearson cheerfully. "Did you sleep well?"

"Yes, indeed," replied Jeannie.

"Lady Helena isn't up," said Pearson. "She left orders to not awaken her afore the decent hour of noon. But when she awakens, she'll be wanting to see you."

"Of course," replied Jeannie, wondering again who Lady Helena could be.

"Pearson, I'm sadly in need of clothes. This," she fingered the nightdress ruefully, "has served me well, but it's hardly fitting for day wear."

Pearson laughed. "You look like a child in it, miss, you being so small."

"But I am not a child," she said, feeling a thrill go through her at the memories those words raised. "And I must have some clothes. Also, I must send a message to my brother."

"Indeed, miss, if it's a message you've in mind, just write it down and the direction, and I'll send it off with a footman this instant. And as fer the clothes, Lady Helena has brought along plenty, I'll wager. She's of a size with you."

Though Jeannie would have preferred to rush post-haste to her brother's side, this was patently impossible. Instead, she settled herself at the small writing table in the corner and composed a short note to him. Wouldn't Jeremy be astonished to find her in London, and able to save him from the hatchet-face? It would be a great surprise.

She purposely made her note as cryptic as possible. "Am in London, staying with the Viscount Trenton, St. James Square. Come soon. This afternoon."

She surveyed her handiwork with satisfaction, sealed it, and wrote Jeremy's direction on the back.

"No doubt he'll be here during calling hours," she told Pearson. "I hope Lady Helena awakens before then."

"Indeed, miss," replied the housekeeper, "Lady Helena will be up and about shortly after twelve. She's that eager to see her brother's bride-to-be. She'd not let a little more sleep delay her."

So Lady Helena was his lordship's sister, thought Jeannie, and was surprised at the relief she felt. Whatever had possessed her to suppose that this Lady Helena might be Trenton's latest inamorata. Even if he called himself the greatest rakeshame in London, he would have a care for her reputation. She felt a blush of shame at this indication of how deeply his words about his former haunts had impressed themselves upon her.

"I'll just take this down and have it sent off," said Pearson. "In the meantime, why don't you drink your chocolate? There'll be a nuncheon later after Lady Helena is up and about."

"Is his lordship still abed?" asked Jeannie as casually as she could.

Pearson chuckled. "Lord no, miss. Why, he's up

bright and early, that one. Keeps us all hopping, he does. Wrote a long letter to your aunt and uncle and sent it right off. Lucky he has the money," she said sagely. "I'd hate to get a letter the size of that. Would empty my purse to pay for it." She smiled. "Here I stand talking and your chocolate's getting cold. I'll be back shortly."

Jeannie poured herself a cup of chocolate. Sipping from the delicate Wedgwood, she settled on the divan and considered her future. This afternoon the tradesmen would come, and she would order new clothes. It would take at least three weeks to read the banns and it was hard to say exactly when his lordship would want the wedding, although probably shortly after that.

Jeannie lost herself in a consideration of marriage and its responsibilities and was unprepared for the brisk knock on the door and the stranger's intrusion. She was small and dark, with perhaps just a trifle more flesh to her than Jeannie possessed. The dark bushy brows would have made her known instantly to Jeannie, even if no other evidence had been forthcoming. This was Lady Helena, his lordship's sister.

"So, you are the bride-to-be."

"Yes, milady," answered Jeannie meekly as the small figure practically scurried from one end of the room to the other, her eyes quickly noting all there was to see.

"Well, everything seems to be in order. I have to say this for my brother. His servants know their business. Best run establishment in London. Yes, it is. But come, let me see you." Lady Helena's birdlike eyes flitted nervously over Jeannie. "You are young, but healthy. That counts for something. And your blood's good. Trenton wouldn't go off with just anyone." She shook her head in exasperation. "God knows, we've been trying to get him to tie the knot these many years."

Under this barrage of words Jeannie could only remain silent. What a veritable whirlwind this sister was.

"Get dressed and come down," Lady Helena continued. "We'll have a passable nuncheon. Trenton always provides a good table." She scurried toward the door.

"But Lady Helena," cried Jeannie, loath to interrupt but afraid not to. "I've no clothes. None at all."

Lady Helena looked suddenly surprised and then laughed. "Of course, of course. The elopement. Don't you worry. The tradesmen will begin arriving before long, and we'll order you an entire wardrobe." Her eyes glittered. "Ah, that will be capital fun."

"But the expense—" Jeannie had a sudden vision of the Viscount in a towering rage. This had been no part of their arrangement.

"Nonsense," insisted Lady Helena. "Trenton has more money than he can possibly use. Besides, he has his reputation to preserve. He insists you be turned out as nicely as any lady of the *ton*."

"Th-that's very kind of him," murmured Jeannie.

To her surprise, Lady Helena laughed. "I'm not one to ask what a woman sees in a man, or vice versa. Partialities seem to me to be strangely peculiar, and God knows, my Charles—bless his departed soul—was not a man easy for me to deal with. But kindness is not a word I often apply to my brother. If he is kind to you, it is because it serves his purpose. He is an eminently selfish man."

Her dark eyes laughed at Jeannie's startled reaction. "Oh, he is charming—devilishly handsome and a prime article with the ladies. But I'm his sister, and

57

I'm not blinded by infatuation. Yes, Trenton is eminently selfish, but that needn't distress you, of course. He is not a pinchpenny."

She turned to go. "Oh, I almost forgot. I'll send along one of my gowns with my maid and the extras to go with it. It may be a trifle large, but it will certainly fit you better than that—that tent." Then, with a swift clatter of heels on the floor, Lady Helena was gone.

How very like her brother she was, Jeannie thought. Just as arrogant and overbearing, and yet in some strange way just as appealing.

She shook her head. There was little time to consider the matter, however, for Pearson reappeared bearing a pitcher of water, and while she was helping Jeannie off with the nightdress, a shy young maidservant entered, silently laid an armful of clothes on a chair, and silently departed.

"Well," said Pearson approvingly, "her ladyship's thought of everything. You'll be turned out as fine as any lady in town."

"My note?" said Jeannie, realizing again how events had taken her thoughts from her brother and his problems.

"Don't you worry none, miss. Your note's on its way. He'll be here in calling hours, I've no doubt."

Jeannie had been of this opinion herself, but as the day wore on her hopes began to dissipate. As she turned this way and that, was measured, complimented, and talked about as though she were not there, and then appealed to by sundry merchants to approve their muslins, bonnets, boots, or capes, she was confident that Jeremy would at any moment appear. In fact, she had left word with Budner that on her twin's appearance she was to be notified immediately.

When they held up the swaths of white satin and rolls of Brussels lace for her wedding gown, she forgot Jeremy for a while. In a few short weeks she would marry. It all seemed unreal and yet here were people who acted as though it were the most natural thing in the world. Jeannie had a sudden picture of herself in a gown of the materials before her, standing at the altar with Trenton. Her heart began to thud in apprehension. How could she do this? How could she promise to spend the rest of her life with this stranger?

After all the tradesmen had gone and she had done some figuring, she was appalled by the enormity of their purchases. She had quite failed in her efforts to hold the new wardrobe down to reasonable size. "But I don't need a dozen pair of white kid gloves," she had cried, only to be met with Lady Helena's look of bewilderment. In Lady Helena's world every woman needed a dozen pair of white kid gloves.

Reluctantly, Jeannie was forced to concede that Lady Helena advanced good reasons for purchasing every item. Indeed, she was so like her brother that there was no gainsaying her. Nevertheless, the amount of their purchases frightened Jeannie. Papa had been extravagant, certainly, but this—this far surpassed any of his expenditures. She simply could not see how the Viscount could fail to be furious at this frivolous waste of his substance.

Jeannie said as much, but Lady Helena only looked at her in dismay. "Frivolous?" she declared in a voice of amazement. "You are his bride—the future Viscountess. It is no waste to have you suitably attired. If he did not— Why the whole *ton* would talk. You don't want that, do you?"

"Of course not," Jeannie replied, remembering

the days when the *ton* had found her desertion food for gossip.

"Don't be so down in the dumps," urged Lady Helena as they sipped tea together later in a drawing room, a beautiful room furnished in deep shades of blue. "Your brother will arrive. Perhaps he was on a spree last night and has not yet recovered from being in his cups. Or perhaps he is out of town on business." She smiled cheerfully. "After all, my dear, when one runs off to elope, one can hardly expect that people will be awaiting one's arrival."

In spite of herself, Jeannie smiled. She knew that Lady Helena was right. Any number of things could be delaying Jeremy. But another part of her insisted that her twin must be in some danger or he would have come to her immediately.

She paced to the window and back so many times that Lady Helena finally remarked in exasperation, "Mercy, Jeannie, do sit down. At this rate you'll wear a hole quite through Trenton's carpet. He'll not like that a bit, I can assure you."

There was a respectful tap on the door and Budner opened it to announce, "A young man, milady. Says he's Miss Burnstead's brother."

Jeannie turned from the window, her hands flying to her cheeks. "Oh, show him in."

Lady Helena rose. "I'll leave the two of you alone," she said. "You must have a great deal to discuss."

"Th-thank you." Jeannie's eyes remained glued to the door through which moments later her twin entered.

"Jeremy!" She threw herself into his arms. He gave her a slight hug and then held her away. Jeannie blinked rapidly to hold back her sudden tears. Then she managed a smile.

"What has happened to you?" her twin asked, his

eyes quickly surveying the room. "What are you doing in Trenton's house? Have you no care for your good name? Trenton's reputation—"

Jeannie laid a finger against his lips. "Ssssh. You must not speak so of my husband-to-be."

Both of Jeremy's eyebrows shot up, and his mouth fell open. For a moment he just stared at her. "Trenton! Your husband-to-be?"

Jeannie nodded. "We're to be married shortly after the banns have been called."

"But what are you doing here now? Where's Aunt Dizzy?"

"It's a long story, Jeremy." Jeannie led her brother toward the divan. "Come, sit down and let me tell you."

She had already decided that Jeremy should have no more of the truth than the others. He, too, must think her union with Trenton a love match.

Jeannie focused her attention on her twin. He was well-dressed, but he looked very thin, and there were fine lines of fatigue in his face. Jeannie did not like what she saw.

"Tell me," said Jeremy. "I can't believe it. Trenton! The biggest rake—" He stopped suddenly.

"I know about his reputation," said Jeannie calmly, although her heart thudded rapidly at this confirmation of his lordship's own words. "It doesn't matter to me."

"Doesn't matter?" Jeremy appeared stunned.

"It doesn't matter," Jeannie said simply, hoping her twin would not dig deeply into the subject. He had always been able to tell when she was lying.

"You can't—" Jeremy cried, as though not believing his ears.

"Yes, I love him," insisted Jeannie. She was nettled by Jeremy's behavior. "I *am* a grown woman," she reminded her twin. "Even though I've been stuck in Shropshire while you were on the town, I *have* grown up."

Jeremy gave her a long look. "I suppose you have, but I can hardly believe it. I think of you still as that scrawny schoolroom miss who followed me everywhere."

"I am not scrawny," said Jeannie, conscious of a rising indignation. What was wrong with these men that they could not see she was a woman?

"But why are you here now?" asked Jeremy.

Jeannie took a deep breath. This was where she must be careful. If Jeremy ever supposed that this was *not* a love match, that paying his debts had been part of the bargain, he might well refuse his lordship's aid. "I—I eloped," she said.

"Eloped! My God, Jeannie, have you lost all your wits?"

"Indeed not!" she replied hotly. "It was exceedingly dull in the country. I was afflicted with *ennui*."

"And you eloped to combat *ennui*?" Jeremy's tone carried sarcasm.

Jeannie nodded. "Yes, in a way."

Jeremy shook his head. "I thought you had better understanding than that."

Jeannie found herself bristling up, but there was no way to defend herself without telling him the truth. "I read about such things all the time in Aunt Dizzy's novels," she added, aware that this would make her look even more silly.

Jeremy just shook his head. He seemed past speech. "But tell me about yourself," urged Jeannie.

Jeremy sighed. "Things are not good. I'm in debt to a moneylender. Play's been going against me. It looks as if I'm going to have to take on the hatchet-face. There seems no other way out."

"Maybe there is," said Jeannie, slowly feeling her way.

"What do you mean?" Jeremy asked gruffly.

"Well, the Viscount has asked me what I want for a wedding present."

"So?" replied Jeremy.

"I could ask him to pay your debts."

Jeremy laughed harshly. "This is not some paltry sum," he observed.

"The Viscount is a man of means," returned Jeannie stiffly, rather surprised to find herself offended by this slur on her intended husband.

"Do you think he'd stand for a thousand pounds?" asked Jeremy with a brittle laugh.

Jeannie hid her fears. A thousand pounds seemed like a tremendous sum to her, especially on top of the day's purchases, but the Viscount *had* promised. "Of course he will," she said sharply. "He loves me." She held her breath, but Jeremy was so taken with the prospect of his deliverance that the lie passed unnoticed.

"Really, Jeannie? Do you really think he will?"

Jeannie nodded firmly. "I know him," she said with more conviction than she felt. "He is not like you think."

A dazed Jeremy shook his head. "I can scarcely believe it."

"He wants me to be happy," she said, wishing that were the truth. "Bring me a list of your debts, and I'll give it to him."

"That's wonderful, Jeannie. You're one of a kind." He glanced at the clock. "Listen, I've got to go now. I'm meeting someone for dinner."

There was a strange glimmer in his eyes that made Jeannie uneasy. There was something threatening about it, something that made her heart lurch in her breast. She found herself clutching her twin's arm. "Jeremy, you won't—You won't get in more debt, will you?"

His eyes clouded suddenly, as though to shut her out. "Don't worry yourself about me. I'll manage very well."

He rose abruptly, shaking off her hand. "I've got to go. I'll bring the list tomorrow."

"Yes." Jeannie bit her bottom lip to keep from crying as her twin made his way out. Jeremy had changed, she thought, as she fought to control herself. This foppishly turned out man with the hard, glittering eyes did not seem like her twin at all. He was a stranger who had not even said thank you before taking such an abrupt departure.

What had life done to the carefree boy who had once meant so much to her? Recalling that cold glitter in his eyes, Jeannie shivered. If gaming were really in Jeremy's blood, this was only the beginning of his indebtedness.

Suddenly unable to sit still any longer, she rose and hurried from the room. Upstairs, in the privacy of her peaceful green bedroom, she would have time to compose herself, to consider how best to meet the Viscount's surprise at the extent of her brother's debt—and the bills for her wardrobe.

CHAPTER SIX

The sun was moving down the sky when Jeannie descended the great staircase and approached Budner. "When his lordship has a moment, I should like a word with him," she said, striving to keep her anxiety from her voice. She had heard his carriage and could not wait any longer.

"I'll see, miss," Budner replied, moving toward the library.

She was not really afraid of the Viscount, Jeannie told herself, but she was deeply distressed over the amount of Jeremy's debts—and the day's purchases. That she had won the better part of the deal she was now more or less convinced, but she did not, of course, intend to let *him* know it. He was arrogant and top-lofty enough as it was.

But Jeannie was a truthful person, even with herself. It did not take a great deal of understanding to realize that she was not the biggest matrimonial bargain of the year. Her dowry, aside from her mama's jewels, was quite small. Uncle Obadiah had always said that her blood would have to count, but after that mess with Atwood—

If it were not for Jeremy, Jeannie thought, she would offer his lordship a way out. Certainly the inauspicious beginning of this marriage did not hold out much promise for its future.

"His lordship will see you now," Budner said. "In the library."

"Thank you."

Jeannie took a deep breath as she paused before the library door. Then she squared her shoulders under Lady Helena's gown and entered.

The Viscount was standing with his back to the door. He swung around to meet her. He was smiling and, with a sinking heart, Jeannie realized that he had not yet had a report on the afternoon's purchases from Lady Helena.

"Good day, Jeannie."

"Good day, milord." Jeannie was dismayed to hear how thin and weak her voice sounded. She swallowed several times.

"Budner said you wished to speak to me." His lordship raised a quizzical eyebrow.

"I—I do." Jeannie found herself unable to go on.

"Come, come, Jeannie. You've never been loath to speak your mind before."

She raised her head. "I know. I—" Finally she plunged ahead, hardly knowing what she was saying. "My brother was here. I told him ours was a love match, that—that you had told me I could have whatever I wanted for a wedding gift."

The Viscount nodded. "An excellent idea. I take it the boy is proud. Wouldn't like the truth, would he?"

Jeannie nodded. "No, he wouldn't."

"So. Did he tell you how much he's in for?"

Jeannie nodded, but did not continue.

"Well?" He eyed her expectantly.

"It's—it's a thousand pounds. I didn't know it was that much." She clasped her hands nervously as he frowned. "Please, milord. I didn't know. You've every right to be angry." She took another deep breath. "And—and we've spent a terrible sum this day. Why

66

don't you cancel those orders? I don't need those things. I did try to tell Lady Helena, but she thinks it's a love match, and she kept insisting—"

Jeannie stopped. She had said all she could and at every word his face had darkened even further. "I—I am sorry," she faltered, her eyes dropping away from his thunderous face.

"Jeannie!" The sharpness in his voice brought her head erect. "You are shortly going to become a Viscountess. Kindly behave like one."

She stared into the hard black eyes that met hers.

"I do not intend that my wife should ever come crawling to me abjectly."

Jeannie's face flamed. "I did not crawl!"

His eyes taunted her. "But you were abject."

"No!" Jeannie's back was up now. How dare he speak to her like that? "I was not abject. I merely sought to apologize for having obligated you for a larger sum than we had originally bargained for."

Something flickered in Trenton's eyes and was gone. "I am not a tradesman," he said curtly. "Nor am I a man of so little substance that a thousand pounds is a matter of great import to me." His mouth curved in a sardonic smile. "You are more the country girl than I expected. I had thought that by now you would be more cognizant of the extent of my fortune."

For just a moment Jeannie stared at him in surprise. Then the sharp thrust of pain in her heart exploded into a wild, surging anger. She drew herself up to her full height. "Milord, if you truly believe that of me, I suggest that you send me back to Aunt Dizzy. I will thank you to remember that this marriage was *your* abominable idea."

He drew closer to her and smiled down at her cynically. "That's more like it! You've the temper of a lady. You'll do quite well."

"Oh!" The sardonic look in his eyes quite infuriated her and before she knew what she was about, she raised angry fists to flail at his chest.

"Jeannie!" Hard hands grabbed her wrists and held them immobile. Tears of rage filled her eyes and blinded her as she struggled with him. But of course he was too strong for her. Then all the tensions of the day, all her worries over Jeremy, seemed to deprive her of her strength. Her knees weakened, and she began to sink.

"Here, here, none of that," he cried, sweeping her up into his arms and carrying her to the divan. In spite of her anger at herself for allowing her weakness to betray her like this, Jeannie could not stop the tears that continued to flow. To her surprise, the Viscount did not speak more angry words to her. He simply held her against his waistcoat, put a clean handkerchief in her hand, and waited until her sobs subsided.

"I—I am sorry," she finally managed, wiping at her eyes and blowing her nose.

"I expect the apology should come from me," said his lordship in a strangely rueful tone. "I will only remind you—again—that I have been on the town these sixteen years, and I have had little commerce with young women of your kind."

"But the young heiresses?" said Jeannie. "The ladies of the *ton?*"

The Viscount shrugged. "No young woman remains innocent for long in the city. If I spoke harshly to one of them, they would give me cut for cut. They've double-edged tongues, the lot of them."

"I see," Jeannie replied. She had certainly experienced those tongues after Atwood's desertion.

"Now," said his lordship firmly, "we must talk. I will take care of Jeremy's debts, but you must tell him that this is the extent of my generosity. Since I refuse to game excessively myself, I do not intend to continually pay the debts of others."

Jeannie nodded. "I will tell him."

"Good. Now as to the clothes, I fully instructed Lady Helena as to how I wanted you turned out. My name as well as yours is at stake here. I have never been known as a pinchpenny, and I do not intend to begin now. Besides"—his dark eyes sparkling into hers seemed to hold her spellbound—"you forget that this is a love match. To convince the *ton* that I have lost my heart will not be an easy task. They have long been confident that I have none to lose."

Jeannie felt her own heart thudding painfully in her breast. It was strange how being so close to him made it beat louder.

She pushed at a strand of hair which had escaped its knot. It was just because she was unused to men that he affected her so.

"When will your brother return?" he asked.

"He said he would bring the list tomorrow," Jeannie replied.

"Very good. Did you order a riding habit?"

"I believe so."

"You don't know?" Trenton raised a bushy eyebrow.

"We ordered so much, and Lady Helena kept wanting more, and I kept wanting less. It's difficult to remember."

"I see. Where did you get the gown you are wearing now?" His eyes slid over her with a look of speculation, and she wondered if he thought the neckline too low or the sleeves too long.

"Lady Helena loaned it to me. My own things will be completed very soon, they said."

69

The Viscount looked thoughtful. "I wonder if Helena has a bonnet to spare."

"A bonnet?"

Trenton nodded. "Yes, a bonnet. I've an urge to take a turn in Hyde Park to show off the bride-to-be. How does that strike you?"

"I'd like some fresh air," said Jeannie candidly, "but I don't much want to be gawked at like some freak in a raree show."

Trenton broke into laughter. "I'm afraid there's going to be a lot of staring, my dear. Better to get used to it now rather than on our wedding day."

Jeannie felt a shiver of apprehension. Could she really be going to *marry* this man? Just a few days ago she'd been in Shropshire, complaining to herself that life was exceedingly dull. Now—now she was to become a Viscountess, and even more exciting and frightening, she was to become the wife of the tall, dark stranger who faced her. He was a stranger, yet not a stranger. With her eyes tight shut, she could see his face quite clearly—those dark, probing eyes under bushy brows, that proud, aristocratic nose, the stubborn mouth and chin. She knew exactly how his dark hair curled over his collar and how his broad shoulders stretched the material of his jacket.

"Jeannie?"

His words brought her out of her contemplation. "Yes?"

"I said—run up and get a bonnet and shawl from Lady Helena, and we'll go for a spin in Hyde Park."

Confusion suddenly came over her. "Do—do I look all right?"

His lordship's mouth curved in amusement. "Of course you look all right. If you did not, I would hardly suggest taking you. I've no mind to become a laughingstock."

"I should hope not." Such an event was difficult for Jeannie to imagine. Anyone who laughed at his lordship was certainly likely to regret it.

"You played the runaway to perfection," said the Viscount with a chuckle. "But can you play a young woman in love?"

"I rather think so, milord." Jeannie managed a slight chuckle. "After all, I *have* read French novels. They are drivel, no doubt, but they contain information useful in these circumstances."

Trenton laughed. "Just so. You must hang on my arm, look up at me with adoring eyes, and color up when I look at you."

Jeannie suppressed a sigh. There was nothing difficult about any of that. It was exactly how she had behaved with Atwood. "Yes, milord," she replied, so demurely that his lordship cast her a look of suspicion. Jeannie pretended not to notice. "And how will *you* behave?"

"Oh, I shall reach often for your hand, look long into your eyes, and sing your praises to all who will listen. I shall play the lovesick swain quite admirably."

For some reason Jeannie's excitement at the prospect of the ride faded. She no longer wanted playacting from his lordship.

"Come, your bonnet." Trenton rose and pulled her to her feet. For a moment their eyes met, and Jeannie saw a flicker of something in his. But then it was gone and she could not say what it had been—or that it had really been there.

His lordship was looking at her devilishly. "Hurry, youngster," he urged. "It's getting on to five o'clock."

"I'm not a—" Jeannie stopped suddenly, recognizing the mischief in his eyes, and, lifting her skirts, she ran for the staircase. As she reached the upper landing, she felt her heart pounding in her throat—but not from exertion. As she composed herself before knocking on Lady Helena's door, she knew that her heart was thudding in this mad way because his lordship had looked at her with his devilish black eyes.

He had wanted her to insist that she was not a youngster, a child. He had wanted her to provoke him into—into kissing her. Jeannie's heart thudded again. Had he really wanted to kiss her, or had he only wanted to tease her, to watch her blush in confusion? There was no way of knowing. Jeannie shook her head; she was going to marry an impossible man.

She took a deep breath and knocked on Lady Helena's door. It was opened by a pert little maid who ushered her into an adjoining sitting room, where Lady Helena lay artfully relaxing on a divan, a French romance in one hand and a chocolate in the other.

"*Ma petite,*" Lady Helena cried, "you must read this romance. It is absolutely breathtaking."

Jeannie smiled. Right now life was more exciting than any romance she had ever read. "His lordship sent me to borrow a shawl and a bonnet. He wants to go driving in Hyde Park."

Lady Helena smiled. "Of course, of course. I should have known. He was always one to show off his newest possessions. I remember when he bought his first pistols. But here, I rattle on."

Lady Helena rose from the couch and hurried to the wardrobe. She drew forth the largest bonnet Jeannie had ever seen. It was a bright, bright green, shaped like a shovel, and boasted a gigantic assortment of artificial flowers.

"Lady Helena, I cannot—"

"Nonsense." Lady Helena herself settled the bonnet on Jeannie's knot of golden curls and tied the strings. "Trenton wants people to notice you. This bonnet is all the newest fashion. My *modiste* assured me so just yesterday. And here—" From a drawer she pulled a cream-colored cashmere shawl fringed in gold and a pair of stone-colored gloves. "Now you are ready to face the *ton*. Remember, hold your head high. Trenton has chosen you and that is something to be proud of. And do not be surprised if some dowager mamas, or even some respectable wives, give you the cut direct. Trenton has had great popularity with the frail ones, too. Many of them will be disappointed to see that he is no longer available."

She shook her head as though still marveling. "Trenton to marry—and for love! Someday you must tell me how you did it."

"Yes, of course," Jeannie mumbled, and, clutching shawl and gloves, made a hasty retreat.

As she hurried down the stairs, she saw that his lordship was already waiting. He had picked up his curly-brimmed beaver and his York tan riding gloves. He was really a fine specimen—this man to whom she would soon be joined for life.

"You took rather a long time," observed his lordship dryly. "I suppose Helena was busy giving you advice."

Jeannie shook her head. "No, it's just that—well—"

His lordship chuckled and the warmth of the sound was pleasant. "She talks a lot," he finished for her.

Conscious of Budner's dignified stare, Jeannie managed a nod. "But I am ready now."

"Good," said his lordship. "I have ordered the barouche brought around. You will show off to advantage, though I must say that I consider that bonnet somewhat excessive. Those flowers appear almost dangerous and the whole thing looks as though your neck cannot support it. Quite a slender neck," he added approvingly.

Jeannie flushed at the compliment, but felt a certain dismay rising in her at the assessment of the bonnet. "Maybe I should run up and ask for another, though Lady Helena insisted that this was the latest style."

"And what do *you* think of it?"

"I'll change it if you think I should," she continued, quite ignoring his question.

His lordship's face clouded, and his eyebrows met darkly. "I did not ask for a sweet echo," he observed caustically. "I thought that I was betrothed to a woman of some sense. I find the always-acquiescent type quite cloying."

Jeannie felt herself bristling up, and she ignored Budner's presence and let her anger go. "I am not acquiescent, nor am I cloying. I simply do not know much about current London fashion, so I am unable to make a sound judgment on the matter."

Her back was really up now and the gathering thunderclouds on his lordship's face did not deter her. "However, I did trust your sister's judgment, most especially as *you* instructed me to consider her my mentor."

By this time Jeannie was breathing heavily, her breast rising and falling under her thin muslin gown as she glared her defiance at him. Just because she was to be his wife he needn't think he could take such a high and mighty tone.

His lordship's dark brows were drawn together in a heavy line. For long moments he glared back at her. Then, as by an effort of will, his brows smoothed, his lips curled in a cynical smile, and he observed dryly, "Your observations are quite correct. I *did* give you into Lady Helena's keeping, and it *is* unfair of me to expect you to know London fashion." His eyes sparkled, but whether with mischief or anger she could not tell. "Above all, you are definitely *not* acquiescent. And now, since I have tendered my apologies in the best possible fashion, shall we proceed on our ride?"

Jeannie could only nod and put her hand through the arm he extended. What a strange sort of man he was, she thought—so stern sometimes, almost angry, and so caustic. No wonder young ladies spoke to him with tongues like double-edged swords.

They reached the barouche and with the utmost solicitude his lordship handed her in and climbed up himself.

As the barouche rumbled off, Jeannie waited for his lordship to say something, to comment on her angry outburst at him. But he remained absolutely silent and Jeannie, her mind filled with memories of their last painful scene together, could only wonder why the man should so insist that she voice her opinions. This was entirely unlike any man she had ever known.

CHAPTER SEVEN

The barouche moved through London's busy streets with its occupants sitting in silence. To Jeannie, however, the silence was not oppressive; she was intrigued by the busy city around her. It had been three years since she and Jeremy had come to London for her coming out.

Her heart gave a lurch at the thought of the different Jeremy she had spoken to that afternoon. He had changed, had grown into a stranger. At times he had seemed like the twin she knew, but then, unexpectedly, she had seen the glitter that even the *mention* of gambling had put in his eyes. And the harsh way he had spoken to her—the old Jeremy had never been like that.

She swallowed hastily and turned her attention back to the city. It looked very much the same. There were still pretty shopgirls loitering in front of the windows, while shopboys paid more attention to them than to the errands their employers had sent them on. There were still old women selling hot tea and pastries, girls with watercress, though sadly wilted by this time of day, and butcher boys careening through the crowds with little regard for the people they jostled. Here a young girl was selling summer flowers and there another hawked mussels.

Yes, thought Jeannie with a satisfied smile, it was the same old city—noisy, dirty, often foul-smelling, but full of people, full of life.

She turned toward his lordship and found him watching her thoughtfully. "Your eyes are sparkling," he observed dryly. "Does the prospect of showing me off intrigue you that much?"

Jeannie noted the spark of mischief in his eyes and returned in kind. "Indeed, milord, I have been told repeatedly that you're the catch of the season. Unfortunately, I have not previously been able to make an adequate comparison. But today, if I am to meet some Corinthians, I shall be able to see whether you puffed yourself or not."

His lordship chuckled. "Surely you can hold your own with venomous-tongued mamas. You have ample wit for it." He looked suddenly concerned. "You will not burst into tears if some dowager mama or her angry chit of a daughter cuts you dead? My friends would never let me live it down if I married a watering pot."

"I am not a crybaby," said Jeannie.

She saw the disbelief in his eyes. "I—I was tired and upset before. Now I'm curious to see Hyde Park and the young gentlemen." Her eyes danced. "I want to see if you are as great a bargain as you set yourself up to be."

His lordship chuckled, but a strange look flickered in his eyes and was quickly gone.

As they approached the entrance to the park, the press of carriages grew greater. "Goodness," declared Jeannie, "everyone seems to have the same idea."

"Of course," said his lordship. "If you were to come here in the morning, you would see the entire park practically deserted."

"Why don't some people come then?" inquired

Jeannie. "It would be much pleasanter without all the dust."

"For my sake," said the Viscount sardonically, "kindly do not make such a remark within the hearing of my friends."

Jeannie stared at him. "And why not?"

One of his lordship's dark eyebrows rose dramatically. "Five is the fashionable hour for riding in Hyde Park. Fashionable people seldom rise before noon. Such a remark would brand you instantly as a country miss. I do not intend to become the laughingstock of the *ton* for having betrothed myself to a bumpkin."

For a moment Jeannie thought he must be joking with her, but his expression was entirely grave. Suddenly she found herself bristling again. What an arrogant, toplofty creature he could be! "May I remind your lordship," she said stiffly, "that to all intents and purposes I *am* a country bumpkin. Perhaps you had best go back to the unfortunate lady your family picked for you. Undoubtedly she knows how to behave properly and perhaps her double-edged tongue would not be used against you except in private."

His lordship cast her a stern glance. "You are behaving like a schoolroom miss," he observed evenly. "I ask you to consider that the name I bear is soon to be yours. Any disgrace that falls upon it will ultimately be shared by you." His dark eyes probed hers. "I sought not to insult but to forewarn you. I, of course, have no control over your actions. If you choose to disgrace us, there is little I can do."

The words were spoken quite evenly, but Jeannie felt a shiver run down her spine. There was little doubt in her mind that anyone who deliberately crossed the Viscount Trenton would have ample cause to regret it.

"I assure you, milord," she replied with all the conviction she could muster, "that I shall do everything within my power to preserve our good name." A memory of his boastful history of his conquests suddenly entered her mind and, before she stopped to think, she added, "Whatever is left of it, that is, after *your* history as the greatest rakeshame in London."

For a moment she was aghast at what she had done, but his lordship merely smiled derisively. "You will soon see that my reputation is an enviable one. These days any lord who has not such a name cannot hold up his head."

Jeannie frowned. "Are you telling me that having the name of the greatest rakeshame in the city is good?"

His lordship nodded. "Of course it is. I told you so before. I am sought after by heiresses and incognitas alike. Everyone knows I am a prime article."

Jeannie suspected that he was teasing her, but by this time she didn't care. He was excessively toplofty and needed taking down a peg or two!

"Do they also know that you are insufferably toplofty?" she inquired sweetly.

His lordship's expression did not change except for a tightening at the corners of his strong mouth. "Perhaps," he replied, "but then, I have cause to be."

Jeannie shook her head in exasperation. "So I am in an enviable position because I am to marry *you*?"

The Viscount nodded.

"And how would the *ton* regard your marriage to a lady with a similar reputation?"

The Viscount scowled, as she had known he would. "Kindly do not behave like a ninnyhammer. As you well know, the rules are different for women."

"Yes," cried Jeannie, "they are, and it's entirely unfair."

His lordship shook his head. "Those who insist on going against the dogmas of society inevitably suffer for it." He eyed her quizzically. "Don't tell me I am going to marry an incipient bluestocking?"

Jeannie shook her head. "I am not a bluestocking, incipient or otherwise. I am merely stating facts."

Trenton gazed at her sardonically. "I trust I have not betrothed an advocate of free love."

"I—What if you have?" asked Jeannie, driven by some insane demon within her to provoke him further.

His scowl deepened. "There is no room in my life for such a notion. I trust you are not foolish enough to believe that I would allow my lady to follow such an unwise course."

Jeannie shook her head. "Don't fret yourself about your precious name. I am not going to stain it." How could he be so arrogantly sure that he was right? Had the man never made a mistake?

The crowd of carriages and riders on horseback pressed around them. Jeannie turned her attention to those nearest her. It seemed strange that people should want to ride in such choking dust. It was certainly much more sensible to ride in the country where the air was fresh and clean. But then, it appeared that the members of the *ton* were little concerned with being sensible. Their criterion had to do with fashion, and fashion alone.

Jeannie stared around her with curiosity. Everywhere were well-dressed women, their flimsy muslin gowns clinging to them, their heads hidden by enormous bonnets. She smiled; Lady Helena's bonnet was not much different from those around her. She turned and surveyed his lordship. He was presently looking out over the crowd, and she could scrutinize him unheeded. Her heart beat faster as she took in his aristocratic features.

Suddenly he swung around, and she found his dark eyes probing hers. "I—" Hurriedly she sought for words. "Point out to me the leading Corinthians," she said. "Tell me their names and something about them." She forced herself to giggle. "Then I can see if they are as well turned out as you. Will the great Beau be here, do you think? Mama used to talk about him. I longed to see such a paragon. But Mama did not approve of little girls frequenting Bond Street." Jeannie realized that she was running on and stopped suddenly.

"Your mama sounds like a wise woman," observed his lordship dryly. "Too bad she isn't around now to give you counsel."

Jeannie forced herself to meet his eyes. "Why do I need counsel now?" she asked curiously.

Trenton smiled scornfully. "You are about to marry the city's greatest rakeshame and you ask such a question?"

Jeannie frowned. "I wish you might forget that for a little while. It is not a fact that I particularly like to contemplate."

"But it *is* a fact," Trenton insisted, "and one you must face. Perhaps you have made a mistake in accepting me."

Jeannie stared at him, but he continued gravely. "You are young. I forced you into this." He hesitated, his eyes veiling over. "Perhaps I should not have done so. I traded on your love for your brother to help me out of my problems. That was unfair of me."

Jeannie's heart was pounding in her throat. Surely he could not mean to send her back to Shropshire.

"I now give you a chance to back out of our bargain." He regarded her soberly.

Jeannie tried to laugh, to pretend that he was teasing. "You are funning me," she stammered.

"Indeed, I am not," declared Trenton. "I will send you back to your aunt if you so wish."

"But the clothes—the gossip." Jeannie was clutching at straws.

His lordship shrugged. "Those are matters of little consequence. Clothes orders can be cancelled. And the gossip—I have been talked about before."

"But—"

His lordship's mouth tightened. "I shall not renege on my part of the bargain. I promised to pay your brother's debts and I will."

"No!" Jeannie cried. "That is unfair to you."

Trenton raised an eyebrow. "You are extremely concerned with fairness."

Jeannie managed a small smile, but her heart seemed about to stop. "You have been very helpful to me, and you are still in trouble with your family." The cold hand of suspicion clutched her heart. "Unless—have you decided that *you* wish a different bride?"

"No!" The word burst from Trenton with such vehemence that it startled them both. He continued to face her. "I merely realized that I was behaving rather highhandedly in this case, and I sought to remedy my error."

Jeannie found herself laughing, almost hysterically. "You—you *admit* to being highhanded?"

The Viscount smiled sheepishly. "I must say that this is not a condition that I normally find myself in, but I *am* capable of apology."

Without thinking, Jeannie reached out to touch the Viscount's arm with a gloved hand. "I am sorry, milord, but, now that I have seen that you are human, you cannot expect me to give up the city's biggest catch."

Something like relief flashed over his lordship's face and was instantly gone. "Good," he replied.

"But remember, this was your last chance." His eyes glittered. "I do not apologize twice for the same offense."

Jeannie bowed her head gracefully. "I stand forewarned, milord. Be assured that after our nuptials I shall not abuse you about the manner of our betrothal. You have been exceedingly fair to me."

His lordship nodded. "Agreed. Now that you have made your decision, I shall point out my erstwhile competition."

Jeannie returned his smile and breathed a sigh of relief. She had not dared to surrender to the wave of panic that had engulfed her at his offer. She was appalled at how intense that panic had been. The thought of being sent back to Shropshire had been unbearable. She could not exactly say why, except that now she was alive again, with a future, and she did not want to give that up.

"Over there," said his lordship, inclining his head slightly, "is the first gentleman of Europe—behind the high-stepping Hanoverian creams."

Jeannie tried not to stare at the Prince Regent, but she was curious to see the man who had been Papa's friend. What she saw caused a frown to form on her forehead. She turned unbelieving eyes to his lordship. "That—that is the Regent?"

Trenton nodded.

"But—but he's fat!"

"Softly," said his lordship with a cynical smile. "We do not notice that. It is impolitic to do so."

Jeannie's frown deepened. To her the Regent did not seem worthy of any regard. His waistcoat was so tight that it looked as if the buttons might pop at any moment.

"And here, with the beaky nose, is Petersham."

84

"I do not like big noses," said Jeannie, managing a smile as she realized that the Viscount presented a far more royal figure than the Regent.

"There—with the great smile—is Alvanley of the celebrated apricot tarts."

"Oh yes," cried Jeannie. "I remember Mama speaking of him. She thought apricot tarts every night in the year was a little expensive, but I suppose that Papa lost more—" She stopped suddenly.

His lordship gave her a warm smile. "You forget. I have been on the town these many years. I was acquainted with your papa."

"So you know—"

He nodded. "I know that your papa was fond of gaming—excessively fond. That is why I told you to caution your brother."

Jeannie nodded, suddenly unable to speak.

Her thoughts were interrupted by the sound of a brisk hallo. "Trenton! There you are!"

Looking out from beneath her great bonnet, Jeannie saw a huge man astride a sturdy roan fall into place beside the barouche. He looked around Trenton's age or a little older.

"Verdon!" Intense pleasure was reflected on his lordship's face. This man must be his friend.

"When did you return to the city?" Verdon asked the Viscount.

"Just a few days ago." Trenton looked around. "It's difficult to talk in this crush. Let's move off the road."

Verdon nodded and moved out of the press of people. Trenton lifted the reins and the barouche slowly followed. As they reached his friend, his lordship spoke. "Come into the barouche. It's easier to talk."

With a smile Verdon dismounted and hoisted himself into the carriage. He was a big man, Jeannie saw, much bigger even than the Viscount, but he handled his bulk with grace.

"So you have returned," commented Verdon with a smile, "and are now the talk of the town."

"I?" Trenton's eyebrow shot up quizzically.

"You," replied Verdon.

His eyes met Jeannie's and she felt their friendly warmth. She already liked this man.

"And what does the *ton* find about me that is worth discussing?" Trenton's eyes gleamed with mischief.

"What!" exclaimed Verdon. "You sit here beside this lovely creature—a woman who eloped with you— and you ask what all London is buzzing about?"

Trenton laughed. "I collect that no one expected me to go off like this. But come, it's time you met the object of my affections." He turned to Jeannie with a smile that quite took her breath away. "My love, this is my closest friend, the Marquess of Verdon. Beware of him. His reputation is second to mine."

"Trenton! You will make the young lady afraid of me."

"Indeed not, milord." Jeannie smiled at the great man. "It is easy to see that you and his lordship deal famously with each other. Since you are *his* friend, I shall also take you for mine."

The Marquess bent low over her gloved hand. *"Enchanté."*

"You speak French?" asked Jeannie.

The Viscount scowled and Jeannie realized that again she had said something wrong, but the Marquess guffawed. "She's a rare one, Trenton. A real innocent." He turned to Jeannie. "All the *ton* speak French, or affect to. It marks us as belonging."

Jeannie nodded. "Although I am just a country

86

girl," she said, "I am aware of the current fashion for all things French. My Aunt Dizzy—Desdemona—loved French novels and she insisted that I learn the language. My question to your lordship was merely for the sake of finding a conversationalist. A language left unpracticed is soon lost."

"You are quite right, miss," declared Verdon with a rueful shake of his great blond head. "I fear that whatever French I was once in possession of—Trenton and I made the Grand Tour together—has dwindled to a few pat phrases."

"That's too bad," Jeannie said, swiftly noting the Viscount's look of consternation. "I had hoped to keep my language active."

The Marquess smiled. "Perhaps Mademoiselle will give me language lessons. Thus we might both benefit."

"A famous idea," agreed Jeannie. "But be warned. I am a strict teacher."

"I shall suffer happily at your hands," remarked the Marquess gallantly.

Jeannie stifled a chuckle, feeling suddenly very young and alive. His lordship's friend was an enjoyable companion. Life in London was proving better than her expectations.

The Viscount consulted his timepiece. "I am sorry, Verdon, but we must return home. I have just remembered an important appointment."

Jeannie flashed him a look of surprise, then quickly hid it. There had been no mention of an impending appointment when they had left St. James's Square.

The Marquess either did not notice her surprise or chose to ignore it. "Of course, my friend." He bent over Jeannie's hand. "I shall call tomorrow to begin our lessons."

"That will be great fun," replied Jeannie, giving him a smile.

Verdon heaved himself out of the barouche and swung up onto his patiently waiting roan. "Until to-morrow."

"Until tomorrow," echoed Jeannie, and was rather startled to find that the Viscount had already lifted the reins and the barouche was moving off. She turned to him. "I did not know that you had an appointment."

"You do not yet know everything about me," he said dryly. "Besides, the appointment had slipped my mind."

"I see." Jeannie felt thoroughly subdued. "I—I did not mean to overreach myself."

"My pretense of living in your pocket will hardly pass scrutiny," he said curtly, "if you take so freely to flirtations among the *ton*."

Jeannie stared at him in amazement. "I—flirtation? With whom?"

His lordship laughed, a harsh, almost cruel laugh. "With whom? Did you not offer to teach the Marquess French?"

Jeannie nodded. "Of course I did. You just heard me do so. But it was a legitimate offer."

"And will necessitate his calling upon you daily, I collect."

"Do you wish me to refuse to receive him?" cried Jeannie indignantly. "I shall do so if you wish it."

The Viscount scowled. "Of course I do not wish you to do such a thing. Verdon is my friend. Just do not behave as though you were a schoolroom chit at her come out. Have a little sense of propriety."

"Indeed, milord," cried Jeannie, by now thoroughly incensed, "I am sorry to have offended you by being polite to your friend. In the future I shall attempt to be ruder."

"Nonsense!" The Viscount cast her a bitter glance.

"Stop behaving like a stupid moonling. You are soon to become a Viscountess. Kindly keep that in mind."

"Yes, milord." Jeannie's back was ramrod straight and she faced ahead, but inside she was seething. How could she live with such a man—a cruel, thoughtless brute. Just because *he* had known half the women in London was no reason to suspect her, no reason to behave like a jealous husband.

Huh! Jeannie thought angrily. How amusing! To think that the greatest rakeshame in London should behave like a Jerry-sneak. But of course it was not *her* that he cared about; it was his good name.

CHAPTER EIGHT

By the next afternoon Jeannie's temper had subsided. She supposed that a proud man like his lordship would be touchy about how society viewed him.

She rose suddenly and began to pace about the sitting room. Of course she would never consider caring for any man. Friendship—that was all she had to offer. Friendship—for London's greatest rakeshame?

Aimlessly she paced back and forth, back and forth, across the patterned carpet. Jeremy should be here soon. She wanted to see him, but she dreaded it too. She must tell him very plainly that his lordship would not stand for any more of his debts, but she was terribly fearful of how he would behave.

Why, she thought dismally, did people have to change? She and Jeremy had been so close, almost like one person. Now a part of her seemed to be missing. She sighed.

"Your brother, miss," said Budner, breaking into her reverie.

"Oh! Show him in."

She pulled nervously at her borrowed dress of blue muslin. Then he was in the doorway. "Jeremy!"

He strode across the room. "I have brought my list. His lordship hasn't had a change of heart, has he?" He asked the question jovially, but Jeannie saw the anxiety in his eyes.

"No, he hasn't changed his mind," she hastened to reassure her twin. "Just give me the list, and they will all be paid."

Jeremy reached in his pocket and produced a paper. "It's more like twelve hundred pounds," he said, watching her carefully.

"Give it to me," Jeannie repeated. "He will pay them."

Jeremy laughed. "You have caught yourself a fine one—well-larded, so I hear."

"His lordship has sufficient substance," said Jeannie, wishing she did not sound so stiff. "But Jeremy, you must listen—"

"Yes," Jeremy continued, "how fortunate that so much blunt should accompany love." He sighed. "In my case I fear it's just the opposite."

"You are in love?" asked Jeannie.

Jeremy nodded. "A Miss Nancy Brockton. I met her since my last letter to you. She's an enchanting creature, Jeannie. You would adore her. But her father has fallen into bad times and cannot afford much in the way of a dowry."

"But if you love her," Jeannie began.

Jeremy snorted. "Love is one thing. Money is another. I'll never marry the girl. It'll be old hatchet-face or someone like her, I don't doubt."

"But Jeremy, you can't! Not Lady Margaret."

Her twin rounded on her. "Listen, Jeannie, the world is different than we thought. It's not one great lark like we believed when we were youngsters traipsing around Shropshire. The world is hard, and people are out to get you. They can't be trusted."

"Jeremy!" How could her twin be saying such terrible things? "You don't mean that."

"Don't mean it?" His face twisted in a harsh grimace. "I've seen men who professed to be my best

92

friends set me up as a pigeon for the Greeks to take. I tell you, Jeannie, you can't trust anyone."

Jeannie shook her head. "Jeremy, you mustn't think like that. How about that girl? The one you love?"

Jeremy scowled. "She's just like the others—on the scramble after a fortune. Without the blunt she can't be had."

"Oh, Jeremy, don't be so harsh on her. Girls must be careful when they marry."

Jeremy did not answer her, but she knew that he did not agree.

"There's no point in my talking to *you*," he sneered. "It's easy for you to give out advice. You've got the love *and* the blunt." He started angrily to his feet and made for the door. "Just give your betrothed my thanks."

"Jeremy!" Jeannie knew the timing was all wrong, but she had to convey his lordship's message.

Her twin swung on his heel and glared at her. "I have an appointment."

With difficulty Jeannie held back her tears. "I will not hold you long, Jeremy. It's just that—" For a moment her voice failed her. "That his lordship said—" She took another deep breath. "This is all he will pay. Don't—don't contract any more gambling debts. He won't pay any more." She clasped her hands together to still their trembling.

"I see," said Jeremy, biting off each word. "His lordship's love for you is measurable."

"Jer—"

But he was already gone. For a moment Jeannie sat quietly, in paralyzed silence. If Jeremy knew how near he had come to the truth—His lordship did not love her at all, but he was a gentleman and he kept his word. Harsh and cruel as he could be, he would never behave as Jeremy had.

The tears that she had been holding back suddenly overflowed from Jeannie's eyes. What sort of man had Jeremy become? Her twin was in trouble, a great deal of trouble, and she could not help him this time. For the problem was not the debt, the problem lay deep within Jeremy himself. Only he could change it. She lowered her head into her hands and gave herself up to her sobs.

She was so lost in her grief that she did not know anyone had entered the room until she felt the divan beside her sink under the weight of another body. "Here, here," said the Viscount's deep voice. "I thought you assured me that you were not a watering pot." He pushed a clean cambric handkerchief into her fingers.

"Th-thank you," Jeannie stammered. "I—I really do not cry often."

His lordship's dark eyes regarded her seriously. "Something has upset you. What is it?"

The harsh, brutal man of the previous afternoon might never have existed. This man was gentle and kind.

Jeannie did not hesitate to confide in him. It seemed the natural thing to do. After all, she was to live with him. "It's—it's Jeremy. He's changed so much." She shook her head. "I hardly know him."

Trenton frowned. "He's a confirmed gamester. Once a man falls willingly into the hands of the Greeks— We have extricated him this time, but unless he finds an heiress—and with his reputation he is not likely to—he's going to be in the briars again." He regarded her sternly. "You know that, don't you?"

Jeannie nodded.

"It's for that reason that I told you to warn him that I would only do this once. You did tell him so, didn't you?"

94

"Yes," replied Jeannie. "I told him—"

"But you do not think he will heed you?"

She nodded again.

"Now listen to me carefully. After our wedding you will have some pin money. I forbid you to give any of it to your brother. In fact, to keep you from temptation, I shall open accounts for you. You may order what you please, but you will have no blunt that he can get from you. I do this for your own protection. Do you see that?"

Jeannie nodded miserably. "But he's my twin!"

"And I am to be your husband," Trenton declared firmly. "Your allegiance and your obedience are due me, are they not?"

His eyes held hers and seemed to force her to agree.

His hand reached out to grasp one of hers. A strange sensation raced up her spine at his touch. "Listen to me, Jeannie. Our marriage may be one of convenience, but that does not mean that I shall not fulfill my duties as your husband. One of those duties, as I see it, is to protect you from your brother's importunities. If he knows you have nothing to give him, he will cease asking.

"Now come, hurry along to Lady Helena and borrow another bonnet and shawl. After dinner we are going to Vauxhall. That will brighten your spirits, won't it?"

Jeannie nodded, but then she remembered. "Oh, Jeremy left his list of debtors and—" Her voice failed her once more.

"And they amount to more than he said. Considerably more," he added, watching the expression on her face.

"Yes."

"Forget Jeremy and his debts," said Trenton cheerfully. "Think of yourself for a change. Quick, wash your face and speak to Lady Helena. I will have dinner served early."

Jeannie managed a tremulous smile. "You are very kind to me."

His lordship seemed surprised. "Nonsense. I simply treat you as another human being. One has certain duties to his position in life."

Jeannie bowed her head. Of course. It was his pride in himself rather than any concern for her that had prompted this talk. And of course it was his money in question. Yet, there had been concern in his eyes—

There would be time to speculate later. She rose hastily. "I'll speak to Lady Helena about a bonnet and a shawl. And perhaps another dress."

Trenton smiled. "That dress goes admirably with the gold of your hair, but change if you wish." His eyes sparkled. "Ask Lady Helena for the cashmere I brought her from India, and a smaller bonnet, one that will not make you a hazard to those around you." His smile took the sting out of his words.

Jeannie grinned, feeling suddenly lighthearted. "Yes, milord."

Several hours later Jeannie descended the wide staircase. She was wearing a borrowed gown of pale green jaconet. "To match your eyes," Lady Helena had said. Perched on her curls was a small bonnet of a darker hue. Her hands were clad in a pair of new kid gloves, delivered that day. The cashmere shawl, so soft that she wanted to keep rubbing it against her cheek, was thrown over her arm.

"His lordship is in the library," announced Budner. "I will tell him that Miss is ready."

Jeannie nodded. She could hardly remember their dinner. Puzzling over the nature of the Viscount's feelings for her had kept her quiet and subdued. Fortunately, Lady Helena had been as vivacious as usual, pursuing various topics of conversation as though she were a butterfly flitting from flower to flower.

Now, as Budner disappeared down the richly panelled hall, Jeannie's heart began to thud. How could she spend the evening alone with his lordship? What were they to talk of during all that time? True, she had been alone with him often before, but things were not the same now. He seemed different—a stranger, an enigma, and yet he was to be the center of her life, her husband.

A brisk knock on the door caused her to jump, startled, and without thinking she hastened to open it. A beaming Marquess of Verdon stood there, resplendent in sartorial glory, his cravat a monument to ingenuity. "Ah," he said with an amused smile. "You make quite a charming butler."

"Oh!" Jeannie, now aware of the impropriety of her actions, took a step backward as though to shut the door again.

"Please do not exclude me from your charming company," implored Verdon. "And besides, it is too late. Trenton has already found you out."

Jeannie swung around to discover his lordship and the butler, both wearing expressions of obvious displeasure, his lordship's somewhat more pronounced since he was making little effort to conceal it. She pressed a gloved hand to her burning cheek. Why did she continue to do such stupid things that obviously annoyed a man of Trenton's sophistication?

His lordship chose to ignore her behavior. "Well, Verdon, and what brings you here at this time of evening?"

The Marquess looked surprised. "I have come to call."

"Indeed."

There was a strange tone to the Viscount's voice, a tone almost of—anger? It must be his anger at her, Jeannie concluded. He had no cause to be angry with his friend.

"Sorry," Trenton continued, "but as you see, we are going out."

"Ah yes," said the Marquess, his eyes on the still flushed Jeannie. "You are going out to show off this ravishing creature. Half the men of the *ton* will be cast into despair to think that they did not find her first."

A half-hysterical giggle escaped Jeannie's throat. How silly the Marquess could be! "Really, milord, you are spoiling me."

"What?" cried Verdon with an exaggerated look of surprise at his friend. "Do you mean to say that Trenton does not fill your ears with such delicacies?"

Jeannie was about to shake her head when the scowl on Trenton's face recalled her to the fiction of their love match. She tossed her curls to cover her confusion. "Of course, but then he loves me."

"Ah," said the Marquess, rolling his eyes dramatically. "But he is not alone. Soon all the world—the male world—will love you."

Jeannie giggled again. Verdon was such an extravagant beau that he was amusing. Of course, she didn't believe a word he said, but she certainly liked hearing it.

"Verdon." The anger in his lordship's tone was even more apparent and belatedly Jeannie remembered their quarrel of the day before. But it seemed incredible that this foolish banter should annoy him. If a woman wished to have an intrigue with a man, she would hardly begin it right before the eyes of her affianced.

"Verdon, you must excuse us. We are just on our way and cannot delay any longer."

"Of course, my friend, of course." The Marquess's eyes sparkled at Jeannie. It hardly seemed possible that he was not aware of his friend's anger. Indeed, he seemed to be deliberately provoking it. "How fortunate that I have nothing special in mind for this evening. Therefore I am free to accompany you and the young lady on your excursion to Vauxhall."

Jeannie gasped audibly, and the Viscount glared at her. Her first impulse was to deny that *she* had told Verdon their destination, but it was obvious from the fierce set of Trenton's eyebrows that he would not believe her. However Verdon had discovered it, the Viscount would lay the deed at her door.

"Trenton, the *ton* is all abuzz about you. You are not yet even leg-shackled, and you are literally living in her pocket. What a Jerry-sneak you are becoming. Come now, man, do not glower at me as though you were ready to call me out. You know you will not do that. No amount of passion for a woman will cause you to turn on your oldest friend."

The Marquess's tone was bright and airy. Jeannie saw the Viscount's face lighten slowly, but her shocked heart was pounding so hard that her ears did not register Trenton's reply. Passion! The Marquess *had* said passion. Surely Trenton did not feel passion for *her*.

Her head was in such a whirl that Jeannie hardly noticed as she was helped into the carriage by Trenton. As Verdon settled his bulk on the squabs opposite her, he smiled affably. "How fortunate you are, my dear. Here you are—off to Vauxhall Gardens with London's two most eligible connections. Tomorrow every young lady of the *ton* will sigh to be in your shoes."

Jeannie giggled again, unable to help herself. Some of the tension within her began to fade. "Indeed, milord. You mistake me. I am just a country miss. I'm sure the young ladies are all better dressed and much more sophisticated than I."

The Marquess smiled, a charming smile. "Indeed, sophistication is not always to be desired. Sometimes innocence is quite an interesting attribute. An innocent young woman—ahhhhh!" The Marquess rolled his eyes again, in the French fashion.

"Verdon, you forget yourself. The young lady is not experienced in the ways of intrigue. She *is* innocent." The Viscount looked hard at his friend. "I trust you will do nothing to alter that condition."

The Marquess laughed. "I! Trenton, my boy. You know me better than that. I shall be your little bride's chief gallant. Thus I shall keep all other admirers at a distance and preserve her in her state of purity."

"Indeed, I shall count on you to do precisely that," observed his lordship dryly with another hard look at his friend.

Jeannie, perceiving the exchange of glances, began to bristle. It was annoying to be discussed as though she were not even present. It reduced her to the status of a child—a condition unfitting to her position as the Viscount's bride.

"I will thank you not to put yourself out for me," she said stiffly. "I can quite take care of myself."

The Viscount snorted. "I think, my love, that you have forgotten certain events in your recent past."

Jeannie glared at him. "I am not a green girl, and I'll thank you to remember that."

A strange smile curved the Viscount's mouth, and his hand reached out to cover hers in a warm grasp.

"Indeed, my love. I above all men should know that you are not a child."

. Jeannie felt an insane urge to pull her hand out of his and slap him. He had no right to laugh at her like this. She glared at him.

"Come, my love." His hand tightened on hers and his other arm stole around her shoulders possessively. Jeannie felt a shiver run down her spine at his touch, but with Verdon watching she dared not pull away. She was to be his wife; she must learn to bear his touch.

She decided to change her tactics. She did owe him something; he had helped Jeremy. "Yes, my love." She smiled up at him and leaned against his shoulder. The Viscount's eyes reflected first surprise and then amusement. He squeezed her shoulder.

Verdon laughed. "Come, come, you two. It's quite plain that you're top-over-tail in love. But you needn't be nauseating about it."

The Viscount chuckled. "One of these days," he observed dryly, "you, too, will succumb to Cupid's arrows."

The Marquess smiled enigmatically. "Perhaps," he agreed. "I do begin to think that that possibility exists."

CHAPTER NINE

As they approached the Gardens, more and more carriages surrounded theirs. "It seems that many people are of your opinion that this is a capital night for the Gardens," observed the Marquess.

"Yes," agreed Trenton. "So it appears."

Jeannie looked around her with interest. Verdon alighted from the carriage and reached up a gloved hand to help her down. Unconsciously Jeannie looked toward Trenton for permission and then scolded herself for doing so. He had no right to order her about, not yet anyway. Still, she was pleased to have his almost imperceptible nod before she laid her hand in that of the Marquess. In a rage, he was not pleasant to deal with and since she was to be his wife, it was well to keep that in mind.

In a moment Trenton, too, had climbed down, and, after a word to the coachman, stepped up to them. "Here, my love," he said, his deep voice seeming to caress her. "Your cashmere is slipping. Let me adjust it."

The shawl had not slipped at all as far as Jeannie could tell, but she managed to mask her surprise as his fingers reached under her hair and touched the nape of her neck. Again a shiver traveled down her spine. With greater difficulty she masked her feelings and managed to stand still.

His lordship finished adjusting the shawl and touched her cheek lightly with a finger. The smile that he gave her then was enough to make her bones melt. She knew that all this was for Verdon's eyes and it annoyed her. Trenton was right; he could play the lovesmitten swain to perfection. She did not like it.

Then he tucked her arm through his and turned to his friend. "Well, Verdon, since you have insisted on intruding on our excursion, suppose you direct us now."

"Of course, my friend. I propose that we stroll first to the orchestra. I understand that the musicians are capital this year, and there's a sweet little singer there." He smiled laconically. "She has a lovely voice."

"Oh, of course," observed Trenton. "It is the *voice* that you admire."

"Of course," agreed Verdon, chuckling. "But come you two, let us stroll."

As the Marquess slipped her free arm through his, Jeannie felt Trenton's arm tighten, but he did not comment on this liberty by his friend.

"Look," she cried in an effort to divert his attention. "The lanterns! So many, and so many colors."

"Yes," agreed the Viscount. "They are quite lovely. Thirty-seven thousand of them, so I hear."

"Who is on that one over there?" asked Jeannie. "The pink one with the figure in black."

Verdon followed her look. "That's a representation of Kean as Hamlet. You'll have to see him. He is quite singular in the part."

"I should like that," said Jeannie.

"*I* will arrange it," replied Trenton. Again his tone was angry.

"Come," cried Verdon. "It nears eight. The orchestra will soon begin."

Together they moved down the gaily lit path. As

they rounded the bend and the orchestra stand came into view, Jeannie gasped at the dazzling beauty. The gaily colored lanterns hung everywhere, festooning the rails of the balconies that protruded from the gilded shell, and sending a soft rainbow glow over the scene.

"It is so beautiful," she breathed. "So shining and beautiful."

Before either gentleman could reply, the orchestra began to play. As the strains of the music moved out over the crowd, Jeannie felt the Viscount draw closer to her side. Casting a glance at him, she saw that the line of his jaw had tightened.

Then a pretty young woman with bright red hair and a soft pink mouth moved out to the front of the orchestra. Her dark, sparkling eyes swept over the crowd and seemed to settle for a moment on the Marquess. An engaging smile curved her lips before her glance moved on.

"I see that the lady has already made your acquaintance," observed the Viscount with a cynical smile.

Verdon shrugged. "A man must have his amusements, and she is a refreshing young thing."

"The benefits of innocence?" suggested the Viscount, again in a cynical tone.

The Marquess chuckled. "That piece has not been innocent since she reached the ripe old age of five."

This conversation, thought Jeannie, had gone rather far. "May I remind you, gentlemen, that I am still—innocent?"

The Viscount's grip on her arm tightened almost painfully. "Of course, my love. You must excuse us. We have been on the town so long that we forget ourselves. We shall be more circumspect, shall we not, Verdon?"

"Indeed, I would never wish to offend your bride-to-be. My apologies, Miss Burnstead."

In spite of the grave formality of their words, Jeannie could not overcome the feeling that they were laughing at her. The memory of her conversations with Trenton came back to haunt her.

Fortunately, when the song was over Verdon spoke. "Shall we show your lady the rotunda and the attached rooms and perhaps stroll down to the river?"

"Agreed," said Trenton, and the three of them moved off.

They had not gone far, however, when there was the sound of hurrying footsteps behind them. "Milord!" called a soft, feminine voice. Both men disengaged their arms and turned. Jeannie swung around too.

The little singer was hurrying toward them. Jeannie cast sidelong glances at both men, but their faces remained impassive. She wondered how the Marquess would react to this little chat with his former inamorata.

"Milord," repeated the soft voice, but it was to Trenton that the words were addressed. Jeannie held her breath.

"Milord," repeated the singer. She was even more lovely up close. She laid a small beringed hand on Trenton's arm. Her touch was like a caress, thought Jeannie with a lump in her throat, as if she had touched him before—many times.

Suddenly Jeannie could stand it no longer. Both the Viscount and the Marquess were busy; neither seemed to notice as she slipped down the path, moving swiftly among the slowly strolling couples, driven by blind instinct away from the sight of Trenton and a woman who had been—perhaps still was—his incognita.

As she hurried down the brightly lighted path, Jeannie sought frantically for some place to hide her misery, some place where no one could observe her give way to the sobs of grief that threatened to engulf her. Rushing along, she saw that one of the paths seemed more dimly lit, and without thinking, she turned into it and hurried on.

There were fewer people here. Jeannie's hurried steps slowed. Yes, this was a good place, a quiet place. She had no thought for Trenton's reaction on finding her gone. Her only concern was to compose herself so that the man soon to become her husband would not see her distress. She could not stand there and watch that terrible creature touch him in such a personal way. Yet she had no reason to feel like this. Theirs was purely a business arrangement. It was only the shame, she told herself. When they were married, would she be forced to stand by when his former incognitas accosted him? Had she gone from one bad situation to another?

It was obvious to her what the singer had been—or more likely, still was—to him. She was so beautiful, Jeannie thought dismally as she sank upon a conveniently placed stone bench. There was no way she could compete with such a woman, a woman who knew how to please a man. She let her head fall into her hands as she fought to control her tears.

She was behaving so badly lately. Every day she ended up crying like a baby. She, who hardly ever cried, had become a literal watering pot. It would have to stop, Jeannie told herself sternly. With effort she managed to control her tears. She wiped furtively at her face and pushed at her hair. Hopefully, in this light the Viscount would not notice anything amiss.

She had better make her way back to the others.

Trenton might be annoyed with her for vanishing. The realization threatened to bring fresh tears, but she held them back.

She raised her head and looked around. Two young men were approaching. One smiled at the other. "A lady alone," he observed.

"Yes, alone."

Jeannie rose. It had suddenly occurred to her that this was not a safe place to be. It was too dark, and there were too few people.

She moved back in the direction she had come, but the way was narrow and as she hurried around a bend she almost ran into another man. His beaver was cocked rakishly over one eye, and Jeannie's nostrils told her immediately that he had been drinking.

"Let me by, sir," she implored, but the buck simply smiled at her. It was not a pleasant smile, and Jeannie realized with a sinking feeling that leaving her escorts had been a bad mistake.

She wheeled and started back in the other direction, but the two swells were waiting for her. "Come with us, miss," said one, grabbing her arm in a tight grip.

"No! Let me go!" Jeannie struggled to free herself, but the man's grip on her arm could not be loosened. "Let me go!" she repeated.

The man who held her laughed. "Don't give us any of those Banbury tales. We know your kind—you're just another dasher, that's all you are. We're as good as any other fellows."

"No!" Jeannie protested, her heart in her throat. "I'm not—I'm not one of those."

But the bucks paid her no heed.

As the other man grabbed her free arm, and they began to hurry her off down the path, panic overtook her and a piercing scream ripped from her throat. The two men stopped in surprise at this unusual circumstance. While they stood regarding her in amazement, the Marquess burst from around the turning.

Calmly he regarded the two bucks. "The lady belongs with me," he said evenly. "Do you gentlemen care to dispute the fact?"

Without a word the two dropped Jeannie's arms and scurried off to safety. Jeannie felt her knees begin to give way. The Marquess was there instantly, his arms giving her badly needed support. She leaned thankfully against his bulk. "Thank you," she murmured into his waistcoat. "I was terribly frightened."

The Marquess patted her back comfortingly. "There now, you should know better than to venture into the Dark Walks alone."

"The Dark Walks?" Jeannie repeated in confusion, still leaning against him. "I do not know what the Dark Walks are."

The Marquess chuckled. "You *are* an innocent."

"I trust she will remain that way." The Viscount's voice, loaded with sarcasm, caused Jeannie to jump free of the Marquess's arms. "So this is where you went," declared Trenton, his hard eyes searching her face. Jeannie was about to tell him what had happened when she realized that she could not. How could she say that the sight of another woman touching him had driven her off in a panic? And now he had come upon her in his best friend's arms.

The Marquess regarded his friend with his usual aplomb. "I perceived that Miss Burnstead had been separated from us, and as I was searching for her, I heard her scream. Two rascals were assaulting her here."

"In the Dark Walks," commented his lordship in tones that dripped sarcasm.

"I will remind *you* that she is from the country. She had no idea where she had strayed to."

The Marquess's tone was still calm and even, as though he were reasoning with a recalcitrant child, but Trenton did not seem convinced. "You both disappear while I am being accosted by your former inamorata, and I find you together in the Dark Walks. All this I am to put down to the effects of ignorance."

The Marquess shrugged. "Come, man, have you ever known me to be a liar? The lightskirt thought she could get you to prevail with me to renew our alliance. Or perhaps she thought to find herself a new protector. Rather an original approach, was it not?"

Jeannie held her breath as she waited for his lordship's reply. It dismayed her that she should be the cause of dissension between these two lifelong friends.

She forced herself to move forward and lay a tentative hand on the Viscount's arm. "Please, milord, those men frightened me. Could we go back and rest in a booth for a while? Perhaps I might have a glass of lemonade."

The harsh lines of the Viscount's face softened a little. "Of course. Do you feel able to walk?"

Jeannie nodded. "Yes, milord. I am not hurt, only frightened." She could not prevent a shudder. "I did not know about these walks."

"We will drop the subject," said Trenton in a tone that chilled her. He did not believe her or Verdon—that much was clear from his tone—but he was a gentleman and would concern himself with her comfort.

As they moved back toward the lights, Jeannie railed at herself. What an addlepated fool she was. The girl had not been attached to Trenton, and she had angered him by running off like that. For the hundredth time Jeannie wished she had not lashed out at him as she had that day. She could not really blame him if he

110

suspected her of believing in—free love! After all, she had not denied it.

Trenton led her back toward the pavilion. Fortunately, a look at the Marquess prevented him from taking her free arm. Jeannie found that her knees were still trembling, and she leaned a little more heavily on the Viscount.

They soon reached the rows of booths. "Shall we continue to the pavilion or should you prefer a private booth?" asked Trenton.

"If you please, milord, let us rest here for a little."

"We can go directly home if you are ill," Trenton suggested.

"No, milord. Please," Jeannie forced herself to be calm. "I do want to see the fireworks. After a little rest I will be quite recovered."

Trenton cast her a dark look and Jeannie realized belatedly that she should have asked to go home. That might have convinced him of the truth of her story. But then again, he seemed determined to suspect everything she did. And all because he was so proud of his name.

The men settled her into a seat and seated themselves. "Would you care for anything else?" inquired Trenton politely. "Perhaps some ham or a syllabub?"

"The lady asked for lemonade," volunteered the Marquess, only to be met by an annoyed frown.

Jeannie suppressed a sigh. She much preferred the lemonade, but if it would please the Viscount—"I believe I will try the syllabub. Thank you, milord."

A small band of musicians stationed nearby began to play. As the soft strains of a violin drifted through the summer air, her eyes stole of their own accord to the face of the Viscount, giving the waiter instructions. If only he really loved her, Jeannie thought miserably, then all of this might make some sense. But

111

to get so angry just because he thought his precious name was in jeopardy—what foolishness!

As they waited for their food, Jeannie let her eyes drift over the crowd. Here and there the sight of a young woman leaning heavily on a young man's arm and looking up at him with adoring eyes made her tears threaten again. She turned her attention instead to the fashionable ladies in the throng. She would be expected to move among these ladies—and to hold her own with them.

Jeannie studied them. They moved with grace, their muslin gowns clinging to them. Perhaps some of them actually did damp their petticoats to make their gowns cling. One woman with jet-black hair, her gown of cream color silk, with a low neck, short sleeves, and a draped tunic edged in gold braid, moved with utmost confidence, swaying provocatively. Looking at her, Jeannie was a little surprised to discover that even in her borrowed finery she felt almost dowdy. But this was certainly foolish, she told herself severely.

Then, as Jeannie watched, the woman approached their booth. As she drew closer, it was easy to see that she was no longer young—being nearer thirty than twenty. Yet she was still exceedingly beautiful, and she knew it. The fact was proclaimed by every swaying step she took.

The man on whose arm she was leaning, an older man with graying hair, seemed to be disagreeing with her about something. They reached the booth. "Verdon, you rascal," said the woman, her eyes alight, "don't tell me you have taken up with a new frail. What happened to the tender little singer?"

The Marquess seemed about to make a reply, but he was prevented by Trenton. "Good evening, Lady Frances. Lord Pritchard." The Viscount's voice was evenly polite, as though he had not heard the lady's opening remark. "I wish to present my intended, Miss Burnstead."

Jeannie found herself being regarded by a pair of cold eyes. With effort she forced herself to meet them.

Finally Lady Frances turned to Trenton. "You disappoint me, milord. When I heard you were dangling after a wife, I supposed that you had lost your heart to a charmer, but it appears that you have lost your mind instead. This is an infant."

"Frances, my dear," expostulated Lord Pritchard.

"Be quiet," she snapped. "I did not ask for your opinion. By the way, Trenton, I believe you left something of yours during your last—visit. Perhaps you will stop by and pick it up." Her eyes regarded him with frank invitation, and Jeannie wanted to scream. Here was another woman with myriad ways of pleasing a man. It was plain that Trenton had been hers—and still would be if the lady had her way.

"Perhaps I shall," Trenton observed dryly. "I shall see."

Lady Frances smiled, and Jeannie shivered.

"Until then, milord." Lady Frances's eyes swept idly over Jeannie and settled provocatively on Verdon. "You, too, are welcome to call."

"My thanks, your ladyship, but I have but lately fallen prey to Cupid's arrows and so have deserted my previous regrettable ways."

Lady Francis laughed, a light trilling laugh that struck Jeannie as highly artificial. "Very good, Verdon, very good indeed. That's the most amusing thing I've heard in many months." With a word to her escort, she moved off.

When she was out of earshot, the Marquess chuckled dryly. "Lady Frances, my friend? Whatever possessed you to become embroiled with the likes of her? I suppose you were the one to break it off, too. You should know that the lady reserves that prerogative to herself."

"Verdon," said the Viscount coldly, "I will thank you to leave the subject. Such talk is ill-suited to Miss Burnstead's ears."

The Marquess regarded Jeannie. "I tender my apologies, Miss Burnstead. I had no desire to offend."

"Of course, you didn't," Jeannie agreed. "You are quite forgiven, but if you please, I have heard quite enough of both of your amorous adventures. Could you not speak of something else?"

"Of course," replied Verdon gallantly. "Of what should you like me to speak?"

For a moment Jeannie was nonplussed. She considered suggesting a French lesson, but that too had annoyed the Viscount.

"Have you purchased any good horses lately?" she asked finally.

For a long moment the Marquess stared at her in surprise, and then he burst into laughter. "You are a connoisseur of horseflesh?"

Jeannie smiled. "Not exactly, but my uncle Obadiah loves horses. He taught Jeremy, my twin, and Jeremy taught me. I love to ride."

"Did you observe the Regent's Hanoverian creams yesterday in the park?"

"Yes," Jeannie replied. "Such beauties."

The Marquess nodded. "But I have a roan filly. What a high-stepper. I'd be honored to have you ride her."

Jeannie was about to nod enthusiastically, but a glance at the Viscount changed her mind. He was scowling again. "I think not, milord," she replied as gently as she could. "I believe there are other matters to which I must apply myself before the wedding."

She was rewarded for this sacrifice by a perceptible

lessening of the Viscount's frown. Whatever made him behave so strangely? He seemed quite determined to alienate his friend, for what reason she could not begin to guess.

At this point the waiter arrived and Jeannie addressed herself to her syllabub.

There was little conversation as they ate what was placed before them. They were just finishing when a bell began to ring.

"I collect that is the bell for the fireworks," said Trenton. "Shall we move to where we can see them?"

"Yes, milord." Meekly Jeannie allowed him to help her out of the seat. Again his fingers moved to adjust her shawl and, there was no mistaking it this time, they lingered overlong on the nape of her neck. If she had not known better, Jeannie thought, she might have supposed that touch to be a caress.

Then he was tucking her arm through his, and they followed the throng of people. The fireworks were quite spectacular. Jeannie watched the whirling pinwheels and the brilliant showers of red, blue, green, and gold that fell from the sky, but her senses were still attuned to the touch of warm fingers on the nape of her neck and she remonstrated with herself. This stirring of feeling within her was unwarranted and foolish.

As they made their way back to the long line of carriages, when the men settled her inside, and even during the ride home, Jeannie attended to their remarks with only half an ear. She was busy trying to convince herself of the truth of her former reflections. When they reached the house on St. James's Square, the Viscount handed her out and turned to his friend. "Come inside, Verdon, and have a nightcap. I've a thing or two to discuss with you."

"Of course," replied the Marquess. "Quite at your service."

Jeannie was escorted up the walk and into the house by the two men. At the foot of the stairs Trenton stopped. "I think you had best seek your bed, my love. From the look of your eyes the syllabub was rather strongly laced with wine."

Jeannie was about to argue with him, but realized that this excused her silent behavior. Smiling demurely, she saw him lean toward her and knew his intent. But, perhaps because the Marquess was watching, or perhaps because the syllabub *had* been too heavily laced, or even perhaps—though she refused to admit it—because the place on her neck still throbbed from the touch of his fingers, she did not move to evade him. In the brief moment before his lips covered hers, Jeannie saw something strange in his eyes again. Then he was kissing her, tenderly and persuasively, and all her bones seemed to turn to water.

Finally the Viscount held her away. "Good night, my love. Sleep well," he said in a voice husky with tenderness.

"Goodnight, milord," she replied. Oh, thought Jeannie as she turned and slowly made her way up the great staircase, what a consummate actor he was. But as she donned her nightdress and crawled into bed, she thought only of his lips on hers, of his arms around her.

He knew how to stir a woman's senses, she told herself bitterly. And why not, considering the long years of practice he had had? But the stirring of her senses meant nothing. Surely it was just as well, since she was to bear this man's children, that she should not be repulsed by his kisses. No, thought Jeannie with a tremulous sigh, she did not find his kisses repulsive at all.

CHAPTER TEN

Several days passed after their excursion to Vauxhall and, though his lordship was invariably polite and attentive when Lady Helena or a servant was present, the moment he was alone with Jeannie his manner changed. He was usually only present at dinner. At other times when she inquired for him, she was informed by Budner that his lordship was out on business. This state of affairs left her feeling quite in the dismals and only the arrival of her new gowns served to raise her spirits.

They were beautiful creations, Jeannie realized with a wry smile. She, who last week had had no regard for clothes, now found them of infinite interest. With sparkling eyes she hurried from box to box, examining and exclaiming over them.

There were day dresses of spotted blue and rose cambric, sprigged green and yellow muslin, celestial blue striped silk, pale rose sarcenet. For evening there were the yellow silk, the hunter-green velvet, and the celestial blue satin, trimmed in deep purple. Jeannie ran a hand over the riding habit of blue velvet with its black military trimmings and pert hat of black beaver.

There was also her wedding dress—a robe of real Brussels point lace over white satin—and to go with it a white satin pelisse trimmed with swansdown and a deep lace veil. She stood for long moments, lost in the sight of it.

If it hadn't been for Lady Helena's insistence, she would have hung each gown in the wardrobe herself so as to be able to regard each one a little longer.

"And this," said Lady Helena with a smile, "was ordered by his lordship."

Jeannie found herself suddenly in need of a chair as she took the parcel in her hands. With trembling fingers she tore off the paper. "Why, it's your shawl!"

Lady Helena shook her head. "No. Mine is in my room. This one Trenton ordered especially for you."

Unbidden tears filled Jeannie's eyes. "It's beautiful," she whispered.

"I must hand it to you," said Lady Helena thoughtfully. "Trenton has changed."

Jeannie looked up, startled, the cashmere still against her cheek. "Changed? How?"

Lady Helena considered this for a moment, pulling at one dangling earring. "This gift, for instance. Of course he wants to see that you are suitably clothed."

"Oh!" Jeannie experienced a sense of disappointment. Why, she could not say.

"But I have never seen him so quiet and pensive. Yes, my dear"—Lady Helena smiled—"love is good for him. He will settle down now and think about the future. Soon, I hope, there will be the heirs our family desires."

Jeannie found herself coloring up. The thought of being the Viscount's wife made her breath come faster and her heart pound.

"Ah ha," said a deep voice from the doorway. "The gowns have arrived. Let me see."

Forcing herself to be nonchalant, Jeannie turned toward Trenton. Her heart skipped a beat at the sight of him, so tall and lean. He had evidently been out for a ride, for he wore his blue coat with brass buttons and his leather breeches. His top boots wore a slight film of dust, but his cravat did not seem to have lost any of its starch.

She wished that she were wearing one of the new gowns that she had just been admiring, perhaps the pale blue one. But it was too late to think of things like that.

Jeannie rose to meet him. "I must thank you for the shawl, milord. It is quite lovely."

The Viscount shrugged broad shoulders. "I thought that Helena's shawl was quite becoming to you on our excursion to Vauxhall the other night. And so I wished you to have one of your own. If you prefer another color or a different design—"

"Oh no!" Jeannie found herself clutching the shawl and tried to look more casual. "That is, milord, this one will do quite nicely."

"Good. I am glad it is satisfactory." The Viscount's dark eyes regarded her carefully. "I came to tell you that I have plans for later this afternoon. I want to take you to Bartholomew Fair."

"Oh!" Jeannie barely stopped herself from clapping her hands.

"It appears that you would enjoy our excursion."

"Yes, milord." Jeannie let herself smile. "I would enjoy it immensely."

"Would you like to join us?" his lordship asked his sister with a twinkle in his eye.

"Indeed! I should not!" Lady Helena held herself stiffly erect. "And I must say that I think you entirely mad to take Jeannie to such a place. Why, there are pickpockets everywhere." She wrinkled her aristocratic nose in disgust. "They say nothing is beyond them. They'll take the necklace from your very throat, the earbobs right out of your ears."

Jeannie looked to his lordship for his reaction, but he merely grinned at her. "Lady Helena suffers from the vapors. Besides, there's a very simple solution to that."

"Indeed!" Lady Helena did not look convinced. "And what is that?"

"Leave your necklaces and earbobs safely at home."

His sister sniffed. "You are foolish, Trenton. I'd as soon go about stark naked."

Jeannie turned again to Trenton, but he was still grinning. "I quite believe you, Helena. Therefore I rescind my invitation. Jeannie and I will brave the terrors of Smithfield alone."

Lady Helena sniffed again. "Trenton, I believe your brains are quite unsettled with your new affections." She turned to Jeannie, who, to her surprise, saw that the lady was smiling. But Trenton's sister said no more, simply tossing her head and making her way out the door.

Trenton moved closer to Jeannie, his dark eyes smiling down at her. "Helena and I used to get into the suds when we were young." He grinned wickedly. "*She*, being a year older, usually led the way."

He moved off toward the wardrobe, and Jeannie let out the breath she'd been holding. "But enough of my checkered past. We must find a dress for you to wear. Something old would be best."

Jeannie followed him. "I—I have no old dresses," she said. "I brought no gowns with me, and my things from Shropshire have not yet arrived."

"Ah yes." He turned to regard her with gleaming eyes, and she realized suddenly that he was quite close to her. For a long moment he stood looking down into her eyes; she felt herself being pulled toward him as though by some force outside herself. He seemed to feel it, too, for he leaned perceptibly toward her. Then there was a noise in the hall and he straightened suddenly. "Well, we shall just have to take the most modest of the new lot." He began to move the dresses along, pausing now and then to regard a particular gown.

Jeannie watched him in silence. Finally he drew forth her gray gown and pelisse, those she had worn on the trip. "I suppose this will have to do. It hardly makes you look like a country miss, but then, since I'll be dressed in my usual impeccable style"—his eyes danced with mischief—"it would hardly do for you to look *too* countryish."

"Of course," said Jeannie dryly. "After all, we have your reputation to consider."

His eyes regarded her quizzically. "Indeed, we do. And yours."

He handed her the gown. "Take no reticule or fine lace handkerchiefs, no jewelry, nothing detachable. Helena was right about the flashcoves."

Jeannie nodded. "But—if it's so dangerous, ought we to go at all?"

He grinned at her wickedly. "Have you any doubt that I can take care of you?" he asked, one of his dark eyebrows lifting.

She found herself smiling. "No, milord. I am not afraid."

"Good. Then get dressed and come down. We'll have a nuncheon and leave directly." He gave her another grin and strode from the room.

Ten minutes later she made her way down the great staircase. She had also put on her old bonnet and picked up her gloves. At the bottom of the stairs Trenton stood in discussion with Budner. Since he stood with his back to her, Jeannie could let her eyes roam over him. His coat of blue nankin fit so tightly across his broad shoulders that she wondered the material did not split with the movement of his muscles. She let her eyes slip down to where his inexpressibles hugged his strong legs. Even though the fairground would undoubtedly be full of dust, his top boots shone brilliantly in the sunshine. In one hand he held his curly-brimmed beaver and his gloves. He was a fine figure of a man, thought Jeannie with a sigh, as undoubtedly every woman at the fair, from high-born lady to lowly servant girl, would be sure to note immediately.

She cleared her throat. "Milord?"

He swung around to regard her, his eyes sliding over her attire. Then he smiled at her and her heart seemed to rise up in her throat. "Miss Burnstead." He nodded briefly. "You look quite well."

Jeannie felt herself coloring up. "Thank you, milord. You are most kind."

He shook his head. "I am most grateful. Helena will be the first to tell you that kindness is not one of my stronger characteristics."

A small smile lit Jeannie's face. "But, milord, Lady Helena is your sister, not your intended. She is bound to regard you differently."

A strange expression, almost of surprise, crossed his features and was gone. Then he shrugged. "Perhaps so. I have not considered such things."

"Perhaps," said Jeannie, "you should." She said no more but saw from the quick change of his expression that he had understood her intent. He must not forget the fiction of their love match.

They exchanged no more words as he helped her out the door and into the waiting carriage. As the horses moved off, Jeannie felt suddenly embarrassed. She was no longer certain how to conduct herself with Trenton. The ease of their rational arrangement had vanished, and she was not sure why.

She turned toward Trenton. "Milord," she asked in an effort to move her mind into some other channels, "do you know anything of the beginnings of such fairs?"

The Viscount smiled at her. "To the best of my knowledge the fairs first began as gatherings of worshippers and pilgrims about sacred places, especially near the walls of abbeys and cathedrals on the feast days of the saints enshrined within them. Since there were many people, tradesmen soon appeared to sell them food, drink, and eventually other things as well."

Jeannie nodded. "That seems most logical. Do you know anything of the beginnings of Bartholomew Fair?"

The Viscount's dark eyes sparkled. "It just so happens that I do, having just been witness to some lords at White's who had a wager as to which knew the most. It seems that Bartholomew Fair began with a grant from Henry the First to a monk who had formerly been his jester."

"His jester?" Jeannie's wide eyes reflected her disbelief.

"Yes. It appears that the man, Rayer by name, had attached himself to the King's court and was quite popular there in the capacity of jester. Later in life, having been vouchsafed the knowledge of the wickedness of his ways, he hied himself to Rome on a pilgrimage. In the holy city he nearly died of some strange fever and subsequently had a vision of St. Bartholomew in which he received instructions as to how to build the saint's church. Upon his swift recovery, he returned to London, told his story to the King, and was given the land."

Jeannie shook her head. "Truly a marvelous story."

"Not nearly as marvelous as the miracles later ascribed to him," commented Trenton dryly. "But then, in the twelfth century people were more easily duped."

"Yes, I suppose so."

The Viscount smiled. "I fear the fair gives many people the opportunity to represent things as they are not."

Jeannie smiled. "It will be enjoyable anyway," she said, then had to wonder at the sudden trembling in her limbs as his lordship gave her a dazzling smile.

CHAPTER ELEVEN

The crowd grew bigger as they neared Smithfield. Jeannie remembered the throngs of London from her coming out days, but she had never seen so many people in one place. Trenton smiled reassuringly as he helped her down from the carriage. "You'll be quite safe with me," he said cheerfully, cocking his beaver at a rakish angle. He led her toward the uncovered stalls that began at the Skinner Street corner of Giltspur Street beginning with the churchyard. Jeannie gazed around her at fruit, oysters, cheap toys, gingerbread, small wicker baskets, and other trifling articles. One man had covered twenty feet of the roadway lengthwise with discontinued woodcut pamphlets and large folio Bible prints.

Further in from the road were lines of covered stalls, their open fronts opposite the fronts of the houses toward the pavement, their enclosed backs to the road. In these covered stalls, formed of canvas stretched tightly on light poles, venders offered gingerbread, toys, hardware, garters, pocketbooks, trinkets, and articles of all prices.

They walked for some time through these, threading their way among the paths. The smell of frying sausages hung in the air as they moved—past the open-sided tents that held the tables of roast duck and pork, past the stalls with tarts and gingerbreads, past the booths with lemonade and cider.

Other little stalls showed rows of pins and amber bracelets, as well as knives, combs, and thimbles to catch the female eye. Jeannie, her attention elsewhere, paid little heed to such gewgaws.

Then Trenton said, "Enough of this. Let's move on to the shows."

Jeannie nodded. Even to her untrained eye it was plain that the merchandise in these stalls was generally of poor quality. She gazed around her with interest as Trenton led her to the center of the carriage way where shows of all kinds were set up. The late August sun was warm and dust was everywhere, but Jeannie paid it no mind. She was fascinated by the tents and the painted canvas showbills advertising various strange and wonderful attractions.

"Oh?" She caught her breath at the picture of the fat lady painted twice lifesize, great mounds of pinkish flesh rolling out of her garish green gown.

Besides Jeannie, Trenton laughed. "I trust you will never achieve such great proportions."

"I should hope not!" she cried. "My word, what great amounts she must eat."

The clamor of the crowd around them made it necessary to speak loudly. Trenton pointed to a showbill. "Perhaps she eats the skeleton man's share, too."

Jeannie suppressed a shiver. Painted on the black canvas, the skeleton man quite lived up to his name.

Outside the next tent, Jeannie and Trenton stopped to watch a strangely dressed man bang a drum. "Come in, folks, come in," he roared over the noise of the fair, his round belly shaking with the effort. "Come in and see the world famous Madame Giradelli, the Fireproof Lady. She puts melted lead in her mouth, she do! And she spits it out again with the marks of her very teeth bit right into it! She do! She do indeed!"

This startling announcement was followed by several vociferous rolls on the drum. Then, apparently having recovered his breath, the man tipped his hat—a particularly ratty beaver—jauntily over one ear and continued. "See the lady put red-hot iron on her body, on her limbs, on her tongue, on her hair! Watch her wash her hands in boiling lead or boiling oil! All this fer sixpence yet!" He produced another loud roll on the drum. "Only sixpence. Just to begin."

The Viscount looked down on Jeannie. "Would you care to see the famed lady who is on such intimate terms with fire?"

Jeannie shook her head. "I think not, milord. The thought of it makes me shiver with apprehension. What if the poor woman should be burned?" She shuddered.

Trenton put his gloved hand on her arm. "There's no need to be alarmed. These people are in no danger from what they do."

He moved her along to where there hung a great canvas advertising Richardson's Theatre. "A Change of Performance Each Day" it proclaimed in large letters. Across a platform lined with green baize, festooned with crimson curtains, and lighted with variegated lamps, marched a gaily costumed band, playing as loudly as possible and followed by actors and actresses in costume. Jeannie smiled at the clamor and the richly colored outfits.

A tattered urchin circulated through the crowd, thrusting playbills into willing and unwilling hands alike. Trenton glanced at his. "Monk and Murderer," he read aloud to her. "Or the Skeleton Specter. A veritable theatrical treat," he added with a grin, "featuring Mohammed the Persian and Ronaldo the Mysterious Monk. With a gothic hall, a mysterious forest, a gothic chamber, a grand combat with shield and battle-axe. The piece terminates with the fall of the murderers, the ascension of the specter monk, etc." His eyes twinkled down at her. "What do you say?"

Jeannie smiled at him. In his present mood the Viscount was fun to be with; she could almost believe in the fiction of their love match. "If you please, milord, I think I should like best to simply walk about."

"Very good," agreed Trenton with a nod, taking a grip on her elbow. Further on, a great tall man in very short breeches and an enormous hat was standing on a wagon, loudly shouting his wares. They stopped a moment to listen.

"This here elixir, the best of its kind ever made. Green's Compendium, that's what she's called." He waved the rather ordinary-looking bottle in his hand. "Green, that's me! Stumbled on this great secret. Never told to another living soul. Only place to get it, right here from the hand of him as made it."

He paused to take a deep breath and adjust the hat which had fallen over his eyes. "Good fer all as ails you. Good fer warts and corns, stomachaches, weak blood, anything as ails mankind can be fixed by Green's Compendium."

Jeannie turned to Trenton, laughter in her eyes. "One medicine to cure everything?"

He grinned back at her and leaned closer to whisper, "There are always those who believe the impossible."

On the next platform a rope had been strung at shoulder height. Jeannie caught her breath as a young rope-dancer in pink tights stepped out on it, took several running steps, then turned quickly and ran back.

"Step right in," shouted a strange woman. "Beginning soon. See the rope-dancer do amazing things. See the tumbling boys. See the boy who twists hisself in knots." The woman had a deep voice like a man's, and was dressed in a huge skirt of brilliant red satin and a blouse of glaring purple. Two acrobat boys came running out and performed a series of somersaults across the platform. Then each stood up and walked off—on his hands.

Jeannie turned to Trenton. "I can't imagine being able to do such things. It's truly amazing."

Trenton smiled. "The human body can achieve great things with practice. These people are raised to their stunts. They know nothing else."

The crowd of laughing, chattering fairgoers swept them along for several paces. When they halted again, they stood in front of another platform where a small brown man stood patiently waiting. He wore no shirt, just some sort of cloth twisted about his loins. "Walk in, walk in!" called a scrawny, shabbily dressed boy on the platform. "Just going to begin. See this yere Hindu fellow from India. Sherem, he be called. He takes these here fearful snakes. Treats 'em like pets. Wears 'em like clothes. Dangerous snakes they be. Their bites is death!"

As the snakes curled themselves around the smooth brown flesh, Jeannie drew closer to Trenton.

"Don't be frighted," he whispered. "The snakes cannot really harm him. Their poison has been removed."

Watching the snakes slither around the man's neck and raise their heads to gaze into his impassive black eyes, Jeannie shuddered. "I can't help it," she said. "Snakes are—"

"Woman's mortal enemy," said Trenton with a wicked grin. "If it hadn't been for snakes—and women —there would be no evil in the world. We'd all still be in Eden."

Aware that he was roasting her, Jeannie held her temper. "I don't think Lady Helena would take kindly to such talk," she said with a mock frown.

Trenton pretended to shudder. "Indeed, she would not. Helena would be far more apt to lay all the world's ills at the doorstep of men."

"Perhaps there would be some justice to such a thing," Jeannie replied, not quite able to keep from breaking into a smile.

Trenton glared at her in mock anger. "Enough, woman," he said. "We will get into no debates of this nature if I can help it." His face sobered. "I daresay men should bear their share of the guilt. Come, let us move on to Miss Biffin."

Jeannie smiled in compliance. "Of course, milord. But who is Miss Biffin?"

"I must remember to point out to Helena the edifying nature of Bartholomew Fair. Where else could you learn about London's most celebrated persons?"

"That is all well and good, milord, but you still have not told me who this Miss Biffin is." Jeannie's face reflected her happiness.

"Miss Biffin," said his lordship, putting on the airs and tone of one of the shouters around them, "is an armless, handless painter. She does amazing likenesses of those who sit for her."

"But how?" asked Jeannie in surprise.

"With a brush tied to her shoulder."

Jeannie felt herself coloring up. "Really, milord, I may be a country girl, but to expect me to believe such a Banbury tale—"

The Viscount grinned. "It's God's truth. You'll see. The Earl of Morton befriended her and, to prove that she wasn't tricking anyone, he had her do his own likeness. He took it home with him every time to forestall any chance of cheating. He was convinced her talent was real."

Jeannie sighed. People sometimes did great and wonderful things under the most difficult circumstances. Imagine someone without arms even *thinking* of painting portraits. "The poor lady has my admiration," she said.

Trenton nodded. "And rightly so." He gave her a slight smile. "In this next booth is displayed Mr. Simon Paap."

"And what does he do that is special?"

His lordship drew her on. "He does nothing but exist. He's billed as the Dutch Dwarf." He pointed up to the showbill, which showed a very small man. "He weighs 27 stone and is 28 inches tall."

Jeannie shook her head. "How very small."

Trenton nodded. "I saw him once before." His features darkened. "It must be very difficult to face life in such a handicapped condition."

His lordship turned to Jeannie and forced a slight smile. "Come, my dear, there is no need to sadden ourselves. Undoubtedly these people take their joy in life, too." He grinned at her. "Come, let's go see Wombwell's Menagerie. We have yet to try the rides as well."

"And a Punch and Judy show?" asked Jeannie eagerly.

"Of course."

As they moved off through the chatter and noise, Jeannie smiled happily.

"What sort of animals has Wombwell in his Menagerie?" she asked.

"All sorts of foreign ones," said Trenton. "Especially those great gray beasts, the elephants. They say some are trained to carry people in their trunks." He stopped before the painted showbill and gestured to the great beast painted there.

"Really?" asked Jeannie. "Wouldn't that be dangerous?"

"I should think not." The Viscount smiled. "I understand the beasts are quite gentle. Come, I'll take you inside." Grabbing her hand, he led her up to the line and paid their fee.

As they wandered from cage to cage, Jeannie realized that the animals looked much smaller than they had on the showbill. She admired the great white polar bear, shivering as Trenton said, "He comes from the cold northern region." She looked at the wild asses, the different kinds of monkeys, the strange and exotic birds with their unfamiliar plumage, the lion and tiger who lived together in the same cage, but especially the great elephant who stood silently munching hay.

She turned to Trenton. "I have never seen an elephant before. Thank you, milord."

"You are quite welcome." Trenton pulled her closer. "Do you see the little man over there? The wizened, sharp-faced one by the lion's cage?"

Jeannie nodded. "I see him."

"That's Wombwell himself," said Trenton. "He began as a cobbler in Monmouth Street and started his show with two snakes."

As Jeannie watched, the little man extended a rough red hand into the cage and began to rub the lion's back. "Oh!" Jeannie caught her breath.

Trenton squeezed her hand. "It's not really dangerous, pet. Wombwell has the reputation of having the keenest interest in his animals. Obviously, he and the lion are friends."

Jeannie could only shake her head. That lion did not look friendly to her!

As they left the row of cages and reentered the carriage way, Trenton grabbed her hand and began to pull her through the throng.

"Milord!" cried Jeannie, her bonnet knocked askew by his haste.

He turned to her with a boyish grin. "We are going to the roundabouts. I must take you for a ride on one."

"But, milord—"

He shook his head. "I concede to no protests. I insist that you experience that."

Laughing and panting, Jeannie was dragged after him into the line where smiling, happy couples leaned close to each other while they waited. Bright flags flapped in the breeze and the music of assorted bands filled the summer air. "But I have never ridden one of these," she said between waves of laughter. "It looks dangerous."

His lordship pulled her closer to his side. "My dear Miss Burnstead, how can you even mention danger when *I* am here? Did I not rescue you from the dangers of a certain dark stretch of woods?"

His eyes twinkled with merriment and hers danced too as she nodded. "Oh yes, yes, you did, milord. Indeed you did. It was a great rescue, very dramatic."

He grinned at her. "I am a famous rescuer."

Jeannie giggled. The fair and the excitement were making her light-headed. She no longer considered her words before she spoke. "I think it was not only *that* wood from which you rescued me."

His lordship's eyes brightened as he picked up the

sense of her words. "Indeed, my dear. I take your drift. Atwood presents a far worse danger than any stretch of trees." He shook his head. "The man defies description." He grinned at her brashly. "I have not yet contrived to have you concede that I am exceptional, but you must admit that I outshine Atwood."

Jeannie giggled again. "Indeed, milord, that I concede quite freely."

In the press of people she was crushed quite tightly against him, and the sudden realization hit her that their faces were only inches apart. Color flooded her cheeks at the thought.

"Do not concern yourself with that part of your life," said the Viscount with a tender smile. "That misery is over." He gave her a quizzical smile. "Is it not?"

"Oh yes, milord!" Jeannie nodded vigorously. Only a fool would prefer the weak-chinned Atwood to the strong, determined Trenton.

The roundabout stopped and laughing people began to climb down from its gaily carved animals and out of its gilt coach seats. Trenton pulled her after the others as they piled onto the platform. "Here!" Before she knew what he was doing, he had grabbed her by the waist and swung her up onto the back of a brightly painted wooden steed.

Jeannie grabbed automatically at the pole in front of her. "Milord!"

"Don't be frightened," he said, stationing himself beside her and slipping an arm loosely around her waist.

She felt her heart begin to pound under her gray gown, but she tried to look as though the touch of his arm were simply an everyday matter. As the music began its happy melody, the carved horse under her began to rise. "Oh!" Jeannie grabbed the pole with both hands and Trenton grinned.

"I guarantee that this steed will not run away with you. I have him well under control."

Jeannie, her eyes bright and cheeks flushed, grinned down at him. "Indeed, milord, I should think that you always have everything under control."

A strange look flickered across his face momentarily. "I am no longer as sure of that as I once was," he said quietly.

Jeannie wondered at this, but she did not pursue the subject further.

As the roundabout continued on its way, her thoughts went to the future. If only they could continue as they had today—in friendly companionship. The color flooded her face again. Perhaps in time he might even begin to care about her.

Jeannie pushed away the thoughts that common sense insisted on presenting. London was full of incognitas, beautiful young things who knew how to give a man pleasure, and beautiful older ladies, like Lady Frances, whose principal occupation in life seemed to be the acquisition of new admirers.

The roundabout stopped, the ride over. Jeannie found the Viscount regarding her soberly and summoned a bright smile. It had been very kind of him to bring her to the fair.

His hands encircled her waist again, and he lifted her easily to the ground. "Now, let us try the ups-and-downs," he said, and, taking her firmly by the hand, he led her through the throng.

As she was jostled from both sides by others seeking the same destination, Jeannie was reminded of Lady Helena's remarks about pickpockets. Certainly in this kind of crush they would have little trouble practicing their profession.

Trenton drew to a stop in the ticket line for the ups-and-downs. She tilted her head to look up at the top. The wheellike structure supported four wooden seats into which passengers were locked by a tablelike contrivance across their laps. As the wheel turned, each swinging seat moved up the circle and down.

"Are you quite sure such a machine is safe?" she asked timidly. Horses did not frighten her and in her younger days she had followed Jeremy up many a tree, but this great machine did not strike her as particularly trustworthy.

"Of course, it is. Don't worry. They are much better built than the one that collapsed last year."

"Milord!" Jeannie found herself drawing closer and then recognized the glint of merriment in his eyes. "You're funning me!"

Trenton laughed. "I am, indeed, Jeannie my pet. And I must admit that it's great sport."

She smiled back at him and when it was their turn to enter one of the swinging seats she forced herself to sit bravely still.

Trenton looked down on her with sparkling eyes. "You may clutch my arm in panic," he said with a wicked smile, "or squeal a bit, if you like. That seems to make it more pleasurable."

Jeannie shook her head. "I am not frighted, milord." That was only a small lie. "And look, we shall be able to see out over the fair."

"We shall, indeed. And, since you are so brave, perhaps you'll hold *my* hand."

She met his eyes in surprise, saw the laughter there, and from somewhere within her came the gay answer, "Of course, milord. If you wish it."

"I do wish it," he replied, his hand closing over hers. "I wish it devoutly."

Just as she was puzzling over his words, the wheel

began to move and a little squeal escaped her unaware. The machine creaked ominously as their seat moved upward, and Jeannie held her breath. Gradually she became accustomed to the movement and when they reached the top and could truly see the fair spread out before them, her fear dissolved. She turned a radiant face to his lordship. "Just look! Isn't it glorious?"

Trenton nodded, his eyes never leaving her face. "Yes the sight is glorious," he said, but the compliment was lost on Jeannie, who had turned back to savor the colorful panorama before her.

Their ride was over all too soon and Jeannie, following Trenton from the seat, cast a wistful look behind her. "Now for Punch and Judy," he said. "They're always fun."

Jeannie, her hand still in his, was led back toward the booths. Soon they stood before the Punch and Judy show. Trenton slipped an arm around Jeannie and drew her closer to him. No wonder, she thought briefly, that the Viscount had such luck with women. He had quite a way about him when he chose to use it.

Then her attention was drawn to the puppets. On the elevated stage the Judy puppet shouted at her hooked-nosed mate. Punch, dancing up and down in his bright red and yellow suit and his dangling cap, turned leering eyes toward a young woman in the front row of the audience. His outraged spouse promptly swatted him with her trusty rolling pin.

Jeannie burst into laughter with the other spectators and turned to find the Viscount smiling down on her. "It's plain to see that old Punch doesn't live in Judy's pocket," he said. "He has a real eye for the petticoat line."

"Like the rest of you," Jeannie said without thinking.

But Trenton merely continued to smile and turned his attention back to the stage.

Standing there with his arm around her, Jeannie scolded herself for behaving foolishly. One did not engage a man's respect by reminding him of his old haunts.

When Punch and Judy had retreated behind the closed curtain, his lordship turned to her. "I don't know about you, but I have discovered a thirst that calls for lemonade and a hunger that demands gingerbread."

"That sounds like just the thing," replied Jeannie.

His lordship tucked her arm in his and moved off through the crowd toward the painted canvas showbill that proclaimed gingerbread. The crowd was heavy, but they seemed to be moving along easily enough, when suddenly Trenton staggered and fell against her. He righted himself immediately and looked at her with concern. "Are you hurt?"

"No, milord." Jeannie watched as his hands went to his pockets and his mouth tightened grimly.

"Just as I thought," he said. "A flashcove on the lay. That's one of their favorite tricks—to knock a man off balance and then relieve him of his blunt. It must have been that scrawny boy." He looked around them. "I don't see him now. He's long gone."

"Did—did you lose much?" asked Jeannie in dismay.

He shook his head. "No. I had only a pocket handkerchief there, a cheap one. My blunt I keep in a different place. Come, don't look so worried. No one will get it. Let us onward and find our gingerbread."

"Yes, milord." Jeannie gave him a timid smile and then, as a sudden thought struck her, she burst into laughter.

"What is so amusing?" asked his lordship, raising a dark eyebrow.

"I was just thinking of Uncle Obadiah," said Jeannie. "If this had happened to him, he would have been quite red in the face by now, puffing and popping waistcoat buttons and roaring about. All to no end, of course. Uncle Obadiah is a dear soul, but he does sometimes carry on."

"He sounds like the choleric type to me." The Viscount regarded her quizzically. "And you, my bride-to-be? Are you given to roaring and popping buttons?"

Jeannie shook her head. "No, milord, I am not a roarer. When I have something to say, I say it. But quietly."

Trenton smiled. "That bodes well for our future. Any roaring and popping will remain in my department." He puffed out his cheeks in an imitation that sent Jeannie into gales of laughter. By the time she had recovered, Trenton was holding two pieces of gingerbread. He offered her one.

"It looks very good," said Jeannie.

"Tastes good, too," said the Viscount, who was already sampling his.

They finished the gingerbread quickly and went in search of a lemonade stand. Jeannie found its sour wetness particularly refreshing. The crowds had raised a deal of dust and her throat felt quite parched. She drank hers quickly down and turned to find that Trenton had emptied his glass, too.

"Now," he said, "we have almost made a complete circuit. Let us continue on our way until we have finished the round. At the entrance, unless you wish to revisit something, we can seek our carriage."

"That is very acceptable to me," replied Jeannie. "We must have been gone a long time."

"I cannot say exactly," returned Trenton, casting

an eye upward at the sun. "I left my timepiece at home so as not to tempt the divers. But I agree that we have been gone for some time."

They did not hurry, but neither did they linger before any platforms, except for one quite near the entrance. Here was advertised a conjuror. Jeannie gazed up at the showbill which depicted a man with a knife stuck in his hand but no blood flowing. In one corner of the canvas was painted a man with flames shooting out of his mouth. Another was shown with cards spread out before him. On the platform itself stood a man juggling brightly colored balls with studied ease. Trying to count them as they whirled through the air, Jeannie could not tell if there were three, four, or even five.

Trenton returned her smile, and put his hand around her elbow. "If you're ready, perhaps we should head for home now."

"Yes, milord." Jeannie found that she was more tired than she had thought. "It has been a most pleasant afternoon. I wish to thank you for thinking of it. It has been an experience I shall not forget. Ever." The last word was uttered so softly that she did not think he would hear it. Since she had felt color flooding her cheeks, she had lowered her eyes and did not see the strange look that crossed his features as the word registered.

He was silent as he guided her expertly through the crowds to the neighboring street where the coachman and horses waited patiently. After he assisted her into the seat, Trenton settled beside her with a smile. "A very pleasant afternoon," he said. "We shall do it again next year, unless something better prevents it."

For a moment Jeannie did not understand and then color flooded her cheeks again. The Viscount was considering the possibility that by this time next year she would have just had a child. Certainly she knew this. It was silly that now it should cause her embarrassment. She forced herself to raise her eyes to his. "Yes, milord. That would be very nice."

He nodded and they sat in companionable silence for some moments. Jeannie was lost in contemplation of the afternoon. If the future were only to be like this. But of course it wouldn't be. After their marriage the need to convince the *ton* of their fictional love match would be lessened and eventually—Jeannie swallowed over the sudden lump in her throat—Trenton would return to his former haunts. She might as well accustom herself to the fact. After all, Trenton did not love her, nor she him. But there was respect between them and Trenton, at least, would be discreet about such things.

Lady Helena was nowhere in sight when Jeannie and Trenton entered the front door of the house on St. James's Square. Trenton turned to Jeannie. "Perhaps you would care to wash up a little before dinner." His eyes twinkled. "Would you like to put on one of your new gowns?"

"Oh yes, I should like that," said Jeannie calmly, wondering at the joy she felt at the prospect of dinner with Trenton. After all, she still had no partiality for his lordship, but it was certainly pleasant to consider that she could deal so well with him, that they could spend a lovely afternoon together. She gave him a timid smile before she turned and made her way up the stairs.

CHAPTER TWELVE

A week passed after their excursion to Bartholomew Fair, and Jeannie spent the time pleasantly, chatting with Lady Helena about their Smithfield adventures, learning the newest gossip about the outlandish doings of the *ton*, giving Verdon his occasional French lessons, and listening to the plans for her forthcoming wedding. Although the banns had already been called twice, the wedding still seemed unreal to her, something that was going to happen to someone else, not to her. It seemed incredible that only a few weeks ago she had been living placidly, if rather dully, in Shropshire, the most exciting thing in her life the next French novel.

Dressed in a new morning gown of yellow-sprigged muslin, her hair piled high on her head in the style called Roman, Jeannie sat reading aloud to Lady Helena in the little sitting room next to her bedchamber. The novel was interesting enough, she supposed, but Jeannie had trouble keeping her mind on the story. Trenton had been absent a great deal since their excursion, and she missed his company.

When a brisk knock sounded on the door, Jeannie turned toward it happily. The knock had a certain sound of authority to it. "Come in," she called.

The door swung open, and his lordship stood there. "Good morning," he said.

"Good morning, milord." Jeannie found herself smiling happily and strove to compose her features.

"Good morning, brother," said Lady Helena, waving a beringed hand.

"Good morning, Helena. Whatever are you doing inside when the weather is so lovely?"

"We are reading the latest French romance." Lady Helena cast her brother a suspicious glance. "And we had just reached a most exciting part."

Trenton grinned. "Come, Helena, why don't you put this drivel aside and look for a real man?"

Jeannie colored up. Sometimes she found the freedom that he took with his sister embarrassing.

Lady Helena, however, merely smiled. "Trenton, my boy, you are just as abominable as ever. I *had* a husband, if you remember." She gazed at him critically.

"Of course I remember." Trenton winked at Jeannie. "Though how the poor man could manage living with you—"

Lady Helena gave her brother another hard look. "My Charles was an exceptional man. It is not easy to find another to take his place."

In spite of the frosty tone in Lady Helena's voice, Jeannie thought she detected a note of pain in it. Evidently his lordship noted it, too, for he changed the subject. "I have come to tell you that tonight we go to Covent Garden."

Jeannie caught her breath as he swung around to look at her. "What play are we to see?" she asked, excited.

His dark eyes glittered and the strong lines of his mouth curved into a smile. "Young is playing Hamlet. Kean will not return to the city till later in the season."

"*Hamlet*. Oh, that sounds grand." Again Jeannie was conscious that she had overreacted. Everything seemed to make her happy these days.

Trenton turned to his sister. "We must select a gown, Helena. Something special for Jeannie's first night at the theater."

"Of course." Lady Helena rose from the divan with such alacrity that Jeannie was startled. "Let us look now."

Jeannie followed the two of them to the wardrobe and watched as he began moving the gowns aside, considering each one. After much discussion of the niceties of fashion and holding up each gown to see if its color was becoming to her, his lordship settled on the gown of celestial blue, gathered high under the bodice with strands of deep purple ribbon. The same ribbon decorated the little puffed sleeves and the scooped neckline and hung in two long strands down the front.

"I hope you ordered matching slippers," said the Viscount.

"Trenton," replied Lady Helena with an attempt at a frown, "you forget yourself. You are talking to one of the most fashionable women in London. I did not forget the shoes or the gloves. Jeannie's outfit is quite complete."

The Viscount's eyes danced mischievously. "And did you order matching ostrich plumes for her hair?"

"But of course." Lady Helena gave her brother a sour look. "I attended to all these things."

"Fine. You will accompany us, I trust."

"Indeed I shall. I have been wanting to get out again."

The Viscount nodded. "Fine. I shall look forward to it. Unfortunately I have a previous engagement for dinner." He smiled at his sister. "I want to see the entire play, including the first act, so please be prompt."

Lady Helena grimaced. "How unfashionable, but if you insist."

"I do insist," declared Trenton. "I want Jeannie to see the whole play. And now I must be off."

Jeannie, watching him stride across the room, felt a sudden sense of pride. At the door he turned and blew her a kiss. *"Au revoir,* my love."

Then he was gone, and she was conscious of a feeling of emptiness inside her. Lady Helena soon began to chatter away and, when a footman knocked at the door to inform her that Lord Verdon was below, Jeannie had almost recovered her spirits.

"Verdon?" said Lady Helena after the footman had closed the door and departed. "What is he doing here?"

"I suspect he may have come for his French lesson," Jeannie said, aware that a few hours in the company of the Marquess would serve admirably to pass the time before dinner.

A peculiar expression crossed Lady Helena's face at this information, but she did not comment.

"Do come and join us," cried Jeannie. "The Marquess is great fun, and he says the most lavish things. It's all a lot of flummery, of course, but it's fun to hear."

Lady Helena smiled and seemed to relax. "Well child, I was about to lie down on my bed for a spell. A trip to the theater can be rather fatiguing. And, in fact, I am not quite up to facing Verdon's eagle-sharp eyes."

Jeannie's face reflected her bewilderment.

Lady Helena laughed. "Jeannie, my dear, I am getting on in years. I cannot appear in the company of a discerning gentleman like Verdon without spending considerable time on my toilette. And today I have been quite lax."

"But Lady Helena, you look thoroughly presentable," said Jeannie sincerely.

Her ladyship smiled. "You are a dear sweet thing, Jeannie, but you are still a child. When you look at me, you see a friend. Verdon, however, sees only a woman, and he sees her with eyes that note every flaw. Since today I am not quite flawless, and, since I am not yet ready to have that information bruited about the *ton,* I shall stay in my room while the Marquess takes his lessons."

"As you wish, Lady Helena," Jeannie replied. "But his lordship—"

"Nonsense. Trenton and Verdon are best friends. You are quite safe in Verdon's company."

Of this Jeannie had no doubt. Yet she did not see how to discuss with Lady Helena his lordship's strange behavior toward his friend. So she smiled, smoothed down her gown, and hurried down the stairs to the drawing room.

The Marquess was seated in a chair contemplating the hearth, but he rose when she entered. She noted that he looked his usual elegant self in a coat of brown nankin, pantaloons of ribbed buff kerseymere worn with Hessian boots, a waistcoat of blue-striped twill and a cravat sporting the Mail Coach tie.

"*Enchanté, mam'selle,*" he said.

Jeannie dropped a small curtsy. "*Bonjour, monsieur.*"

Verdon laughed. "I am making famous progress in my lessons, am I not?"

Jeannie had to laugh, too. "*Au contraire, monsieur,* you are only beginning."

The Marquess grinned ruefully. "You are quite

right. I'm afraid it will take me a dreadfully long time to manage the language. It will take daily lessons, for years no doubt." His eyes laughed at her. "Do not look so startled, *ma petite*. Is not that an admirable excuse for a daily call?"

Jeannie shook her head. "You forget yourself, milord. A *daily* call?"

"Of course." The Marquess's eyes glittered with amusement. "Didn't you hear me promise Trenton that I would be your chief gallant and keep the other beaux at a distance?"

"Yes, I heard you," replied Jeannie, "but I do not know that Trenton will appreciate your offer."

The Marquess chuckled. "I have never seen the man so possessed with love. Trenton and I have been on the town these many years. We have on occasion competed for the same lightskirt and neither of us has ever had the least hard feelings about it. But now, when I compliment him on his choice of a wife, he flies up in the boughs. It's the most amusing thing I've ever seen."

"It is not amusing to me," cried Jeannie, feeling genuinely distressed. She could not disclose to the Marquess that it was not jealousy that motivated his friend's peculiar actions. "His lordship gets very angry."

The Marquess's eyes hardened. "I hope he does not vent his anger on you."

"No, no, of course not," Jeannie hastened to add. "But you must see that I do not wish to upset him."

The Marquess shrugged. "I believe you have as bad a case as his lordship. He shook his head. "May I always be fortunate enough to escape such absurdity.

"I can forego my French lessons," he told Jeannie soberly, "but be assured there will be many young men hanging about you after your marriage. It is the fashion these days. And how will you keep them away? It would be far better to have *one* official admirer. I quite assure you that if *I* hold that office, no one will bother you."

"But why must I *have* admirers at all?" asked Jeannie. "I will have a husband. I will be a married woman."

The Marquess chuckled. "My dear innocent, those are the best kind. They are protect—"

Jeannie clapped her hands over her ears. "Enough, milord, enough. I will give you French lessons until or unless Trenton forbids it. Does that satisfy you?"

"Quite." The Marquess looked around the drawing room. "No doubt you will soon redecorate."

Jeannie, too, looked around the room. She liked its dark blue tones, its stately furniture. "Whatever for?" she asked.

The Marquess smiled laconically. "I believe it is an affliction that attacks new brides. They find suddenly that they must change the rooms about."

"Nonsense," said Jeannie. "I like this room as it is."

The Marquess nodded. "That is good, but there is another affliction of new brides, one of an even worse nature. Right after the ceremony they discover a deep desire to make changes in their husbands."

Jeannie burst into laughter. "Verdon! Excuse me, milord, but that is the funniest thing I have heard in ages. I? To change Trenton? Such a thing is impossible. Besides," she dropped her voice, "I like him the way he is." She was surprised to find that this was true.

The Marquess beamed. "You are a diamond of the first water, my dear. If I could discover a gem like you for myself, I might even be tempted to try matrimony."

"I should not advise it, milord," replied Jeannie

with a smile. "Remember the afflictions that strike new brides and count yourself fortunate to have escaped their results."

The Marquess smiled ruefully, his fingers moving to his cravat. "I expect you are right, my dear." He consulted the clock on the mantel. "In fact, one of my friends is awaiting me at this very moment. I should not like to disappoint the dear little thing. *Au revoir.*"

"*Au revoir,*" replied Jeannie, watching him out the door. How strange, she thought, as the Marquess's footsteps receded down the tiled hall, that Verdon should really believe his friend to be in love. His lordship's behavior was puzzling, as she well knew, but it had nothing to do with love. Whatever it was that motivated his strange behavior—Jeannie leaped to her feet. Of course! That was it! His jealousy was all part of the fiction of the love match. It was part of his plan to convince the *ton* and his family that his preference for her was firm and unshakable. Well, thought Jeannie with a great sigh, it was good to understand that anomaly at last. But certainly he needn't carry this charade to such extreme lengths. He should be able to trust his friend Verdon.

She sighed again and moved toward the stairs. Perhaps she would lie on her bed and rest a while. She wanted to be fresh and rested for her first evening at the theater.

When she descended the stairs later in the evening, Jeannie felt entirely unlike herself. She had given herself into the hands of Lady Helena's dresser, and the results had been far above her expectations. A look in the cheval glass had disclosed a beautiful young creature in a gown that fit perfectly. Her blond curls were tumbled in an artful confusion that had taken the dresser almost an hour to achieve. From their planned unruliness issued a great ostrich plume. Jeannie was almost afraid to walk. In fact, she had protested to Lady Helena, "How will I keep my neck straight?"

"It's not heavy, child. Simply forget that it is there. Carry yourself with grace—and pride." Lady Helena's eyes glowed. "After all, you are the beloved of the most eligible man in the *ton*."

Jeannie managed a small smile at that, but now, on her way to stand the scrutiny of his lordship's sharp eyes, she wished for Lady Helena's companionship. But his lordship's sister had sent her on. "I am not going to be ready quite on time. You must distract him for me, my dear," she pleaded. "I shall be down as soon as I can."

As Jeannie reached the middle of the stairs, his lordship emerged from the library and stood watching her descend. How well turned out he was, she thought. His broad shoulders stretched taut the cloth of his coat of blue superfine. His cravat was tied with the utmost precision in the Mathematical style, his knee breeches of cream kerseymere and his white stockings clung to a leg fit for the finest actor, and he carried his *chapeau bras* with great *élan*.

His eyes sparkled as she reached the bottom and looked up at him. "Excellent," he said. "The dress was a wise choice. I see you have your white kid gloves, but you have forgotten your cashmere."

Jeannie flushed. "I will get it."

"No." His tone stopped her as she was half-turned. "Budner, send one of the maids for Miss Burnstead's cashmere. Jeannie, come with me."

As she followed him down the panelled hall, Jeannie wished she knew what was on his lordship's mind. He had not seemed angry with her, but it was not always easy to tell; his moods were so changeable.

The Viscount unlocked a drawer in his desk and took out a box. "I put your mama's jewels here for safekeeping. I thought perhaps you might want to wear some of them tonight. Or—perhaps, if they please you, you might wear these."

He put a velvet-covered box in her hands. Jeannie opened it and gasped. Against the white satin lining nestled a necklace and bracelet made of alternating sapphires and amethysts set in filigreed gold.

What an unusual combination of gems, Jeannie thought. They matched her gown so well. Then the realization hit her. His lordship had ordered these jewels made especially. He had checked first with Lady Helena and planned the little scene about choosing the dress. But why had he gone to so much trouble?

"They are far too lovely for me," she said over the lump in her throat.

"Do not talk nonsense. They are just a few trinkets I picked up to amuse myself. They are of no real value. Here—" He took the bracelet from the box and clasped it around her wrist. The white kid glove set off the dark stones admirably.

Gazing down at them, Jeannie did not believe his words about trinkets. These jewels had cost a great deal of money.

Then he reached for the necklace. "Allow me." He had not yet donned his gloves and his fingers were warm on her neck as he fastened the clasp.

With his hands on her arms he turned her around. For long moments his eyes swept her from head to foot. Coloring under the scrutiny of those dark eyes, Jeannie fought to keep her own from revealing her embarrassment.

He nodded. "Yes, they were a wise choice." His hands pulled her closer, and his lips brushed hers in the lightest of caresses. She thought he was going to pull her closer still, perhaps to kiss her again, when suddenly from the doorway came Lady Helena's chuckle.

"Well, Trenton, *I* am ready. Are we to be on time for the first act or not?"

"Yes, Helena, we are," declared the Viscount. "We were just coming, weren't we, my dear?"

Jeannie turned with Trenton and stopped suddenly. Previously she had seen Lady Helena dressed to receive callers. She had not seen her dressed to go out in the evening. The sight was one not soon to be forgotten. Lady Helena's gown of silk was a shade of deep and vibrant yellow. Its square-cut neck admitted an extensive view of Lady Helena's throat and upper bosom and its little puffed sleeves showed her upper arm. From slightly above her elbow her arms were encased in long gloves of white kid. From directly below the bodice her gown fell to the floor in shining waves of bright color. Around the hem and for several inches up it was ornamented with large rosettes of white silk. Around her neck Lady Helena wore a necklace of emeralds, and matching stones hung in her ears and were clasped around one gloved wrist. The *pièce de résistance* of the outfit was a turban of matching yellow silk set with a great emerald and from which towered two gigantic green ostrich plumes.

Surveying this sight, Jeannie found herself thinking that the effect was overwhelming. Lady Helena looked much nicer in her morning dress, but of course Jeannie did not say so.

His lordship made no comment on his sister's attire but simply swept Jeannie along to where Budner waited with the cashmere. There he shawled her with charming solicitude and turned to his sister.

Lady Helena laughed. "Do not waste your charm on me, Trenton," she teased. "I know the ways of you beaux."

"So you do, sister dear," agreed the Viscount laconically. "But come, we have delayed too long already."

A bemused Jeannie was led out and handed into the carriage. As the horses moved off toward Covent Garden, her hand stole often to her throat and her eyes to her wrist. Trenton had bought her jewels.

CHAPTER THIRTEEN

As the carriage moved through the London streets, Jeannie tried to keep her mind on the present. "How is Covent Gardens these days?" she asked.

"It is its usual self," said Trenton dryly. "Smirke's design is holding up reasonably well, disallowing the regrettable fact of the Bow Street facade."

"What is wrong with the facade?" asked Jeannie, grasping at any subject which might keep her mind occupied.

"Those who know architecture say that the facade with its Greek Doric portico is unsatisfactorily related to the side and rear elevations."

"I think that is silly," interjected Lady Helena. "One seldom looks at the outside, and the inside is quite marvelous. The grand staircase, for example, is superb."

There was something in Lady Helena's tone that indicated she was waiting to be refuted, but his lordship merely added dryly, "It is copied after Chalgrin's staircase for the Paris Directorate at the Palais du Luxembourg. One must admit to Smirke's ingenuity in placing it alongside the auditorium. Since one can scarcely envision an opera house without a grand staircase and, since his site allowed him no room for one leading directly to the auditorium, he did the best he could. Of course, the fact that so monumental a staircase leads to nothing and opens into a corridor on one side may be considered an anomaly."

Lady Helena snorted. "There are always those about who are anxious to criticize. Covent Garden serves its purpose admirably well. As long as one can see and be seen, it is unnecessary to quibble over trifles."

Trenton exchanged a wry glance with Jeannie. "The finer points of architecture are lost upon my sister. As long as there are velvet-covered sofas and gilt boxes she is content."

Lady Helena threw her brother a hard look but did not answer.

Fortunately, the carriage drew to a halt and they were occupied with alighting. Jeannie studied the crowds of people—all members of the *ton* it seemed, from the dazzling array of diamonds that blazed on the throats and wrists of the fashionably dressed women. Jeannie's fingers stole unconsciously to her necklace of sapphires and amethysts. She would not trade her beloved gems, for the crown jewels themselves.

Trenton alighted and offered his hand, first to his sister and then to Jeannie. "Goodness," said Lady Helena with a sniff, "the crush is dreadful tonight."

The Viscount gave her a devilish smile. "It seems that a great many people prefer to see *all* of the performance."

Lady Helena cast her brother a look of disgust and then smiled at Jeannie. "I counsel you, my dear, to keep this man in line. He is absolutely abominable once he gets the upper hand."

Jeannie managed a small smile. Lady Helena did not know—and Jeannie hoped that Trenton didn't either—that his lordship had already taken that position of ascendancy. Oh, she might come to cuffs with him; undoubtedly she would assert her opinion, but when it came to the final decision, that would be his lordship's, always. He had so much strength, so much power, that she knew she could not stand against his wishes.

The Viscount, guiding them both through the crowd, smiled down at Jeannie. "My sister is on her way to becoming a dowager," he said, quite ignoring the outraged gasp that this comment brought from Lady Helena. "Dowagers in general give very poor advice. The best way to keep a man in line is to submit to his every wish."

"Submit!" sputtered Lady Helena, and Jeannie felt her own backbone stiffen.

"What's the matter, sister dear?" inquired his lordship. Jeannie, seeing the light of mischief in his eyes, was glad she had not yet spoken.

"The matter!" cried Lady Helena. "Trenton, you are a wretch. I should never agree to being submissive."

"Ah, but you do not have *me* for a husband," replied his lordship with a superior smile.

Lady Helena sputtered again, and before she could speak, Trenton turned to Jeannie. "And you, my love, what think you of submissive wives?"

Jeannie was aware that he was roasting her and his sister and she determined to give him back in kind. "Well, milord, I am only a poor country girl and don't know much of city life." She lowered her eyes demurely. "But it does seem to me, human nature being such as it is, that if *I* were a gentleman and *my* wife *always* submitted to me, I should begin to wonder about her."

"Well said, Jeannie. Oh, well said," crowed Lady Helena.

His lordship did not look pleased. In fact, his grip on her arm tightened painfully, and his mouth tightened also.

"Of course," continued Jeannie, perversely wishing now to make him smile again. "Any woman so fortunate as to be his lordship's wife—"

He looked at her quickly and caught her grin. His mouth relaxed then and he grinned in return. "You have a quick wit, my love." He winked at her. "But then, of course, how could it have been otherwise with *my* chosen bride?"

More sputtering was heard from Lady Helena's direction, but Jeannie was lost in the sparkle of the Viscount's eyes and could no longer continue the game. He *was* the most eligible man in the city, she told herself with a secret smile, though there was no reason she had to admit it to *him*.

By this time they were inside the great theater and moving up the staircase. Jeannie would have liked to have time to look around, but now there were too many people in the way. A great many of those people seemed to know his lordship. Fat mamas, in glittering diamonds and ostrich plumes twice as high as her own, nodded and smiled fetchingly at him. Behind or beside them came their daughters—shy, simpering, or proud. All of them had one thing in common—they lavished languid looks upon her husband-to-be.

All of this Jeannie found amusing. After all, the mamas and their daughters were no real threat to her happiness. But occasionally in the throng there would appear a beautiful woman nearer the Viscount's age. She, too, would cast him inviting looks. These women, Jeannie was quite certain, were leaning on the arms of their husbands. It was women like this who frightened her. They recognized no rules; they simply took what they wanted.

Also among the crowd were flocks of younger, beautiful women. Jeannie was quick to notice that although they, too, sent smiles his lordship's way, he offered them no smiles in return. Jeannie was about to ask him why when one of them went boldly up to a man and slipped her arm through his. Jeannie bit back an exclamation of surprise as the truth hit her. The beautiful young women must be incognitas, lightskirts, available to any man with the necessary blunt.

By this time they had reached their box. Trenton settled them in seats on each side of him, then leaned toward Jeannie and whispered, "My idiot sister will think I am whispering sweet words of love in your delicate pink ear, but that is not my intent. Play the game well, Jeannie, and let us not have any arguments where the *ton* can observe. And be sure of it, we *are* being observed."

Before he straightened, his lips brushed her ear. Jeannie colored up immediately and saw his approving smile. For some reason that smile made her extremely angry. Did the fool think a woman could color up at will? Or—and this made her even angrier— had he known what effect that brief caress would have on her?

In either case she was angry with him, but she realized that her anger went far deeper than the matter of a kiss. She was angry that he did not love her and yet could so confidently convince the world that he did. She was angry with herself for having succumbed to his charm. However, there was no point in spoiling her visit to Covent Garden.

"Look!" cried Lady Helena. "Prinny is coming in. The Duke of York is with him."

Jeannie looked, but found it difficult to generate much pride or respect in the royal brothers. Jeannie's small nose wrinkled in distaste. The rumor that the Regent wore stays must be true, she thought sadly. He walked with the careful gait of a man who could not bend properly.

"They say Prinny's latest is a grandmother," Lady Helena began and was silenced by a look from her brother.

"And there," whispered Lady Helena, "is Harriette Wilson. For a woman who's not really beautiful she has such *élan*."

Jeannie looked toward where the auburn-haired woman was being seated by a crowd of admiring beaux.

"They say she always wears cream satin—and only earrings. Rubies tonight, I think," continued Lady Helena.

Jeannie leaned forward to get a better look.

"Too bad we weren't able to see her carriage." Lady Helena shot her brother a sly look. "It's upholstered in blue satin, they say."

Jeannie's heart thudded. Blue satin! Like Trenton's carriage!

The Viscount stiffened perceptibly. "Really, Helena, I think it highly out of place for you to be speaking of London's leading demi-rep to my intended."

"She will see plenty of demi-reps in London," said Lady Helena nonchalantly. "I am merely continuing her education."

Trenton glared at his sister. "I am aware that I asked you to direct Miss Burnstead's entry into society. I am not aware that I asked you to point out to her women of whom it were better she know nothing."

Lady Helena snorted. "Come, come, Trenton. Certainly Jeannie will not hold your previous alliances against you. After all, you are a man of years and experience."

"Helena!" The Viscount's dark eyebrows drew together in a heavy frown, and his lips grew tight.

Jeannie laid a reassuring hand on his arm. "Please, Trenton, do not be angry with your sister. I certainly do not intend to make the acquaintance of any such ladies. Lady Helena is correct. A man of your years will have made alliances. It would be foolish of me to suppose otherwise. Besides," she gave him a smile that she hoped would convince him, "I like having the carriage lined in blue satin."

For a long moment he stared at her. Then he chuckled. "You see, Helena, what a gem I have chosen. Every day she amazes me in some new way." He reached out and took her hand. "Your vote of confidence is much appreciated, my love."

Jeannie, whose eyes had suddenly filled with tears, looked quickly out over the theater. The last thing she wanted was for his lordship to become aware of her growing feelings for him. Indifference she could stand. Even derision. But pity? Her blood ran cold at the thought.

Gradually her vision cleared and just as she was about to look back to Trenton the orchestra began. Jeannie fastened her eyes on the stage. She had not seen a play for such a long time and she had never seen Young do Hamlet.

As the curtain went up, Jeannie saw a man of medium stature. His dark eyes and dark complexion gave added strength to his portrayal of the gloomy Dane. With a slight smile, she noticed that this Dane was a trifle heavy in the midsection, but when he began to speak, she forgot about his figure. His voice was admirable and his delivery a melodious chant. When the sorrowful Hamlet sighed, Jeannie thought she had never heard such sweet sound, and when he vacillated in indecision, the quality of his voice conveyed his emotion beautifully.

As the curtain fell for intermission, Jeannie turned with shining eyes to Trenton. "He's very good, milord. Such a voice."

Trenton nodded. "The critics speak kindly of his Hamlet. He's also rather good at proud soldierly characters and testy philanthropists with a vein of kindness."

Jeannie leaned forward to look at Lady Helena. "Are you enjoying the evening?" she asked.

"The play is bearable," said that lady, "and the crowd is rather dull."

Jeannie stifled a smile. Lady Helena affected to be bored with the world, but her bright eyes darted everywhere. Surely she would know the name of every person of quality who had attended the performance.

As Jeannie settled back into her chair, her cashmere slipped from her shoulder. She was about to reach for it, but his lordship was quicker. "Allow me, my love," he said as he rearranged it carefully.

Jeannie sat stock-still, amazed at how she enjoyed his nearness and the feel of his fingers on her neck. Gloved though they were, they seemed to send sparks down her backbone.

Finally he had adjusted her shawl to his satisfaction. "Helena," he said, "I see someone with whom I must speak. Will you remain here and protect Jeannie from the beaux that will soon be arriving?"

"Of course, brother dear," said Lady Helena with an artful smile. "I will promise to protect her if she will promise *not* to protect me."

"Helena."

"All right, all right, run along. I will keep watch over your little bird. Go! Go!"

The Viscount made his departure. Without him, Jeannie grew suddenly nervous. "Lady Helena, must we admit the beaux?"

The lady looked shocked. "My dear! Of course we must. Why else should we come to the theater?"

"To see the play?" ventured Jeannie timidly.

"Of course not, my dear child. We come to see and be seen."

"Yes, but—"

"No buts," said a voice from the door of the box. "Lady Helena, my dear, do introduce me to the young lady."

"Come out of the shadows, then, Beau. Certainly you've no reason for standing there."

A small man, very well turned out, stepped forward and raised Jeannie's hand to his lips. "Beau Brummell," said Lady Helena with a smile. "London's best-dressed man." Jeannie regarded him curiously. She had heard a great deal about him.

"I deserve the title," said the Beau, "for I work very hard to keep it." He shook his head. "I wager I spend more time in the hands of my valet than you do in those of your dresser."

Lady Helena laughed. "I'd not be so foolish as to make such a wager with a man of your reputation, Beau. For you would surely win it. This is Trenton's intended, Miss Burnstead."

The Beau smiled. "I see that Trenton has chosen wisely. The lady has a certain freshness not often seen in London women."

Jeannie felt the color rising to her cheeks. Would she never get used to the compliments that London men handed out so easily?

"Ahhhhh!" The Beau's eyes had alighted on her necklace. "Sapphires and amethysts. What an unusual combination. I wager Trenton had them made especially to go with that gown."

Lady Helena smiled. "Of course. You know how Trenton is."

The Beau smiled too. "It appears that he is top-over-tail in love. As I recall, his taste in jewelry has always been rather conventional—diamonds and such, that appeal to—" He stopped suddenly and paused. "I admire your choice in a husband as I admire Trenton's in wives. You must have exceptional talents to have snared such a paragon."

Jeannie smiled. No wonder the Viscount was puffed up. Everyone seemed to concur with his high opinion of himself!

"Thank you, Mr. Brummell," said Jeannie demurely, "but I do not quite know how it happened."

"Love is like that, so I've been told," observed the Beau laconically. "I myself have never been one of its principal sufferers. Fashion is my first love, and women, being notoriously jealous creatures, do not take kindly to second place."

His glance moved out over Jeannie's head to the boxes on the other side of the theater. "Nor do they take kindly to being supplanted," he added, almost to himself.

There was a strange tone in the Beau's voice and, even before she had turned, Jeannie had an idea of what she would see—Lady Frances and the Viscount engaged in conversation. The Viscount's face was impassive, but Lady Frances's was by turns amused, seductive, and angry. This evening she wore a dress of silver lamé cut very low. Its little cap sleeves clung precariously to the very edges of her bare shoulders and from under her scantily covered bosom the gown fell away in long silvery folds. Her shining black curls peeped enchantingly from beneath a small lace cap.

She had removed one of her long kid gloves and her hand was very white as she placed it on Trenton's sleeve and looked up at him intimately.

There was no doubt then in Jeannie's mind. Lady Frances had been his lordship's inamorata before his trip to Shropshire, and she fully intended to resume that position now that he had returned to London.

Jeannie admitted to herself that she liked seeing the anger on Lady Frances's face. That might well mean that Trenton had ended their alliance. But as she watched the lady's expression became exciting and seductive again, all Jeannie's elation fled. Perhaps he had told her that he would not see her for a little while—until after the wedding.

Jeannie fought to keep her feelings from showing on her face. Why had she been so stupid as to agree to marry this man, knowing all the time what he was? How could she walk around London with her head held high if Trenton continued this kind of flirtation? But perhaps he wouldn't. He *had* promised discretion.

There was a great deal of confusion at the door of the box and then a crowd of men entered in a rush. Though Lady Helena faithfully introduced each one as he bent over her hand, Jeannie had only a blurred recollection of a series of faces above high starched cravats. Indelibly printed on her mind was the sight of Trenton bending over Lady Frances's bare fingers.

Then Trenton was entering the box again, and there was a chorus of exclamations about a sly fellow, hiding such a gem, and a diamond of the first water.

Trenton smiled as he moved to stand beside Jeannie's seat and laid one hand possessively on her shoulder. "Gentlemen, I am quite pleased that you concur with my opinion. Besides all her physical attributes, my Jeannie has a very good understanding."

The rest of what he said was lost to her ears. "*My* Jeannie," he had said. The words echoed and reechoed in her head. What had he meant by them? But of course it was simply another lie to convince his friends.

Then the friends were gone and Trenton settled himself for the rest of the play. Jeannie's thoughts were in a whirl and it took her a while to focus her attention once again on the play. Gradually its magic took over. Poor Ophelia, she found herself thinking. Love was not an easy thing. To love a man like Hamlet—or his lordship—might easily drive a woman to bedlam. But, thought Jeannie, automatically stiffening her backbone, she was not the kind to give in easily. No one was going to find Jeannie Burnstead, or the Viscountess of Trenton either, bedecked with flowers and lying drowned. When she realized quite suddenly that she was thinking of love and his lordship, her cheeks flushed scarlet. She, of course, never intended to love anyone.

In spite of the fact that she perceived Ophelia as giving up too easily, Jeannie found herself in tears as the young woman's body was lowered into her grave and Hamlet discovered her death. At least he had some feeling for Ophelia, she thought, as the tears slid down her cheeks. At least it wasn't all pretense on his part.

Suddenly Jeannie found that his lordship had taken her hand in his and was squeezing it gently. Without a word he handed her a fresh cambric handkerchief. Jeannie accepted it silently and wiped at the tears on her face. What a ninny he must think her.

Jeremy would certainly scoff at such infantile behavior. But the thought of Jeremy brought her fresh pain. There had been no word from him since he had brought the list of his debts. True, that hadn't been so terribly long ago but, still, he was her twin, and he

166

could have sent a word of thanks. Jeremy had not always been so thoughtless. Jeannie took a deep breath. There was nothing more she could do to help her twin.

As the curtain fell she found Trenton gazing at her with concern. "I hope the play has not upset you."

Jeannie shook her head. "It's just sad. Love like that—"

The Viscount shrugged. "Those who give themselves up to love must be prepared to pay the price—which is generally too high."

Jeannie nodded. He was obviously thinking of her experience with Atwood, but he had forgotten his sister or he would never have voiced such a cynical opinion.

Lady Helena did not let this remark pass. "Trenton," she said pointedly. "I do not understand you. Earlier this evening you were quite put out with me for pointing out to Jeannie Harriette Wilson—who can be considered one of the city's landmarks. And now you make such a cynical statement about love that your bride-to-be may well think you have regretted your choice."

"Nonsense, Helena. My Jeannie is no such featherbrain. Are you, my love?"

Jeannie could only nod as the Viscount continued. "She knows me quite well, Jeannie does. There will be no terrible surprises in store for her. She knows exactly how deeply I am in love with her." The words hit her almost like a blow.

It took Jeannie a moment or two to marshal her thoughts. Obviously he expected her to agree with him. "Yes, milady, his lordship is right." She took a deep breath and hoped to keep her voice steady. "The understanding between us is quite clear."

Lady Helena shrugged. "This was not the way of

love when I was a girl. But then, the world is changing."

"Indeed," observed Trenton with a wink at Jeannie, "we are all growing older."

"Trenton, you abominable man!" Lady Helena threatened him with her fan. "Must you continually remind me of that?"

It was Trenton's turn to shrug. "The family has certainly been after *me* on the matter. It appears that six and thirty is but one step from the grave, and you are a year older than I."

"Trenton! Be still!" Lady Helena glowered at him, but it was clear to Jeannie that both brother and sister were enjoying themselves.

The Viscount rose. "I believe some of the crush may be over by now. Shall we continue our discussion on the way home?"

"Of course." Lady Helena rose and was shawled and then the Viscount turned to Jeannie, expertly assisting her.

The crowds on the great staircase were still heavy and Jeannie was pressed hard against his lordship's side. His arm went out to circle her protectively, and she felt a wave of the same feeling that had swept over her at his use of the term "my Jeannie." It was pleasant there in the circle of his arm, and to her chagrin Jeannie suddenly remembered how she had enjoyed lying against him during their ride to London.

All too soon Trenton was handing her and Lady Helena into the carriage, and they were homeward bound. Jeannie found herself still yearning for the feel of Trenton's protective arm. Indeed, she must stop this yearning. It was one thing not to feel repulsed by his touch and quite another to actually long for it. The first spoke of duty and respect. The other of— Jeannie did not allow the word to form in her mind.

She was silent on the ride home. Lady Helena seemed determined to discuss the gowns and jewels of every woman in the theater. How she had seen and remembered so much Jeannie could not imagine.

Once at the house on St. James's Square, the Viscount helped them both to descend and guided them up the walk to where the ever attentive Budner stood by the open door. At the foot of the stairs his lordship paused. "There is less than two weeks until our wedding, my love." He spoke for Lady Helena's benefit, Jeannie knew, yet her heart seemed to leap into her throat.

"Yes, milord," she replied. "Less than two weeks."

Something strange flickered in his eyes, something that Jeannie could not put a name to. Could he be having second thoughts? It must be difficult for such a man to contemplate marriage.

"Good night," said his lordship.

"Good night," replied Jeannie over the thudding of her heart.

As they stood looking into each other's eyes, Lady Helena snorted. "For mercy's sake, Trenton, kiss the girl. I'm here to protect her good name, not her *lips.*"

Slowly his lordship bent and brushed her mouth with his. It was a light kiss, fleeting, and infinitely sweet. Jeannie's legs trembled as he straightened.

"Now, Trenton," said Lady Helena, "we will bid you good night. Your bride-to-be needs her rest."

"Helena," said his lordship briskly, "you grow more acerbic every year."

Lady Helena chuckled. "And you, my dear Trenton, are growing positively pettish." With this last word, Lady Helena swept grandly up the stairs, gesturing to Jeannie to follow her.

CHAPTER FOURTEEN

The sun woke Jeannie toward mid-morning the next day. She stretched luxuriously and smiled to herself. "My Jeannie," the Viscount had said. The words had a pleasant sound. Of course, there was no great passion between them, but surely they shared friendship. Everyone knew that friendship lived longer than passion.

Jeannie pulled back the bed curtains and climbed out of bed. First she peeked lovingly in the drawer where she had put her new jewels, and then she went to lean out the window and sniff the fragrance of the late summer flowers. Then she pulled the bell for the maid and hurried to the wardrobe. What kind of day was this? Was it a yellow dress day, or perhaps green? Her eyes slid down the row of gowns and came to rest on a bright yellow one. Yes, that was the dress for such a beautiful, sunny day.

Some time later, clad in the yellow gown and with her golden curls piled high, Jeannie made her way to the breakfast room. She did not expect Lady Helena to rise before noon. She had at least an hour to spend by herself, unless she should happen to see his lordship. Her heart fluttered at the thought. If she did, could she hide the joy that seemed to want to bubble out of her?

But the breakfast room was empty and Jeannie

moved on, out into the courtyard where the late summer flowers flourished. Noticing the tall stocks of hollyhocks, her favorite flower, in one corner of the little courtyard, she smiled with pleasure and moved closer to examine their delicate hues.

Lost as she was in her contemplation of them, she failed to hear anyone approach and so was startled to hear the Viscount say, "Good morning. Did you sleep well?"

"Oh, yes indeed," replied Jeannie, turning toward him and trying to hide her pleasure. "I slept very well."

"Good," said the Viscount. "The mail has arrived. I'm afraid I have some bad news."

"Oh, what is it?" Jeannie scrutinized his face carefully. His expression was sober but not alarmed.

"I have had a letter from your Aunt Dizzy. Uncle Obadiah's gout has flared up, and he cannot undertake the trip to London at this time. She begs that we postpone the wedding for several weeks until he recovers his health."

Jeannie nodded, her first fears fading. "Of course, Trenton. Uncle Obadiah often has these attacks. He is somewhat given to excess in food and drink."

His dark eyes probed hers. "So we shall have to postpone the wedding for the time being. They promise to let us know as soon as he can travel."

Jeannie smiled. "Aunt Dizzy will strictly oversee his diet. It should not take him long to recover."

"Good. Then that is settled." His eyes moved over her face. "You seem to be taking well to the city. Your eyes are sparkling and your cheeks are pink. You look most becoming in that yellow gown."

Jeannie flushed even more, and, because she was embarrassed by his compliment, said the first thing

172

that came into her head. "It's a yellow dress day."

The Viscount shook his head. "I'm afraid that is beyond my understanding. Would you please explain?"

"Of course," Jeannie replied. "The sky is blue, the sun is shining, and I am happy. So it's a yellow dress day."

"Ahhhhhh," said his lordship. "The color of your gown reflects your disposition for the day."

"Sometimes."

The Viscount smiled. "If I should ever see you wearing drab brown, I shall know you are sad."

Jeannie nodded.

"And if I see you in red"—his eyes laughed at her— "I shall know you are angry."

"I'm afraid I have no red gown," said Jeannie, "but if I am angry, you will know it, never fear."

The Viscount chuckled. "I have no doubt about it. It's quite the most refreshing thing that's happened to me in a long time—being about a woman who is honest with me and speaks her mind. You'd be surprised at how women—heiresses and incognitas alike—think that the way to a man's heart is by repeatedly agreeing."

"But, milord—" Jeannie's eyes danced with mischief, "you *said* you preferred a submissive woman."

Trenton frowned. "I was roasting you. My sister and I are fond of bickering." His mouth tightened. "But your point was not lost on me. I have told you to speak your mind to me. I cannot abide a mealy-mouthed liar, male or female." His eyes probed hers. "You wouldn't lie to me, would you, Jeannie?"

For one wild moment she thought he had discovered her growing partiality for him. "No, milord. I would not lie to you." She forced herself to say the words calmly. She would not lie to him about anything else, but she could not admit to him that she was learning to care for him.

His eyes still held hers. "That is good. We may not have love—but we shall have respect."

Jeannie could only nod.

The Viscount leaned over and picked a late rose. "Be careful of the thorns," he said as he handed it to her.

Jeannie nodded. "Thank you, milord. And thank you for the lovely jewelry last night."

The Viscount smiled. "They were nothing really. It amused me to have your jewels match your gown. I'm glad they pleased you. We should put them away, too."

"Oh, must we?" Jeannie found herself covered in confusion. She wanted to have the jewels by her, to look at them, to touch them.

Trenton shrugged. "I suppose not if you want them at hand." He looked at her questioningly.

"Oh, I do! You see, milord, these are my first jewels, the first of my very own."

The Viscount smiled. "There will be many, many more."

"But I don't need—" Jeannie protested.

"You forget yourself." His smile took the sting out of the words. "Of course a Viscountess needs jewels. Would you have all London brand me as a pinchpenny?"

"Of course not," declared Jeannie, "but to spend so much!"

"I have plenty of blunt," replied his lordship. "There is no need to concern yourself about it."

"But I feel guilty!" blurted Jeannie.

The Viscount raised a quizzical eyebrow. "Guilty of what?"

"We made a bargain," Jeannie stammered, "and you have been paying ever since. It does not seem right."

The Viscount regarded her for a long moment before smiling. "You are truly a remarkable child."

"I am not a—" began Jeannie and stopped. She was not going to fall into that trap again. "What is remarkable about me?"

Trenton smiled again. "You must be the only woman in London who is not eager for all the money she can get."

Jeannie shivered. "You don't make London sound like a very nice place."

"It is not," declared his lordship. "And it is certainly not the place for an innocent heart such as yours. Perhaps—perhaps I should not have asked so much of you."

A vision of Lady Frances smiling seductively up at Trenton flashed into Jeannie's mind. He could not send her home now!

"The banns have been called twice," she reminded him, "and many of your friends have seen or met me. The scandal would be terrible if we parted now."

Trenton shrugged. "I have borne scandal before. It passes and is forgotten. But we are discussing the rest of your life. I do not wish to see your life spoiled."

"*I* wish to stick by our bargain," said Jeannie as firmly as she could. "I will do all in my power to make you a good wife."

His lordship patted her hand. "A man can not ask for more than that." For a long moment he stood looking down into her eyes. It seemed almost as though he were about to kiss her again. Jeannie found that she was holding her breath in anticipation. But then he straightened. "I must go. I have business to attend to. Have a pleasant day."

"I shall see you at dinner," replied Jeannie.

Trenton shook his head. "I'm afraid not. I'm having dinner out tonight. Amuse yourself with Helena."

Then, before she could say another word, he was gone.

Jeannie looked down at her gown and sighed. It was not a yellow gown day after all. What was she to do with herself for a whole day?

Perhaps she would send a maid to the lending library for a new French novel, she thought as she returned indoors. Drivel or not, she must have something to occupy her time.

She reached her room and threw herself rather petulantly into a chair. This business of wanting his lordship's company was getting out of hand. Certainly respect did not call for such strong feelings on her part. She must not begin to expect too much of this marriage. It was probably all right to enjoy his lordship's presence, but to be yearning after it—and find her whole day ruined without it—this was surely not wise.

A brisk knock on the door jarred Jeannie from her reverie. "Come in." She turned to discover Lady Helena standing there in disarray.

"Jeannie, my dear," said Trenton's sister, "I must ask a favor of you."

"Of course. What is it?"

"I simply must go to Bond Street this morning. I need a new gown for the evening. Something outstanding."

Privately Jeannie was of the opinion that a gown any more outstanding than that of the previous evening would be far beyond the bounds of good taste, but she did not say so. "Of course, I'll go shopping with you."

"Fine, fine." Lady Helena beamed. "You're a dear girl, Jeannie, a very dear girl. It was such a blessing when Trenton decided upon you. When I think of the women who have been after him. It's simply appalling what might have come into the family." Lady Helena paused. "Yes, yes, we can count ourselves quite fortunate that Trenton's eye fell upon you."

Jeannie did not quite know how to respond to this. Lady Helena's words had raised some appalling pictures in her own mind—of Lady Frances with her soft white hand grasping Trenton's sleeve or Harriette Wilson's auburn curls shining against the voluptuous shoulders rising out of her gown of cream-colored satin. Of course, Trenton would never have brought either of them *into* the family. Jeannie pushed such thoughts from her mind and turned toward the wardrobe in search of a gown. "How soon shall I be ready?" she asked.

"We shall leave as quickly as possible so as to be back before calling hours." Lady Helena's pert face was lit by a mischievous smile. "After all, I should not want to miss any gentlemen callers." With that she scurried out to finish her dressing.

Jeannie simply shook her head. No wonder Trenton and his sister quibbled so often. They were proud and stubborn, with a broad streak of mischief running through them both. She pulled out a walking gown of celestial blue and a gypsy hat adorned with blue cornflowers and tied by a blue scarf. This outfit should be admirably suited to a shopping trip on Bond Street. After all, she told herself, she now had to consider her looks. Being Trenton's future Viscountess meant that many eyes would be upon her—and they would not all be friendly ones.

Some time later, with her gypsy hat securely tied under her chin, Jeannie stood in the hall while Lady Helena gave Budner last-minute instructions for the day. That patient butler received all her flurried orders with dignity and a look of long-suffering patience. There was no doubt in Jeannie's mind—nor in Budner's it seemed—that the house would continue to run in its usual well-ordered fashion without any intervention from Trenton's sister, but Lady Helena evidently thought differently.

Finally, after having exhausted every possibility in which Budner might conceivably find instruction necessary, Lady Helena turned to Jeannie. "Come, my dear. We must hurry."

Jeannie nodded and followed Trenton's sister out to the waiting carriage. "What color gown have you in mind to order?" she asked.

Lady Helena sighed deeply. "I really cannot say. I have so many gowns, yet I find none of them sufficient. I shall have to see what stuffs Madame Adelaide has received recently from France."

Jeannie nodded. She found all this business of clothes fatiguing. It was true that she no longer went about clad in drab gowns with no thought to her appearance, but she could not help thinking that Lady Helena's interest in clothes, as well as her taste, was somewhat excessive, although Jeannie would never have admitted to such a traitorous thought. Fortunately Lady Helena's dark complexion and hair could withstand the assault of such flamboyant colors as she sometimes wore. On the other hand, sometimes the styles she chose were inauspicious, as well. Take, for instance, the walking dress that Lady Helena now wore—of white muslin with a pleated foot-wide flounce around the bottom and a matching pelisse with close-fitting long sleeves and a round yoke below its high collar all edged with ruffles. It seemed better suited to a far younger woman. And her bonnet, with its high crown trimmed with green feathers and its lace-edged brim, did not seem to do her features justice. But this, of course, was Lady Helena's affair, not Jeannie's.

"I do like that new shade of blue," said Lady Helena. "Or perhaps I shall try a tunic gown of gold lamé. Lady Frances looked quite the thing in silver the other night, don't you think?"

Jeannie found a lump in her throat and had to swallow twice before she could answer. "Yes, yes, she looked quite the thing."

Again, Jeannie's thought was that such excessive dress detracted from its wearer's natural beauty. Now for real elegance—she started slightly and smiled as she realized the model that her mind had presented to her. For real elegance she much preferred the simplicity of Harriette Wilson's cream-colored satin. There was nothing in Harriette's mode of dress to detract from the shine of her gorgeous auburn hair, and the cream-colored satin was the ideal color to show off the milky white of her shapely shoulders. Even in the matter of jewelry, thought Jeannie, the demi-rep was far wiser than the ladies. She wore no heavy necklaces to hide a slender throat. Harriette Wilson, Jeannie told herself thoughtfully, was not only beautiful; she was wise.

"Perhaps an emerald green silk to be worn with my rubies," said Lady Helena aloud.

Jeannie shuddered inwardly at the proposed combination, but made no comment. It was unlikely that Lady Helena would care to receive advice in matters of fashion from a miss newly in from the country.

"Perhaps you should order a new gown or two," said Lady Helena suddenly.

"Oh no! I think not. I have so many new ones just come. My things have arrived from Shropshire, as well."

Lady Helena shook her head. "You are not natural, my dear. It is the nature of every young woman to want as many gowns as possible."

"But I can only wear one at a time," replied Jeannie reasonably. "And think of the cost."

Lady Helena's bushy black eyebrows, so like her brother's, shot skyward. "Cost? My dear, what is cost to you? Let Trenton worry about trifles like that."

It was clear to Jeannie that Lady Helena's family had never suffered for lack of substance. It seemed useless to try to explain her very real distress at the idea of wasting her husband-to-be's substance.

"Or perhaps the new purple," continued Lady Helena, Jeannie's conversation already forgotten. "Although generally I abhor purple. It's such a dowagerish color, don't you think?"

Jeannie could only nod to this since Lady Helena did not pause long enough for anyone to interject an answer while she continued to think aloud. Thank God, Jeannie told herself, that Trenton did not hold his future wife responsible for his sister's mode of dress. Crossing Lady Helena might be nearly as difficult as crossing his lordship himself.

The carriage stopped, and Lady Helena turned to Jeannie. "Here we are. Madame Adelaide will have all the newest fabrics and fashions from France. She is one of London's most fashionable *modistes*."

Jeannie stepped down from the carriage and paused to gaze about her. Bond Street had not changed in the two years she had spent in Shropshire. Young ladies, and older ones, in pairs or accompanied by demure maidservants, moved from shop to shop or strolled casually along the pavement, nodding and being nodded to by the well set-up dandies and exquisites who also strolled there. Jeannie sighed. Surely there were more important things to be done in this world than strolling about simply to see or be seen.

Lady Helena had not paused as Jeannie had and so was just disappearing through the door of the *modiste's* establishment when Jeannie felt a hand on her arm. "Jeannie Burnstead," said a familiar voice that caused her heart to sink heavily. "What a fool you two took me for."

Jeannie felt the red flood her cheeks as she looked up to meet the gaze of Lord Atwood. His chin seemed weaker than ever and his eyes were unnaturally bright. He was already in his cups, she thought, and this early in the day! She wanted to move away from him, but her legs refused to move, and Lady Helena was out of sight.

"Yes, yes." Atwood nodded with the exaggerated sagacity of the inebriated. "You really put one over on me." His face took on a pained expression. "You could have told an old friend, a good old friend like me."

Jeannie could feel the eyes of passersby regarding her curiously, and she took a step to move away from him, but his hand retained its grip on her arm.

"Mustn't run away from me," he said, slurring his speech. "Pretty young thing. Got plans to make."

Jeannie tried to gather her wits. "Please release me, sir." She wanted her voice to be cool and firm, but it had a most disconcerting tremble in it. "Lady Helena is waiting for me."

"Ahhhh! Helena. Trenton's sissssster. Little old. But still kicking."

"Milord!" With her other hand Jeannie tried to pry his fingers loose from her arm, but without success.

"Be nice to me," he murmured. "Pretty little thing."

Jeannie fought down an urge to scream. The man could not really hurt her physically, not here on Bond Street in full view of passersby. But already her face was flaming from the embarrassment of such a position and she still did not know how to effect her release.

Then a sweet, low voice came lilting through the air. "Atwood, my boy. Where have you been keeping yourself?"

Jeannie looked up to see the auburn hair and delicate features of Harriette Wilson. As her gaze met that of the demi-rep, Jeannie saw compassion and understanding. Then Harriette's gaze returned to Atwood, and Jeannie watched in surprise as the fingers fell from her arm and Atwood muttered, "Lil Harry. 'Pon my word. Lil Harry."

Jeannie waited no longer but made her way as quickly as possible up the walk and into Madame Adelaide's dress establishment. As the door closed behind her, she leaned back against it, the color beginning to fade from her cheeks. What a terrible scene! To be accosted so by a drunken lord right on Bond Street where everyone could see. Gossip would be all over London by nightfall. She shivered. The *ton* was seldom noted for its kindness, and malicious tongues would wag madly at the news that Jeannie had been seen in conversation with her former intended.

Her knees felt so weak that she doubted she could move, but she knew she could not continue to stand with her back against the dress shop door. She looked ridiculous, and Lady Helena would soon note her absence. She forced herself to move away from the door and smile at the young shopgirl who approached her.

"Lady Helena is this way," said the girl. "She sent me to fetch you." Jeannie nodded and followed her toward the back of the establishment, where she found Trenton's sister ensconced among bolts of fabric.

"Jeannie, where have you been? Just look at this array. I am having the most difficult time deciding. Do sit down and help me make up my mind."

Even in her flustered condition, Jeannie was aware that no one could help Lady Helena with that kind of task. Still, she settled into the proffered chair gratefully. This was not the time, with Madame Adelaide and her girls standing by, to inform Trenton's sister of the scene that had just taken place. Later, in the carriage on the way home would be more auspicious. She turned her attention to the material surrounding Lady Helena. Bolts of silk, satin, lamé, and crepe tumbled in gay profusion.

"I simply cannot make up my mind," said Lady Helena petulantly. "This emerald silk now—" She rubbed it speculatively between her thumb and fore-finger. "Or this gold lamé." She turned to the *modiste* with a frown. "Really, Madame Adelaide, I had hoped for a better selection."

The *modiste,* a drab, spinsterish woman, trembled visibly. "Her ladyship has seen all the latest fabrics."

"Have you nothing else?"

"Well—there is just come, the new muslins from France. The very sheer muslins."

With a start Jeannie was reminded of Trenton's words about damped petticoats.

"Very sheer?" asked Lady Helena with a mis-chievous smile and the *modiste* nodded.

"I will have some brought. Does your ladyship favor a particular color?"

Lady Helena shook her head, which still wore the white lace-edged bonnet. "No, no. If I wanted a particular color, I should ask for it. That is precisely the problem. I have no particular color in mind."

The *modiste* nodded and scurried off, rather like a little mouse in search of something to placate the cat, thought Jeannie with an inner smile.

Lady Helena sighed again. "I think perhaps I shall have to search out a new dressmaker. Why, would you believe that creature tried to persuade me out of having this gown made? She said it was too old for me. Imagine!"

Though Jeannie quite concurred with this opinion, she did not care to say so and contented herself with nodding in commiseration. By this time Madame Adelaide had returned, followed by several shopgirls burdened with bolts of fabric.

"Now this," said the *modiste*, with the merest of glances at Jeannie, "is the newest of French muslins. Very sheer."

She held up one end of a length dyed a deep blue and Jeannie gasped as she saw the clear outline of Madame's face through it. "Women *wear* that?"

The dressmaker bowed her head. "Indeed, miss, they do."

Jeannie could not imagine going forth in a gown of such material, not even over a heavy petticoat, but she knew that Trenton's sister had no such scruples.

"And what sort of petticoats are worn under these?" asked Lady Helena, her eyes dancing.

"That depends, milady." The *modiste* seemed rather embarrassed by the whole subject and Jeannie saw two of the shopgirls exchange glances and smother giggles. "Some wear heavy petticoats and some wear light."

"And some who wear light ones damp them," said Lady Helena.

Madame Adelaide nodded. "But I should not advise—" She stopped, obviously aware that she had erred.

Lady Helena turned critical eyes upon her. "That is just as well," said she with a sharp smile, "since I rarely take advice." She turned back toward the patiently waiting shopgirls and eyed the bolts they were holding. Then she motioned to one. "Bring that bolt here."

Obediently a girl stepped forward. Lady Helena reached out to feel the material. It was the same sheer muslin in a shade of coral. "This!" she cried triumphantly. "I shall have a gown in this and one in gold lamé. The lamé is to be a tunic dress and this one is to be well-fitted and with a suitable petticoat."

The dressmaker nodded. "And of what weight does your ladyship desire the petticoat?"

"The lightest, of course," replied Lady Helena sharply and the *modiste* bowed her head.

Jeannie found herself at a loss. She did not think Trenton would approve of his sister going about in garments that left her halfnaked, yet Jeannie could not do anything. The little dressmaker had tried, quite unsuccessfully, and Jeannie could sympathize with her. She did not want to risk bringing Lady Helena's displeasure down upon her own head, especially when she knew her efforts would be futile. Instead, she sat quietly by while the rest of the business was transacted.

When they left the dressmaker, Jeannie felt some trepidation. What if Atwood were still hanging about outside? But fortunately the pavement outside the shop was empty. She followed Lady Helena to the carriage and settled in her seat with a deep sigh.

The sigh brought Lady Helena's attention to her. "My word, Jeannie," she said, "you're pale as a ghost. Are you ill?"

Jeannie shook her head. "No, no, milady. It's just—before—when you had gone inside—Lord Atwood accosted me."

"Atwood?" Lady Helena looked bewildered. Plainly she did not remember the facts of Jeannie's past life.

"I was once promised to him," Jeannie explained, "and he threw me over for an heiress."

"I remember now. I know the man. He has a weak chin and a character to match."

Jeannie nodded. "I know that now. He—he was in his cups, and he laid hold of my arm."

Lady Helena raised a shocked eyebrow. "Why didn't you scream? The coachman would have come."

Jeannie sighed again. "I was so frightened, I couldn't think. I didn't want to make a public scene." She felt tears rising to her eyes. "Before—when Atwood left me—the talk was awful. The *ton* whispered for weeks." She swallowed. "I couldn't stand it anymore, so I went back to Shropshire."

Lady Helena frowned, bringing together the black brows so like her brother's. "The *ton* is always talking. Gossip is its food and drink. You must not let such things bother you. Just go merrily on your way."

Jeannie nodded. "I know that. But—but—I couldn't stand their whispering about me like that. And now—it will all start up again."

"Nonsense!" Lady Helena said the word quite firmly. "You forget that you are now Trenton's intended. This meeting was only an accident, a trifling thing. Forget it."

"But—shouldn't I tell Trenton?"

"Well, if you should like to see Atwood killed, go ahead. The laws against dueling are still evaded."

"You mean Trenton would—"

Lady Helena nodded. "Unless I miss my guess, Trenton would call him out immediately."

Jeannie raised a gloved hand to her burning cheeks. "Oh no! Atwood is despicable, but I should not like to be the cause of his death. And Trenton—dueling. If he should be hurt—"

Lady Helena snorted again. "By Atwood? Don't believe it. Trenton is one of the best shots around. No, it would be Atwood's demise, no doubt of it."

Still Jeannie could not be satisfied. Bullets could go astray and if one found its way into Trenton's person, she would never forgive herself. "No, no. He must not. Please, don't you tell him, Lady Helena. Please!"

Lady Helena shrugged. "It was just a trifling occurrence. I counsel you to put it out of your mind completely."

Jeannie nodded. Lady Helena's advice made good sense; it was just quite difficult to follow.

By this time they had reached St. James's Square. Once inside the great house, Jeannie went up to her room. Despite Lady Helena's advice, some nagging voice kept insisting that she inform Trenton, no matter the risks. What if someone else told him, she thought, her breath catching in her throat. But then she realized that such a thing was unlikely. No one would be foolish enough to invite his anger by such a deed.

CHAPTER FIFTEEN

Some time later Jeannie was able to take her place in the drawing room, even to chat amiably with the several elderly women who called briefly. Those dowagers, after a spirited exchange of descriptions of every pain experienced in the last month, finally departed, leaving Jeannie to say, with a shake of her blond curls, "I do not see how any living person can survive such suffering."

"Survive?" said Lady Helena dryly. "They live on it. You must understand, Jeannie"—the lady's bright eyes fixed themselves upon her—"that their ailments are the reason *for* their survival."

"For?" asked Jeannie in bewilderment.

"Precisely," replied Lady Helena. "Their ailments are by far the most interesting aspects of their lives. Cure them and they would have nothing of which to speak."

Jeannie shook her head. "I find this very difficult to understand."

Lady Helena's dark eyes sparkled. "Has your aunt no ailments?"

Jeannie considered this, then shook her head. "No, Aunt Dizzy—Desdemona—is quite healthy. She devotes most of her time to reading French novels."

"Ahhhh!" said Lady Helena. "Now you see. Your

aunt's romances serve the same function as these ladies' illnesses. They give her something to think about besides the emptiness of her life."

"I believe I begin to understand," said Jeannie. "Still, I hope I shall not be driven to such lengths."

Lady Helena smiled. "As long as you have Trenton, my dear, you will have little time for such amusements. A husband can put a great deal of demand on a woman's time."

Jeannie found herself smiling at the thought. "Isn't that as it should be?" she asked.

"You have been reading too many romances yourself," said Lady Helena, but her smile took the sting from the words. "Seriously now, my dear, marriage is a sober business, and living with Trenton can be trying." She sighed. "However, my brother does have his better side, as I'm sure you are aware."

Nodding at this, Jeannie could not help but wonder what would be Lady Helena's reaction if she were to discover the true nature of this alliance between Jeannie and her brother. Would she recoil in horror at its business nature or simply smile cynically? Certainly Lady Helena's outward attitude was one of worldliness, but certain things had led Jeannie to suspect that her heart was much softer than it appeared.

"I'm sure there are things I shall have to learn," began Jeannie, only to hear a cough behind her.

She turned and Budner spoke. "His lordship has returned, miss. He says he wishes to see you in the library."

"Yes, Budner."

"Do you see what I mean?" Helena said. "He comes in and immediately calls for your presence, as though you exist only for his pleasure."

Jeannie smiled at this. "But you must admit, milady, that it is pleasant to have someone call for you."

A sudden spasm of pain crossed Lady Helena's features. "You are quite right in that, my dear. Now run along. We don't want to keep Trenton waiting."

"Yes, milady." Jeannie smoothed down her blue gown and moved toward the library. She would be glad to see the Viscount again, she thought as she moved down the hall.

She paused before the library door to pat at her hair. Then she smiled and stepped into the room where Trenton stood, his back to the door. "Milord, you asked for me?"

As he swung around to face her, her smile faded. "Yes, I asked for you," he said. There was no expression of greeting on his face, only a stern frown.

"Is something wrong?" asked Jeannie, moving timidly forward.

"I believe so." His dark eyes bored into hers, and Jeannie began to tremble.

"W-what is it?" she asked.

"Are you aware of nothing wrong?" His eyebrows met in one thunderous line.

Jeannie put a hand to her forehead. Her heart was pounding in her throat, and she could not think. She recalled the scene with Atwood, but that could not have put Trenton in such a temper. "I—no," said Jeannie, crossing the room to sink into a chair. "Please, milord. Tell me what is wrong."

Trenton moved closer until he stood towering over her. "I thought that we had an agreement to speak clearly to one another, to tell no lies. Was this not the case?"

"Yes, milord." Jeannie forced herself to meet the blazing black eyes. "But I have not lied."

"Oh? Are you quite sure?" His mouth tightened into a thin stubborn line.

"Yes, milord." Jeannie clasped her trembling hands in her lap.

"I suggest you review the events of the day."

"Today?" If only she could keep her voice from quivering in that disgraceful fashion.

"Today." He stood quite still, looming over her, his hands clasped behind his back.

"Today I went shopping with Lady Helena on Bond Street."

"Continue."

"She went to order a gown for the opera." Jeannie dropped her eyes.

"And—"

It must be the meeting with Atwood, she thought. But why should that make him angry with *her?*

"I was stopped outside the dressmaker's by Lord Atwood."

"I see." His voice indicated his barely controlled rage.

"He was in his cups, and he laid hold of my arm." Jeannie made herself go on.

"In his cups? In the morning?" His face reflected Trenton's disbelief.

"Yes," said Jeannie firmly. "In his cups. In the morning. And he laid hold of my arm. He said we had played him for a fool, you and I." Her voice grew stronger now that she knew the reason for his anger. "He said that we could have told him the truth that day in the carriage." She stopped, hoping he would ask no more questions.

The silence in the room was so heavy that it lay on her like a great burden. Finally Trenton spoke again. "And what else did he say?"

Reluctantly Jeannie raised her eyes to his. "He—

he made some advances to me, as he did in the carriage that day." She paused, unable to continue because of the ferocity of his frown.

"What was my sister doing all this time?"

"She had already stepped inside the dressmaker's and was not aware that Atwood was there."

"Then what did you do?"

"I tried to follow her, but I could not get my arm free from his fingers. And then, just as I thought I should scream for the coachman, Harriette Wilson came along and spoke to him. He turned away from me, and I hurried into the shop."

"Is that the complete story?"

"Yes, milord, except that I feel sure Miss Wilson knew my dilemma and wished to help me." She might as well tell him everything, she thought.

"How do you surmise this?"

"It was the way she looked at me, with so much friendliness—and—and compassion." Jeannie waited for the storm to break. Surely Trenton would not approve of her finding such qualities in an incognita.

But surprisingly his features began to clear. "Little Harry's a trump, all right. I wager she did rescue you on purpose. It would be just like her."

He swung on his heel and began to pace back and forth in front of her. "So, you were relieved of Atwood's importunities."

"Yes." Jeannie began to relax, but it was too soon.

"Why wasn't I informed of this?" he asked, his features again contorting into a scowl.

"Really, milord, you've only just arrived home. I had no time to tell you anything." Jeannie hoped her bluff would work, but it did not.

"As I recall—and quite clearly—whenever you have had any matter to discuss with me, you have informed Budner of that fact. You left no such information with

193

him today. Come, Jeannie, tell the truth, all of it—no more half-truths."

Suddenly Jeannie felt her anger rising. He was creating all this furor over something that wasn't even her fault. "The truth is, milord, that Lady Helena advised me not to bother you with such a triviality."

"Triviality! My bride-to-be is accosted and insulted by a drunken dog, and this is a triviality?" He stopped again in front of her, his chest rising and falling with his efforts to contain his rage.

"It was exactly this kind of attitude that we hoped to forestall," said Jeannie. "The incident was small, my embarrassment momentary. Lady Helena and I feared that you might think it your—your duty"—for some reason the words caught in her throat—"to avenge such a slight. I—I do not want you on the dueling field. I've no wish to be a widow before I'm a wife."

The Viscount suddenly burst into rollicking peals of laughter. Jeannie stared at him, considerably affronted by this reaction. "Atwood could make no woman a widow," he said finally. "Atwood can't hit *anything* with a pistol."

"But I was afraid. Accidents do happen."

A strange expression crossed Trenton's face. "Your concern for me is very sweet," he said in oddly formal tones. "Very sweet and very misplaced. There is no man in London that I can't best on the field." His eyes watched her narrowly as he spoke, and they noted the color that flooded her cheeks.

"I—I hope that you are not fond of dueling," said Jeannie. "I should not like that."

"And why not?" His features were very serious, and his eyes bored into hers.

"I—I—" Jeannie cast about in her mind for some answer that would not reveal her feelings. "That ought to be apparent," she said finally. "All things considered, I am not likely to find another husband I can respect. And then, of course, there will be the little ones to consider. They are the real reason for this marriage. And children need their father."

"Of course," replied his lordship, a hint of sadness appearing around his eyes. "We must think of the little ones."

A persistent fear still nagged at Jeannie. "You will not—call Atwood out, will you?"

"Dueling is illegal," Trenton replied. "You know that."

"But that would not stop *you*," Jeannie cried.

The Viscount smiled wryly. "Now I am not only London's greatest rakeshame, but a man who flouts the law with impunity."

Jeannie rose hastily to her feet. "Milord!"

Trenton grasped her arms and pulled her close to him till their eyes were only inches apart. "Tell me, Miss Burnstead, how can you consider marriage to such a person?"

Under the scrutiny of those dark eyes, Jeannie felt the blood racing to her cheeks. She must keep him from learning her secret, she thought, and yet she could not withdraw her gaze from his. "I—can consider marriage to a man I respect," she faltered. "And that—that is enough."

For another long moment he looked into her eyes and then he shrugged, the nonchalant shrug of the affirmed rake. "Of course. We must stick to our bargain. Respect—that is the word."

Jeannie dropped her eyes, unable to bear his look any longer. Then suddenly he shook her lightly. "But hear me, Jeannie. To keep respect we must have no more lies. Agreed?"

She raised her eyes once more, meeting his boldly. "Agreed, milord."

There was only one matter on which she would not speak the truth, she thought moments later as she made her way up the stairs to dress for dinner. She would never be able to tell him the real reason she did not want him to risk his life on the dueling field, the reason she had this very afternoon been forced to admit to herself. It was not respect that she felt for his lordship. And it was not just a question of finding that her marital duties would be not unpleasant or difficult to bear because of a growing partiality for her husband-to-be. It was the stark staring fact that Jeannie Burnstead, who had vowed never to open herself to such pain again, had fallen madly and deeply in love with the Viscount Trenton and could not contemplate the prospect of a life without him.

CHAPTER SIXTEEN

More days passed and Jeannie, finding that her love had not been discovered, began to relax a little. Atwood had not reappeared and Jeannie had braved the terrors of Bond Street at the insistence of his lordship without again seeing that creature. No more occasions had arisen upon which to quarrel, and Jeannie was confident that if she could only keep her love from him, they should deal reasonably well together in marriage. She could not believe that she could arouse in him the passions so familiar to Lady Frances or Harriette Wilson, but she would strive to be a good wife, strive with all her heart and soul.

She and Lady Helena were at the breakfast table when Trenton entered the room. He dropped a swift kiss on the top of Jeannie's head. "Good morning, pet."

"Good morning, milord." By now Jeannie was accustomed to being addressed by such affectionate nicknames.

Trenton smiled at them both. "Kean has returned. Tonight he is doing *Hamlet*."

"*Hamlet* again?" said Lady Helena in an aggrieved tone. "Can't we see something light and frivolous for a change?"

The Viscount smiled. "We have the world of the *ton* to offer frivolity. Besides, I thought Jeannie might like seeing Kean do *Hamlet*. Since she has seen Young, she can make a comparison between the two."

"Yes, I should like that," said Jeannie, her cheeks turning rosy as his words about Young recalled the precious gift of jewels he had given her that night. How many, many times a day she opened the drawer to take a quick, loving look at them.

"Well," said Lady Helena, "I suppose I shall survive. I shall wear my new gold lamé. Jeannie can wear her yellow silk." She gazed at Trenton. "I tried to persuade the foolish child to order some new gowns, but she insisted on worrying over your substance."

Trenton favored Jeannie with a smile. "I appreciate your concern, but I assure you that it is unnecessary."

Jeannie nodded. "Yes, milord." But still she did not think she would be wasteful. A good wife should be prudent and saving, a help to her husband.

"Well, Trenton, are you going to breakfast with us or not?" asked Lady Helena.

"Not," he replied with a smile at Jeannie. "I'm afraid there are certain affairs that require my presence today. But I shall return in good time for the theater."

"I suppose I shall have to see this performance from the start, too," lamented Lady Helena.

The Viscount grinned mischievously. "If you intend to go to Drury Lane with Jeannie and me, then you must be ready on time."

"Very well, Trenton." Lady Helena heaved such a sigh of martyrdom that Jeannie was forced to choke back a giggle.

"Now I must run," said the Viscount. "Until tonight."

With a smile on her lips Jeannie watched him stride across the room. In his coat of blue superfine, his light kerseymere breeches, and his top boots, he would catch the eye of any woman he might meet. Jeannie's smile faded. What was the nature of the business that kept Trenton out so often? Was it business with Lady Frances or perhaps Harriette Wilson?

Unconsciously, Jeannie sighed. She could hardly expect his lordship to be unaware of Harriette's charms. And how could she blame anyone for loving Trenton when she herself did so to distraction?

Lady Frances, of course, was another story. Jeannie could not believe that love was the determining force behind any of Lady Frances's actions. What moved Lady Frances was avarice, pride, perhaps even hatred, thought Jeannie. The proud lady liked to own people, as some liked to own things. As the Beau had pointed out, Lady Frances also liked to have the say in disposing of her possessions.

Jeannie sighed again. She was not equipped to battle either of these women for Trenton's affections, and she was doubly handicapped by the nature of their agreement. Unless he flagrantly flouted his amours before the public eye and thus could be supposed to do damage to her pride, she had no call to censure him.

"Jeannie!" Lady Helena's tone made her aware that this was not the first time Trenton's sister had addressed her.

"I'm sorry. I fear I was woolgathering."

Lady Helena smiled. "I hope it was about clothes. You shall have to wear your yellow silk. It is the only thing suitable. We shall have to go back to Madame Adelaide's soon for some new gowns for evening. You cannot always be wearing the same thing."

"I should really like to wear the celestial blue gown," said Jeannie, the thought of her jewels warming her.

Lady Helena shook her head. "No, my dear. I understand your desire to wear your new jewels, but it simply will not do. It is far too soon to be seen again in that gown." The determined look on Lady Helena's face told Jeannie quite clearly that further discussion was useless.

"Yes, milady," murmured Jeannie, a little dismayed to find herself thinking of the day when Lady Helena would no longer be around to issue orders.

"And now I shall retire to my room. I want to look my best this evening."

Jeannie made no comment to this, but as Lady Helena made her way up the stairs, Jeannie sighed. It was now only one o'clock. How Lady Helena could need rest when she had arisen from her bed barely an hour ago, Jeannie could not tell, but she herself felt a terrible restlessness gnawing at her these days and she did not know its cause.

She wandered into the library, thinking perhaps she had left her last romance there, a book by an unknown Englishwoman who wrote under the pseudonym of Lady Incognita. It was called *Love in the Ruins*. But she could not find it.

Jeannie sighed again. She felt like stamping her foot, but of course such behavior was hardly fitting for the future Viscountess. She whirled on her heel and marched to the window. Perhaps if she gazed out on the garden she could alleviate some of this boredom and the anxiety she felt over Trenton's whereabouts. But the late summer flowers, beautiful as they were in their bright array of colors, could not turn her mind from visions of Trenton standing with Lady Frances's white hand on his sleeve or dancing attendance on the lovely Harriette. A tear of frustration rose to her eye and Jeannie dashed it away angrily. She was not going to become a waterworks.

A slight noise at the door made her turn. Budner stood there, his face set in its usual dignified lines. "Your brother, miss."

"Oh, do send him right in." Jeannie composed herself and put a smile on her face. It would not do to let Jeremy suspect anything was wrong.

As Jeremy entered the room, Jeannie moved toward him. "Oh, Jeremy. I'm so pleased to see you. I'm going out of my mind with boredom. Come, do sit down and talk to me." She took his hands in hers.

She was so pleased to see her twin that Jeannie did not at first note the expression of despair on his face, but once they had settled on a divan and she turned to him, she realized that something was very wrong. "Jeremy! Are you ill?"

He laughed harshly. "I suppose you might call it that. I need some blunt and I need it quick. Otherwise it's debtors' prison."

"Jeremy!" Jeannie's face paled. "Trenton said he would pay all your debts."

"He did." Her twin passed a hand over his face. "But I had not yet incurred this debt."

Jeannie's heart began to pound in her throat and her palms grew wet. "It's another gambling debt. Oh, Jeremy!"

He scowled at her, his handsome features contorted. "It's not that much. Only a hundred pounds. But he insists on having it right away."

Jeannie felt tears rising and fought to keep them down. "I can't help you, Jeremy. I have no money."

Jeremy's features hardened. "Ask him for some."

"He won't help you anymore." Jeannie swallowed over the lump in her throat. "He doesn't change his mind about such things."

Jeremy's frown deepened. "Mama's jewels then. Give them to me."

Jeannie shook her head, her lip trembling. "I can't, Jeremy. They're locked up for safekeeping. I can't get them without asking him."

Jeremy's hands clutched at hers. "You *must* help me, Jeannie. Oh, what'll I do?"

Jeannie bowed her head. She had just realized that upstairs in her drawer lay her new necklace and bracelet. *Her* jewels, the ones Trenton had given her. Her heart seemed to break just thinking about giving them up.

Trenton, if he found out, would be furious, but perhaps he would not find out—at least, not until after the wedding. After all, the jewels had been selected to be worn with that one gown, and fashionable ladies did not appear often in the same gown. If she gave the jewels to Jeremy, he could get out of debt. Trenton would find out, in time, of course, but she couldn't ask him for the money—not after what he had said. This seemed the only way to help her twin.

"Jeremy." She raised her head and looked at him from tear-filled eyes.

"Yes?"

"I have thought of a way, but I will never be able to help you like this again. When Trenton finds out what I have done, he will never give me the chance to do it again."

"What is it, Jeannie? How can you get me the blunt?"

"Trenton gave me some jewels. I will give them to you; but, Jeremy, you must understand. He absolutely refuses to pay your debts and when he discovers what I have done—" she could not suppress a small shiver of fear—"he will never leave any jewels in my keeping again."

A strange smile crossed Jeremy's face. "I scarcely think his lordship will be too hard on you—especially if you let drop that you know he's been seen coming out of Little Harry's place."

"Jeremy!" Jeannie sank down into the nearest chair, her legs no longer capable of holding her. "He can't have been there! Please say it isn't so."

Her twin shook his head. "There's no need to get all atremble. I thought you were a woman of the world. Probably every lord in London has been to Harriette's—or wishes he had."

"But Trenton—" Jeannie felt all her hopes shattered. If he had returned to Harriette this soon—even before their wedding—She covered her bowed face with her hands.

"Come now, Jeannie," said her twin impatiently, "I wouldn't have mentioned the thing at all except to give you something to defend yourself with. I didn't expect you to fall apart at the news. It's not such a rare thing, after all."

Jeannie made no answer to this. She was making every effort to control the sobs that threatened to overwhelm her.

Jeremy took her roughly by the shoulders. "Jeannie! I haven't time for this sort of thing now. Come on, get me the jewels. Quick!"

Jeannie raised a tear-stained face. "Jeremy, please. There must be some other way."

Her twin shook his head. "You know there isn't. Just get the jewels. Quick, Jeannie. I've got to meet the man I owe."

Jeannie could withstand him no longer. As she hurried upstairs, she refused to allow the terror in her mind to surface. She loved Trenton and the last thing she wanted to do was to bring his wrath down upon her head. But what choice had she? Jeremy was her twin; she had always looked out for him. Minutes later she put her beloved jewels in her twin's hands.

"Good. These should cover it. I've got to go now." He swung on his heel and was gone.

He wasn't even out the door before Jeannie knew for sure that she had made a dreadful mistake. Jeremy had not said thank you, had not seemed to hear—or to care—that Trenton would be furious with her. Jeremy could think only of himself. Life on the town had made him spoiled and selfish.

Jeannie swallowed over the hard lump of tears in her throat and wished for her beloved jewels back. But there was no recalling them now. A new terror rose up to haunt her. How was she to hide her guilt from Trenton's sharp eyes? Nervously she paced back and forth over the patterned carpet.

When she thought of Trenton's face, of his anger when he discovered the foolish thing she had done— she knew it *was* foolish. Jeremy had not even bothered to deny that this was a gambling debt. He would never stop gaming.

If only Trenton did not make this discovery till after the wedding. She knew it was the wrong thing to do, keeping it quiet, especially after her promise to him. But she could not chance losing him. Thank goodness he would not be home to dinner. That would give her time to settle her thoughts. But if he were not coming home for dinner, where *was* he going? Was he going to meet Lady Frances, to resume their alliance? Or had he gone to Harriette's—again? Jeannie pressed her palms to her cheeks. She must stop this senseless behavior.

Rising from her chair, she saw the book she'd been seeking earlier. With another sigh Jeannie picked up *Love in the Ruins*. Perhaps she could lose herself in the problems of someone else.

* * *

Several hours later, when Budner appeared in the doorway, Jeannie had made very little progress in the novel. The story seemed so foolish compared to the problems in her own life. "Yes, Budner?"

"It's Lord Verdon, miss. He says you are expecting him."

"Yes, of course, Budner, send him in." Jeannie tossed the novel onto the divan and turned expectantly to the door. Verdon was the very man she needed. A little of his fun and exaggerated gallantry would help to divert her thoughts from the terrible thing she had done.

"Milord, how good to see you!" She noticed the slight look of distaste on the butler's face at the heartiness of her greeting, but it was too late to recall it.

"Miss Burnstead." From the expression on his face, Verdon, too, had thought her greeting excessive. He paused in the doorway, elegantly dressed as usual.

"It's the *ennui*," she explained. "Trenton is gone for the day, and I have been so dreadfully bored. You've no idea how little there is to do. I have been trying to read this romance. It's better than the French. Drivel, Trenton calls *them*. But I can't seem to concentrate." She smiled. "But now you are here and things will be better."

"Indeed, they will," agreed the Marquess. "But tell me, Miss Burnstead, how could that wretch have left you to spend the day alone?"

"*Je ne sais pas*," replied Jeannie, determined to be cheerful. "But come, let us not speak of him. Tell me the latest news and then we will commence our French lesson."

"*Oui*," said the Marquess, "but I know very little new scandal. It does not seem to register in my brain." He smiled and Jeannie perceived how he had charmed many a woman. If it were not for Trenton—"Scandal, after all, is very much the same no matter who is involved with whom."

Jeannie nodded. "You are quite right. Sometimes, you know, Lady Helena rattles on and on, and I don't even know the people she's telling me about. Perhaps we had best go directly to the French."

The Marquess shook his head. "As you are aware, I really do not know much French. You must move slowly with me."

Jeannie smiled. *"Oui, monsieur. Comment allez-vous?"*

The Marquess frowned in mock puzzlement. "How—ahhh! *Bien, merci. Et vous?*"

"Pas mal, merci."

"You are only 'not bad'?" inquired the Marquess.

Jeannie dredged up a smile. *"Non-sens!* You are imagining. Come, your lordship, the French. I am trying to keep our bargain."

The Marquess smiled wryly. "I do not care much about my French," he said, his large hand pulling at the top of his cravat.

Jeannie looked at him in surprise. "Then why are you here?"

Verdon appeared a little sheepish and seemed about to clear his throat, but before he could speak Trenton's deep voice resounded from the doorway. "Yes, why *are* you here?"

Jeannie jumped and raised startled eyes to the Viscount. She could feel herself coloring up. Her heart seemed stuck in her throat.

"Come, come, Trenton, do not behave like the jealous hero of some French novel. I am your friend and as such I am concerned for Miss Burnstead's welfare. I do not want her to be lonely and bored." Verdon gave his friend a steady look.

"I see." The Viscount leaned nonchalantly against the doorway, the long length of him so elegantly outlined that it made Jeannie's heart thud. She had not seen him before in his riding coat of Bedford cord atop his buckskins. His eyes slid insolently over the Marquess and Jeannie stiffened. How could Verdon countenance such a look? But he seemed not even to notice it.

"My friend," the Marquess said, rising easily from his chair, "I think you had better consider your future. Perhaps, given the passionate—and jealous—nature of your love, you'd be better off in the country, where there would be fewer rivals for Miss Burnstead's attention."

The Viscount straightened suddenly and his eyes grew even chillier as he gazed at his friend.

The Marquess shook his head. "Trenton, Trenton, come, man. Be sensible. If you've no faith in *me*, you must at least trust *her*."

It seemed to the waiting Jeannie that the Viscount made a great effort. Slowly the harsh lines of his face smoothed out. "Of course I trust her," he said pleasantly. Then he laughed. "The role of lover has never sat so uneasily upon my shoulders before."

"Perhaps," said the Marquess with a chuckle, "you have never played the role in earnest before."

The Viscount smiled ruefully, his dark eyes giving Jeannie a quick look before they moved to his friend. "I believe you are right, Verdon. I quite believe you are right."

The Marquess consulted his timepiece. "I'm afraid I must leave now. I have an engagement." He bowed to Jeannie. "Good-bye, Miss Burnstead."

"Good-bye, milord."

The Marquess made his departure, leaving a trembling Jeannie. With all that talk about jealousy and love, it still seemed to her that the Viscount was playing the role of lover too strongly. Yet his friend had appeared convinced.

"I thought you were going out to dinner," she commented, filling the silence with the first thing that entered her mind.

The Viscount gave her a strange look, his dark eyes grown hard. "Yes, so I told you. But a passing carriage threw mud on my buckskins, and I decided to change."

"I see." Jeannie wished desperately for something to say, but she could think of nothing. She clasped her hands tightly in her lap to stop their trembling.

"Your brother was here," said Trenton sternly. "What did he want?"

Jeannie felt scarlet flood her face. Why had she not realized that Budner would tell him about Jeremy's visit? Now she had no lie prepared for him. "Yes, yes. He was here."

"What did he want?" repeated the Viscount evenly, but his face unpleasant.

Jeannie summoned a smile. "Oh, nothing. He just wanted to say thank you." This lie would make matters worse; she knew that even as she voiced it. But she could not tell him the truth now. She could not risk being sent back to Shropshire.

"I see." Trenton's expression tightened. "I'm glad to know that he has some gratitude. That's a good sign. Perhaps he will be able to give up his bad habit."

Jeannie knew from the sound of his voice that he did not believe what he was saying, but his lie was meant to comfort, not to deceive as hers had been. She forced herself to continue meeting his eyes.

The great clock in the hall began to chime, and the Viscount turned to the door. "I must go."

"But your buckskins?"

He shook his head. "There's not time now. I do

not wish to be late for my appointment. I will see you in time for the theater. *Au revoir.*"

"*Au revoir,*" echoed Jeannie, watching him stride out of the room, his every step speaking of manly grace and power. She loved even the way he walked, she thought sadly. But at least he had not discovered the truth. She was still safe.

Safe. Jeannie laughed bitterly as she moved to the divan to retrieve the romance. This was a precarious safety. It was certain that his lordship would eventually discover the truth. And when he did—

With a cry, Jeannie dropped the book and hurried up the stairs to the sanctuary of her room. Her previous misery over Atwood was nothing to the pain she felt now. She had flagrantly disobeyed the Viscount and had given up the most precious gift she had ever been given, all to help a twin who was now a stranger to her and to whom *she* obviously meant nothing.

She threw herself on the green brocade cover of the bed and burst into tears. It had all been a mistake, a horrible mistake. Her loyalties were no longer to her twin. Her loyalties, her love, and all her hopes for the future were given irrevocably to the dark, handsome man who was to be her husband—*if* he did not discover her terrible secret before their wedding day.

CHAPTER SEVENTEEN

Jeannie rose from her bed in time to bathe her eyes with cold water and erase the signs of her tears. She must be very careful. She must do nothing that would lead Trenton to suspect her of anything. If she were careful, if she managed to keep up the facade, then gradually she would be more at ease. Once her accounts were opened, perhaps she could even commission some jeweler to duplicate the lost jewels. She had looked at them so often that she knew precisely how they looked. She took heart from this hope.

As she drew on the yellow silk, Jeannie considered it. Thank God Lady Helena's taste seemed sound where her protégée was involved. Jeannie shuddered at the thought of being forced to appear in public in Lady Helena's new gown of coral muslin. At least this gown was opaque and its hue muted. She rather liked its cut. Its short sleeves were draped away from the square neckline and the front of the gown fell straight to the floor from the gathering under the bosom. The rest of the material was pulled to the back, where it was gathered into a slight train. The neck and the hems of the sleeves were edged in silver braid and the gown was brocaded with little silver flowers. Staring at herself in the cheval glass, Jeannie had to admit that the gown looked well on her. It seemed to emphasize the slenderness of her form, but did not make her seem girlish. She was also pleased with her latest hair style. It made the efforts of Lady Helena's dresser almost unnecessary since the jumbled mass of curls known as *à la Titus* did not really require her arts. Jeannie picked up the ostrich plume and fixed it in her hair. Though Lady Helena had insisted on the plume, she had at least been amenable to Jeannie's desire for one silver-dyed. The thought of appearing in public sporting one of the flamboyant colors so favored by Trenton's sister was decidedly unsettling to Jeannie. Fortunately, she had also been able to convince her mentor that a turban was not needed. The Viscount did not care for turbans, she reminded her, recalling his exact words.

Jeannie took one last look in the glass and tried a smile. If only she hadn't this dreadful secret hanging over her, how happily she would have looked forward to this evening. Now, however, with her transgression ever uppermost in her mind, and her fear of discovery so strong, how could she enjoy anything?

With a sigh Jeannie turned away. There was no way to undo her wrong deed. She would simply have to live with it until after their marriage when he would be unable to send her away. She swallowed over the lump in her throat and moved toward the stairs.

As she reached the top of the staircase, Jeannie saw Trenton below, deep in discussion with Budner. He turned at the sound of her approach and her heart seemed to leap up into her throat at the sight of him. In his raven-colored coat with covered buttons, a waistcoat of white superfine, black silk florentine breeches, black silk stockings, and black shoes, with his *chapeau bras* under his arm, he made a sight that no woman's heart could resist. Surely in all of London there was no other man quite so lithe and lean, quite so darkly handsome, quite so strong and powerful.

"Good evening, Jeannie," he said, his voice sounding deeper than usual.

"Good evening, milord. Am I ready in good time?"

Trenton nodded. "Yes, but Helena is not." He frowned slightly. "She has always made too much of these foibles of fashion." He consulted his timepiece, set in a handsome gold case. "I shall give her five more minutes, that is all." He turned to the butler. "Dispatch a footman to have the carriage brought round."

"Yes, milord. Immediately, milord."

As Budner turned away, it seemed to Jeannie that his expression changed—to what she could not exactly say as the subsequent glimpse of his features was too fleeting to allow for more than speculation.

"While Budner is gone," the Viscount said, "I have a matter to discuss with you."

For one terrifying moment Jeannie believed that he had learned her secret and the room began to whirl. But then, as she realized that he was smiling at her, everything came back into focus. "Yes, milord?" She forced herself to become calm.

"Budner has informed me that you had a caller today."

"Yes, milord. Two. Jeremy and Verdon." She kept her eyes on his.

"An additional caller."

Jeannie was puzzled. "Budner announced no one else."

"Because he was obeying my orders." His eyes scrutinized her carefully.

"But who could be calling that you would not wish me to see—"

The blood left her face, and he reached out an arm to steady her. "Easy, Jeannie."

"Atwood? Was it Atwood?" she faltered.

"Yes, it was. After the incident the other day, I thought perhaps I should take precautions, so I advised Budner that you were not to be in to Atwood."

"Oh, milord, thank you. I cannot thank you enough. I never wish to see that dreadful man again." Jeannie shivered to think what might have occurred if Atwood had burst in upon her after Jeremy's departure.

Trenton's eyes were still regarding her critically, and she felt the color flooding her cheeks. Was it possible that he could suspect her of wishing to see Atwood? That couldn't be.

"I am glad you approve of my action. Ordinarily I would not take upon myself the liberty of monitoring my future wife's visitors, but I did not wish you to be distressed again."

"I am very glad you did," said Jeannie. "It spared me a great deal of annoyance." She did not know with what warmth her eyes glowed at him or how sweetly her mouth curved into a smile.

"Thank you." Trenton's reactions seemed strange, as though he wished to evade her glance, but she could not think why. She was genuinely grateful for his concern.

She was about to tell him so yet again, when Lady Helena called out from the top of the stairs. "I say, you two. Will you give off casting calf's eyes at each other? I assure you, Trenton, I have gone to considerable travail in order to be ready at the specified time. If we miss one word of the first act, *you* shall never live it down."

The Viscount swung around to face the stairs. "Good evening, Helena." His eyes swept over the gown of gold lamé that fit quite closely to his sister's figure. The neckline, which was cut square like Jeannie's, seemed to be much lower and to reveal a dangerous amount of the lady's ample white bosom.

Jeannie waited for his lordship's explosion of wrath, but after a full minute of complete silence, he merely said, "I trust that you have a shawl."

"Of course, Trenton. Shall we go?"

Trenton shawled his sister and then Jeannie, carefully wrapping her in the cashmere he had given her. Then, giving them each an arm, he escorted them to the waiting carriage.

As they settled into the carriage, Jeannie found her eyes straying to Lady Helena's décolletage. She stifled a gasp. Sitting down, the lady's bosom was even more generously displayed. She turned to Trenton. "I am anxious to see Drury Lane again, especially the great staircase."

Trenton nodded. If he knew her intent, he gave no indication. "I suppose Wyatt was more fortunate in his design than poor Smirke. He had a site which allowed for more room and so could achieve a much grander design. His domed Corinthian rotunda, with grand staircases to right and left, is certainly well done. Unfortunately, the facade to the Lane has the inert heaviness that seems to plague Wyatt's clubs and palaces."

"Really, Trenton. So much architectural knowledge is dreadfully dull." Lady Helena's dark eyes sparkled in the light of the carriage lamps, and Jeannie waited for Trenton to reply.

When he did so, his voice held dry amusement. "A little architectural knowledge hurts no one," he said. "Jeannie's understanding is very good. That pleases me," he added, "since I've no desire to be leg-shackled to a perfect block."

Lady Helena made a face, but did not reply to this. Jeannie turned to his lordship. "I must thank you for your confidence in my understanding," she said. "I do like to learn new things. Although I know little about it, architecture is a very interesting subject."

The Viscount beamed at her. "You are going to make an admirable wife," he said with such warmth that she felt her bones threaten to melt.

"Thank you, milord."

Lady Helena snorted. "What a pair of moonlings you are, sighing over each other."

Trenton smiled. "I should have thought that with your passion for romance you would appreciate a love match."

His sister's mouth curved in a mischievous grin. "Ah, but Trenton, it seems so much more real when I read it on the printed page."

The Viscount chuckled. "Well then, Helena, you must avert your eyes. Jeannie and I *have* made a love match, you know. Since the banns have been called and we only await Uncle Obadiah's good health to proceed with the ceremony, you must not expect us to behave as strangers." As he spoke he put his arm around Jeannie's shoulders and drew her close. "Isn't that so, my love?"

Fighting back a sudden rush of tears, Jeannie could only nod. He could not know how much pain his words were causing her; to him, it was all part of the arrangement they had made.

Fortunately, by this time the carriage had reached the theater. The air was filled with the hoarse cries of coachmen, the jangle of harnesses, and cries of "Playbills, fresh-printed playbills."

Jeannie descended from the carriage and surveyed the scene. Here were the same resplendently dressed members of the *ton* whom she had seen at Covent Garden. Every bosom and wrist, every coat front, seemed to blaze with precious jewels. She thought of her own unadorned throat, but did not lower her head. She was Trenton's intended and if she chose to come to the theater without jewels, there was no one foolish enough to think it was due to a lack of them. She had deemed it safer not to bring up the subject. If she had asked for her mother's jewels, Trenton might have remembered his gift and told her to give them to him for safekeeping. She could not have risked that.

Trenton took her arm and escorted her and his sister toward the entrance. "The crush is just terrible," protested Lady Helena. "Why must everyone come at once?"

"They wish to see Kean," replied his lordship. "The man is all the rage. Everyone is talking about him, and this is his first performance of *Hamlet* this year."

"At least we shall not be pushed and prodded about once we reach our box."

The Viscount made no reply to this, simply guiding them up the righthand staircase. Jeannie risked one glimpse upward at the domed ceiling, then the press of people was so great that she feared falling and so resigned herself to being led to the box.

As the door closed behind them, Lady Helena settled into her seat with a great sigh. "At last," she said. "I simply cannot stand such a great crush of people. The effect on my constitution is just dreadful."

The Viscount's grin at Jeannie indicated that in his opinion Lady Helena's constitution was not in much danger, but his tone was sober. "You are safe enough now, Helena. Relax and do not put yourself into such a taking." He turned to Jeannie. "The theater is quite crowded tonight."

Jeannie nodded. "Yes, the pit appears quite full, too." She looked down to where the benches were beginning to fill up. Some of the exquisites were beginning their nightly strut up and down the aisles, the better to show off their finery. Jeannie could only smile at the strange combinations that some men seemed to think elegant.

She let her eyes move from the assembled masses below up to the tiers of boxes. In the lamplight the many jewels flashed brightly. Jeannie surveyed the boxes for the sight of a familiar face. Only when she came to the conclusion that Lady Frances was not anywhere in the theater did she realize what she had been doing. She would enjoy the performance much more if she knew that Lady Frances was elsewhere. With the terrible secret of her misdeed gnawing at her, she could use a little respite from that elegant lady's presence.

As her eyes continued to scan the crowd, Jeannie bit back a cry of distress. Directly across the theater sat Atwood, his hand resting familiarly on the bare shoulder of a young woman. She was about to move her gaze on, when Atwood's eyes met hers and he nodded cordially. Jeannie shivered and attempted to give the man the cut direct, but she was still upset from their encounter on Bond Street, and her cold stare was not effective. Atwood continued to ogle her.

Finally she could bear no more. "Trenton," she whispered, turning to him and putting a gloved hand on his sleeve.

He turned to her instantly. "What is it, my dear?"

"Across the way, Atwood. He's ogling me." She tried to make her voice calm, but the hand on his sleeve trembled.

The muscles under Jeannie's fingers stiffened, and Trenton drew himself erect in his chair. Jeannie, glancing up at his face, saw a ferocious frown mar his handsome features. His dark brows met over his nose and his black eyes sent deadly rays at the unfortunate Atwood. Shifting her gaze, Jeannie looked toward the box where Atwood sat still ogling her. The girl became uncomfortable under Trenton's stare and paled visibly. Then she extricated herself from Atwood's grasp and slipped from the box. Now that she looked closer, Jeannie could see that Atwood was plainly in his cups. It took some moments before he grew aware of Trenton's gaze. When he did, he started visibly, then attempted to brazen it out. But he was unsuccessful and, as Jeannie watched, his eyes fell away. He fiddled around for some moments and finally he, too, rose and left the box.

Trenton turned to her, only a vestige of his frown remaining. "I trust that Atwood has learned his lesson. I doubt he'll resume his box this evening."

"Thank you," Jeannie murmured. "I suppose it is foolish of me, but the man makes me feel so—so tarnished." Her voice trembled over the last word and Trenton took her gloved fingers in his.

"If anything was tarnished by Atwood's desertion of you," he said softly, "it was Atwood's reputation, not yours. But do not be dismayed. His lady wife will soon recall him to the country. And, since she holds the pursestrings, he will no doubt obey the summons."

A shudder raced over Jeannie's slender frame. What a terrible fate she had escaped.

Trenton grinned at her, mischief in his dark eyes. "Are you ready yet to admit that I am an exceptional man?"

Jeannie summoned a smile. "Yes, milord," she replied, "I am ready to concede that."

He looked down at her warmly. "Good. We shall deal very well together."

"I hope so, milord." She could not help thinking of her missing jewels and another tremor passed over her.

Fortunately their conversation was interrupted by

the raising of the great curtain, and Jeannie turned her attention to the stage. She did not know quite what to expect. She had heard the talk that Kean was just a little man, but they said that he had a noble head and fascinating eyes. He did seem small in his black suit, but Jeannie waited expectantly. When he turned and she felt the power of his dark eyes, she knew that everything they said about him was true. He had tremendous power. Gratefully, Jeannie let herself be drawn into the world of the play.

When the curtain fell for intermission some time later, Jeannie had difficulty recalling herself. The world that Kean created had seemed so real to her. With a start she realized that for the entire space of the play she had not been plagued with guilt over her disobedience to Trenton. For those minutes she had not once been wracked with anxiety over the terrible thing she had done.

"Well?" said Trenton. "Does the great man fulfill your expectations?"

Jeannie nodded. "Indeed, yes, milord. Such a voice! So much power! He is infinitely better than Young. And yet Young was good in the part."

Trenton nodded. "Yes, Kean has marvelous passion, impetuosity, subtlety, and force. I think it probable that he is the greatest actor ever to walk the English stage."

"Really?" Jeannie was relieved that they could talk about something far removed from the matter preying on her mind.

Lady Helena shifted in her chair, putting her décolletage in serious jeopardy. "One thing you must remember, Jeannie dear. Trenton believes that he *knows* the theater. You will never dare hold a differing opinion."

Jeannie smiled sweetly. "Oh, I think I might venture to differ on matters of theatrical opinion. After all, Trenton does not really want a mindless ninny to share his life with."

"Bravo, Jeannie," cried Trenton. "You have stated the point exactly."

Lady Helena allowed herself a grimace of disbelief. "Such talk is all well and good *now*," she remarked, "but wait until you have been married some years. Then he will expect you to accede to his wishes in everything."

The thought of being Trenton's wife of longstanding was a pleasant one to Jeannie, but it also raised the specter of her disobedience. Would their marriage ever take place?

Trenton laughed dryly. "Do not listen to Helena. She is in a dowagerish mood this evening. She forgets that she and I have dealt reasonably well together these many years." His dark eyes gleamed at Jeannie in amusement. "And she and I seldom agree on anything."

Lady Helena's dry chuckle came softly across the box. "Beware, Jeannie. This man is devious. *He* quite forgets that he and I stood in a different relationship to each other than do the two of you. Brother and sister are not husband and wife unless—"

Trenton cut his sister off. "Conceded, Helena. Do not press your point. Still, and as Jeannie well knows, I cannot abide a mealymouthed hypocrite who says one thing and means another. There will be no lies and deceptions between us, only good will and respect. Is that not so, Jeannie?" He looked to her for confirmation.

"Yes, milord. That is right."

Lady Helena was silenced by this, though not beaten, Jeannie was sure.

Then Trenton shifted suddenly in his chair. "I see

someone with whom I must speak," he said. "Excuse me for a moment." Before Jeannie quite knew how it had happened, he was gone. On an impulse Jeannie looked out across the theater. Her heart leaped suddenly into her throat. Just settling into a box was the lovely Harriette Wilson. Again she wore cream-colored satin, though this gown was of a different cut. Her auburn hair shone in the glow of the lamps as several beaux vied for the honor of helping the lady remove her shawl.

They were drawing their chairs close around her when the door to the box opened. Somehow, even before the man stepped out of the shadows, Jeannie knew who it would be. Her heart threatened to choke her as Trenton advanced and bowed low over Harriette's hand. She noted with what deference the other men stepped aside for him and with what a warm smile Harriette raised her eyes to his. Then her own eyes so filled with tears that everything became blurry. Jeremy had been right! Here was proof positive. She could hardly persist in disbelieving what she herself could plainly see.

Evidently Lady Helena could see, too, for she spoke suddenly and motioned to a box in quite a different direction. "Oh Jeannie, do look at the dowager dragon in the gown of striped blue and white silk. See her? She is wearing that monstrous orange turban with the blue and white plumes."

Obediently Jeannie turned her head in the indicated direction. Filmed as her eyes were by tears, she found it difficult to see anything. But she kept her head turned that way and nodded. "Yes, yes. I see." She managed to get the words past the horrible lump in her throat. "It's—it's really dreadful."

It was futile to give way to tears now, Jeannie told

herself. After all, she had her pride. And for Trenton to subject her to the gibes and stares of the *ton* like this was insupportable. Surely he knew how difficult such a thing would be for her. Still, she held her head high. She had let herself be cowed the last time; let the *ton* drive her from London. She would not give them that advantage again. Trenton was far more important to her than Atwood had ever been. And she, at least, would be his wife. She could share things with him that those other women could not; especially the children. She felt the color flood her cheeks at the thought, but it was the truth. Lady Frances certainly would not bother with little ones. Surely Harriette, too, had her ways of avoiding such embarrassments. And even then, should such a thing happen, surely Trenton's legitimate children would be most important to him.

"Jeannie!" Lady Helena's insistent tone awakened Jeannie to the fact that her ladyship had already addressed her more than once.

"I am sorry, milady. I had something in my eye, but it seems to be gone now."

Lady Helena did not remark on this subterfuge, merely saying, "That is well. For unless I miss my guess, Verdon is on his way here."

"Oh?" Jeannie felt her spirits rising slightly. Verdon inevitably made her more cheerful. In the big man's presence she seemed better able to believe in a happy outcome for the future.

Moments later the door opened to reveal the Marquess. His dress was almost an exact copy of Trenton's—raven-colored coat with covered buttons, black silk florentine breeches, black silk stockings, and black shoes, except that his waistcoat of superfine was black instead of white. All in all, he was a fine figure of a man, she thought, though not as fine as Trenton.

"Well, milord," said Lady Helena. "I guessed right."

"How so?" Verdon moved forward into the box and bent low over Lady Helena's hand and then Jeannie's. As he raised his head, she saw the twinkle in his eyes and knew that the lady's décolletage had not been lost on him.

"I saw you leave your box and I thought you were coming to pay your respects."

"Quite right," said Verdon, settling into Trenton's chair. "Two such diamonds of the first water deserve all the praise one can give them."

Lady Helena smiled and Jeannie blessed Verdon silently. His outrageous compliments were too inflated to be believed, but they did wondrous things for a woman's spirits.

"And how are you enjoying our theatrical genius?" he inquired cheerfully.

"He really is quite marvelous," said Jeannie, "the best actor I've ever seen."

"I collect you've seen Kemble in the part?"

Jeannie nodded. "Yes, but that was several years ago. As I remember it, Kemble did not have the same sort of power."

Verdon smiled. "Kean is a magnificent actor. His Shylock will bring tears to your eyes."

Lady Helena nodded to this. "You are quite right, Verdon. And now that I think on it, I suppose his slight stature is to his benefit."

Verdon's eyes twinkled at Jeannie. "How do you come to this conclusion?" he asked.

"Well, it appears easier for a small man to make himself look large than for a large man to make himself seem small." Lady Helena regarded him soberly.

The Marquess, looking down at his long legs,

chuckled. "I believe you have made a point, Lady Helena."

Lady Helena's warm chuckle echoed her agreement.

"Nor, I doubt, would I look well in parts that call for a little, wizened, or misshapen man."

"Indeed not," said Lady Helena. "A fine figure of a man like you. Why, no one would be able to believe such a thing."

The Marquess preened himself, shot his cuffs in an extravagantly ostentatious style, and grinned. "It's only the truth, of course. Nevertheless, it is kind of you to say so."

Jeannie's bright peal of laughter rang out across the theater, but engrossed as she was in the little scene before her, she did not notice the scowl that crossed Trenton's face as he left Harriette Wilson's box.

Lady Helena surveyed Verdon with bright eyes. "How is it, milord, that you have so far escaped the noose of matrimony?" she asked.

Jeannie, by now used to Lady Helena's bluntness, did not color up.

Verdon grinned mischievously. "I am not quite sure, milady. Perhaps the Fates were pleased with me, or displeased."

"I do not understand," said Jeannie.

"Well," replied Verdon. "Seeing Trenton go off like this has changed my outlook." He sighed deeply, but his eyes still sparkled with laughter. "I may perhaps soon desert the single life."

"Indeed?"

There was such a strange expression on Lady Helena's face that Jeannie had suddenly a very odd notion.

"Ah, some young lady will be very fortunate then," said Lady Helena.

Verdon shook his head. "I have had enough of vain young things. They are too frivolous by far. No, I think I shall look for an older woman, perhaps even a widow. I am, after all, not exactly a stripling."

"But your family," said Lady Helena, whose face had colored up like a young girl's. "Won't they expect you to provide an heir?"

The Marquess shrugged his broad shoulders. "My family has learned to expect very little from me. Besides, my brother is quite a sound chap and he has two young boys." Verdon turned to Jeannie and slowly winked. "No, I believe I should like to spend my declining years in relative peace. The patter of little feet is too noisy for me."

"Some sober widow will think herself already transported to heaven," said Lady Helena, with a nervous tug at her shawl.

Verdon laughed. "Lady Helena, please! I did not say that I desired to be bored to death. No indeed. I shall look for a woman of wit and sparkle, one capable of enjoying life with me." The corners of his mouth twitched. "A woman like yourself perhaps."

Jeannie had never thought to see Lady Helena left speechless, but such was now the case. Trenton's sister sat quite silent.

The silence grew oppressive and Jeannie, seeking to do something to relieve the tension, said brightly, "Milord, have you seen Kean do other parts?"

"Indeed, yes. You should see his Othello."

"Or his Iago," said Trenton from the doorway with such vehemence that Jeannie started. "Hello, Verdon." The Viscount advanced into the box. "I hope you are enjoying the play."

"Quite so," replied Verdon. "But I have been especially enjoying the company of two such lovely ladies."

"Indeed." Trenton's voice was flat but it seemed to Jeannie to carry a hint of anger.

Verdon rose slowly. "I suppose I had best get back to my box before the play commences again. *Au revoir.*"

"*Au revoir,*" Jeannie echoed with the others.

As Verdon left the box, she sank back into her chair. It couldn't be, she thought. Verdon and Lady Helena? Yet Verdon was several years older than Trenton and Lady Helena only a year her brother's senior. But what a strange way to conduct a courtship. She cast a quick glance at Lady Helena, who seemed to have recovered her composure and was intent on the stage. Trenton's sister's reaction to Verdon's words certainly seemed to indicate some feeling on her part. Jeannie smiled wistfully. What a grand thing—to have Verdon in the family.

The smile lingered on Jeannie's face and Trenton bent toward her as though to ask a question. But just then the curtain rose and Jeannie once more gave herself up to the magic world that Kean created.

When the curtain fell on the last act, Jeannie found she was holding her breath. Such artistry as Kean possessed must be a wonderful gift. "He's such a talented man."

Trenton nodded. "Yes. Unfortunately, there are rumors around that he is too much given to the blue ruin."

"To gin?" For Jeannie this seemed incredible.

Trenton smiled dryly. "So they say. He likes to relax by going to low dives and drinking himself under the table with the denizens of such iniquitous establishments."

"I should never have thought it," said Jeannie. "He seems such a sensitive man."

Trenton's eyes turned hard. "One need not be sensitive to act so. As one need not be an innocent to put on the airs of one."

That he meant her to get something more from this than the words actually conveyed was obvious to Jeannie. But exactly what his meaning was she could not tell. A sudden sense of guilt washed over her as her misdeed with the jewels again came to the forefront of her mind. But she could hardly believe that Trenton, once apprised of that act, would content himself with veiled references. No, if such knowledge ever reached his ears, the resultant explosion of wrath would be immediately obvious.

She forced herself to act naturally, to smile and reach for her shawl. "It just seems a shame for so much talent to be put in jeopardy."

"I should not worry myself about it," said Lady Helena. "Creative persons are quite often considered reprobates by the standards of society. And besides, there is little we can do about it. If Kean favors such gambols, that is his affair."

"Quite right, Helena," said her brother. "And now shall we find the carriage? This evening has left me rather fatigued."

Jeannie bit her lip to keep back the words that rose unbidden. Obviously his lordship was irritated about something and right now she did not really care to pursue the matter. Between worry over the jewels and wonderment over the affection between Verdon and Lady Helena, she had no more room for concern. And so the ride home was made in silence, each passenger in the carriage lost in his or her own thoughts.

Trenton escorted them up the walk and into the house. At the foot of the stairs he turned to face

Jeannie. "Good night, my love." He said the words softly, but they carried no caress. Indeed, his eyes seemed very hard.

"Good night, milord." Jeannie could not take her eyes from his. Why did he look at her in that impersonal way? At least before there had been friendliness between them. Now she was not sure what it was that his eyes indicated.

And then, much to her surprise, he reached out and drew her to him. It appeared that he meant this kiss to look fleeting and tender, but just as she expected him to release her, his lips grew more possessive and his arms tightened around her. With Lady Helena standing by, Jeannie dared not protest. In any case, there was no part of her left that wished to do so. But still, as his kiss grew more savage, she felt her heart begin to pound with fear. This was a kiss of passion— and punishment. She sensed that he wanted her complete submission—and obviously for some reason other than love. It was this feeling, finally, that kept her from the complete surrender she longed to give him.

When he put her aside, his eyes were still hard and without a smile he turned away. Fortunately, Lady Helena was still in a bemused state and noticed nothing different about their embrace. As she made her way up the stairs, Jeannie was left to her own uncongenial thoughts. Something had angered Trenton, and it couldn't be the jewels because he wouldn't have kept quiet about them.

CHAPTER EIGHTEEN

As the days passed, Trenton gradually grew less stern and, when the letter arrived from Shropshire with the news that they could set the wedding date two weeks hence, he seemed to relax still further.

On Jeannie's part, as the days passed and the jewels were not mentioned, her fears gradually subsided. They did not entirely disappear, but she could speak to Trenton, look at him, without being washed by constant waves of guilt. She did not allow her thoughts to advance past the wedding. That was the day she lived for. After they were married, Trenton would not dare send her back to Shropshire; she would have time to allay his anger.

The Viscount was much away from home and in his absence Jeannie found Verdon's daily visit a great spirit raiser, especially as Lady Helena often joined them. Jeannie took great pleasure in the developing relationship between the two, but somehow she did not mention it to Trenton. Perhaps she was afraid some remark of his might ruin things, or perhaps she was loath to discuss any matters concerning love with him.

And then one evening, an evening when the Viscount had dined in and they were all sitting after dinner before the fire in the library, he turned to her.

"I have ordered you a new dress, my love. It is to be delivered tomorrow."

"But I have so many." Jeannie felt the color flood her cheeks. Guilty as she was, she felt that anything he did for her was too much.

Trenton smiled. "This one is of lavender silk, trimmed in blue. I ordered it especially to go with your jewels. Tomorrow evening we go to hear the Catalani. You can wear it then."

Conscious of his eyes on her, Jeannie fought the panic that threatened to overwhelm her. But in spite of her efforts she was not successful in keeping all expression from her face.

"What is it, Jeannie?"

Her mind did not seem to work. Oh, why wasn't she better at lying? "Oh, it's all right," she faltered. "It's only that I've taken the jewels to be repaired. The clasp was loose and I did not want to lose them."

The Viscount frowned. "I shall have to speak to Kerston. The clasp should have been in order."

"Please," cried Jeannie. "It was not his fault. I—I caught it in my hair."

"Tell me the name of the shop," said his lordship. "I will stop there in the morning and be sure they finish in time."

"I—I cannot recall the name of it. But I know exactly where it is. I'll go there myself in the morning."

Jeannie knew that she was avoiding his eyes and forced herself to look at him. She must not let him suspect.

"Very well," he seemed about to scold her but then merely nodded. "But I want you to have them tomorrow night."

"Yes, of course," answered Jeannie. She took a deep breath. "I've heard a lot about the Catalani. They say she's a marvelous singer. And such a beautiful woman."

"Yes, she is," replied the Viscount, continuing to watch her closely. "Of course she is quite temperamental. Most women—are."

"Trenton," said Lady Helena, looking up from her needlepoint. "I will thank you not to cast aspersions on the whole of womankind." Her affection for Verdon had not at all dulled her pleasure in these little bouts with her brother. While the Viscount and Lady Helena enjoyed a round of bickering, Jeannie had some time to regain her composure.

The rest of the evening was torture to her, but she forced herself to act calmly and to make bright conversation while the minutes slowly passed. When she had bid them both good night and was upstairs, secure in the privacy of her room, she let herself think about what had happened. She *must* have those jewels back by tomorrow evening.

But how? Nervously she paced the room. She had no pocket money, and certainly no way to get a hundred pounds. She would have to send to Jeremy. Surely when he saw her distress her twin would do *something* to help her. Perhaps he could get a loan from one of his friends and get her jewels back. Or perhaps he even had some money of his own now.

There was nothing else she could think of to do. She might lie to Trenton again, but it didn't seem likely he would believe her. No, Jeremy was her only hope.

That thought did little to calm her. She could not forget Jeremy's selfishness. But if she *begged* him, if she told him how very much she loved Trenton?

There was little sleep for Jeannie that night. Her dreams were haunted by visions of Trenton's anger—

233

clouded face. She had done a terrible thing, she knew, yet she loved him so much. In the dreams she tried to tell him so, to tell him she was sorry for disobeying him, but he simply turned his back on her and stalked away. Many times that night Jeannie woke in tears and by morning she was exhausted. As soon as the sun rose, she climbed from her bed and began a note to Jeremy.

Nothing that she put down seemed right and finally she simply wrote, "Jeremy. I must talk to you. I need your help. Please."

As soon as she knew the fashionable world was up and about, Jeannie dispatched a footman to her brother's residence. Then she waited.

She had put on the first dress she came to, an off-brown, and fleetingly she thought that it was a fitting dress for such a day. But she could hardly think of anything but her terror at the coming evening. What lie could she tell the Viscount now?

While she waited for her brother, the dressmaker's girl arrived. As Jeannie unpacked the new gown, her eyes filled with tears. It was a beautiful gown of sheer French muslin. Its lavender shade matched the amethysts perfectly. The long sleeves that issued from the puffed shoulders and a small ruffle around the gown's scooped neck were sapphire blue. To be worn under the dress was a heavy petticoat of matching blue silk. The effect, judged Jeannie, would be one of lovely, changing hues.

The whole was quite beautiful and her tears spilled over and slid down her cheeks. She had no doubt that Trenton himself had been responsible for the design. He had been so good to her. And in return—she had betrayed him!

Sniffling, Jeannie carried the gown and petticoat to the wardrobe and hung them carefully. The sight of the white gown of Brussels lace for her wedding almost caused her to burst into sobs.

But she could not allow herself the luxury of tears now. She must look normal so that she could receive Jeremy when he came.

She made her way back down to the drawing room to wait. Jeremy *must* come, she told herself. She had to have his help.

The hours passed slowly, and as the day drew on Jeannie became more and more distraught. Where could Jeremy *be?* Why didn't he answer her plea for help?

Back and forth she paced, knowing that it did no good but unable to keep herself still. She had forced herself to take nuncheon with a chattering Lady Helena who had then retired to her room with a box of chocolates and another French novel. Hearing that Jeremy was expected, Lady Helena said, "You will want to be private with your brother. I quite understand that, my dear. Besides, my novel is becoming so breathtaking. I simply must finish it before we hear the Catalani."

"Of course, Lady Helena. My brother will be here soon, I'm sure."

But the hours had passed and Jeremy had not appeared. The sun had already begun its downward course when Budner appeared in the door. "A message for you, miss," he said.

"Yes, of course." Jeannie took the message with trembling fingers. "That will be all, Budner."

The butler nodded and left the room. Only then did Jeannie dare to open the letter that bore Jeremy's seal. "Sorry. Can't help. Have my own troubles. Ask Trenton. Love will cover all."

For a moment Jeannie stood unable to move except for her trembling fingers that held the note. Then the trembling seemed to spread over her whole body. She sank onto a nearby divan. Her twin had deserted her. Jeremy had not even come to her. The note fluttered to her lap as she bowed her head in her hands. There was nothing left to do.

It was thus that Verdon found her when he entered a moment later. "My dear, whatever is wrong?" he asked as he put a comforting arm around her shoulders.

This last was too much for Jeannie. Here was someone to help. Wordlessly she pushed the note into his hands.

He read it and handed her his handkerchief. "I do not understand. Obviously your brother has refused to help you. But what trouble can you be in?"

Jeannie sniffled. "He—Trenton gave me some jewels —unusual ones—sapphires and amethysts."

Verdon nodded. "Yes, I heard."

"Today a new gown arrived. We are going to hear the Catalani. And I am to wear the jewels."

"And so what is the problem?"

"I—I do not have them. I gave them to Jeremy. To pay a gambling debt."

Verdon frowned. "You should have asked Trenton."

She shook her head. "I could not. He paid Jeremy's debts once—twelve hundred pounds worth. And I was to tell my twin that he would not pay anymore. He gave me positive orders not to help him either."

"Then why did you?" Verdon asked soberly.

"He's my twin. I've always looked out for him. I know it was a mistake," Jeannie cried. "But I was so used to helping him."

"And now Trenton expects you to wear the jewels?" Verdon's expression sobered.

Jeannie nodded. "I told him that the clasp was

broken and they were at the jewelers. He said to be sure to get them today. When I don't have them tonight, I shall have to tell him the truth." The tears threatened again and she twisted the handkerchief. "Oh, Verdon. I am so frightened. He'll send me back to Shropshire. I know he will, and I love him so much."

"Surely as much as he loves you—"

"But he doesn't! He doesn't love me at all." And the whole story tumbled out.

When she had finished, the Marquess stared at her in amazement. "You mean to tell me that Trenton *doesn't* love you?"

Again Jeannie nodded. "It's all acting to convince his family—and you."

The Marquess seemed unable to digest this news. "I still cannot believe it. But never mind that now. The important thing is to get you out of this fix."

Jeannie grabbed his arm. "You mean you *can?*"

"Of course," Verdon reassured her. "Now, first, give me your brother's direction. If I know to which moneylender he took the jewels—"

"I will give you his direction," said Jeannie.

The Marquess smiled. "That greatly simplifies my task. Now, my dear, you must compose yourself. The jewels will be here in time for you to wear them. But I must leave immediately. There's much to do."

Jeannie grasped his hand fervently. "Verdon, I can never thank you enough for this. He means so much to me."

Verdon smiled. "He means a great deal to me, too. And I believe you are the woman to make him happy."

"Thank you, milord."

Jeannie watched as the Marquess left the room. What a fine man he was, a very fine man. And she had no way to repay him for this wonderful thing he was doing for her. No way at all. Except, perhaps, if she could do it, to make his friend happy.

He had seemed to think that she could. Her heart danced at the thought. And the tremendous sense of relief she felt at the knowledge that this evening she could face Trenton and be wearing her beloved jewels made her light-headed. Perhaps she would not ever have to tell his lordship about this.

In her first flush of relief, Jeannie sped back up the stairs to reexamine her new gown. Now she could enjoy wearing it. The Marquess would return with the jewels. He must. With her own hands she laid out everything she intended to wear that evening. Oh, she would be beautiful. Beautiful for *him*.

When that was done, she returned to the lower floor. "The Marquess had an errand," she told Budner. "He will return later. I shall be in the drawing room."

"Yes, miss," replied Budner, his face strictly devoid of expression, as Jeannie returned to the drawing room—to wait.

At first her spirits were quite high. She had implicit faith in the Marquess. He would not fail her. But as the minutes passed, her imagination began to conjure up various disasters. Perhaps the moneylender had sold the jewels to someone and Verdon could not reclaim them. Or perhaps Jeremy had paid the debt directly with the jewels, not exchanging them first. So many things could go wrong.

And so by the time Budner announced that Verdon had reappeared, Jeannie was again trying to prepare herself for a terrifying evening. "Verdon!" Conscious of Budner's presence, Jeannie tried to keep the apprehension out of her voice.

"All is accomplished," said Verdon with a cheerful

smile, watching the butler leave the room. "And let me tell you something. Your dear brother got considerably more than a hundred pounds for these jewels."

"Oh Verdon, I am sorry. I will repay you. I swear I will."

"Nonsense." Verdon frowned at her. "That was not my reason for telling you. I hoped to open your eyes to your brother's true character."

"There's no fear of me forgetting that," Jeannie cried. "I swear to you that he will never get another tuppence from me."

"It pleases me greatly to hear that," said Verdon as he handed her a small parcel.

With tears in her eyes Jeannie unwrapped her precious jewels. "Oh, Verdon. They were his first gift to me."

The Marquess nodded. "Of course. They have a great deal of meaning—to you—and to him."

Jeannie looked up from the jewels in surprise. "To him?"

"Yes—never before has he had something especially designed for a woman."

"But he has given diamonds and such—to his incognitas. The Beau said so."

Verdon nodded. "Of course he has. It is customary. But diamonds would have been entirely out of place for you—an innocent young girl from the country. To have given you diamonds would have branded you as loose. Instead, he chose something befitting your beauty and uniqueness."

Jeannie sniffed back the tears. "I wish that I could believe you, Verdon. I truly do. But the Viscount does not love me. Whatever he does, he does for himself— for his good name."

The Marquess shook his head. "I think you mistake Trenton. He values his name, but—"

"Well," said Jeannie. "He need not worry about me hurting it. Not now."

"Of course not." Verdon consulted his timepiece. "I must go now. Perhaps I will see you at the Opera tonight. I'm sure you will shine."

Jeannie gave him a bright smile. "Thank you, milord. I'm sure I shall—now."

Then the Marquess was gone again and Jeannie shifted her eyes to the jewels in her lap. How precious they were to her, her first gift from the man she loved.

When Jeannie descended the stairs later that evening, she felt that all her problems were over. She would never help Jeremy again. Her loyalties were entirely given to the man who waited for her at the bottom of the stairs. How lean and handsome he was, standing there so nonchalantly, his dark eyes regarding her intently as she made her way down the stairs.

Jeannie smiled down at him. Now she could meet those dark eyes with confidence. Her hand stole unconsciously to where the necklace nestled against her throat. "Good evening, milord."

"Good evening, my dear. The gown fits well. You look ravishing. And I see that the jeweler completed the repairs."

"Yes, milord. It was only a small repair. He did not even charge for it."

"Indeed. That was most generous of him. We shall have to send some more business his way."

For a moment panic clutched at her. If he should ask the jeweler's name— She reached the bottom of the stairs and lifted her skirt just a trifle. "I wore my blue kid slippers. This skirt is a lovely idea. Look at how the colors flow."

"Yes. The *modiste* assured me that it would have

that effect. She also suggested you damp your petti-coat."

"Damp?" asked Jeannie, the blood rushing to her cheeks.

"Yes, certain ladies are known to do so—as I told you earlier." His eyes danced at her.

"Perhaps so, milord," she replied. "But I do not."

The Viscount smiled warmly. "It pleases me to hear that. By now you might have learned much from the London ladies."

Jeannie shook her head. "You mistake me, milord. I do not care for such things. Look, here comes Lady Helena."

Lady Helena was slowly descending the stairs. She was dressed in her new gown of coral muslin trimmed with chocolate brown. Its neck dipped dangerously low and the sheer material seemed to cling to her every limb as she came slowly and gracefully toward them.

With a start, Jeannie turned to his lordship. "Lady Helena?"

Trenton smiled. "So it appears." He lifted a quiz-zical eyebrow as he greeted his sister. "The air is grow-ing chill these nights. I hope you do not catch a cold in all that dampness."

Lady Helena gave her brother a hard stare. "You manage your affairs, my dear brother, and I shall manage mine. My state of health is of no concern to you."

"Very well, Helena. I shall remember that in the future."

Lady Helena simply smiled at him. "My dear brother, it occurs to me how fortunate I am that you have never before fallen into the throes of passion. It sits uneasily on you."

His lordship looked about to make an acerbic

reply, but then thought better of it. "You have not long to suffer, my dear," he said cheerfully. "After the wedding we will of course enjoy our connubial bliss without the benefit of your company."

The rest of their exchange was lost to Jeannie's ears. In fact, the rest of the evening was a blur of unfocused faces and sounds. She was vaguely aware that the Catalani sang divinely, but she was lost in a vision of herself in the gown of white satin and lace standing before the altar and becoming the bride of the dark, passionate man she loved.

CHAPTER NINETEEN

When Jeannie rose the next morning, her spirits were high. All her problems were behind her, she thought, as she chose a cheerful gown of green-sprigged muslin. As she was making her way to the breakfast room, she was quite surprised to have Budner say, "His lordship wishes to see you in the library."

"Yes, of course. I shall have my chocolate first."

Budner's face became even more dignified. "I believe his lordship's word was immediately."

"Yes, of course." Jeannie's elation faded. There was something in the butler's face that presaged trouble. By the time she had reached the library door, her palms were wet and she found it difficult to breathe. She had to force herself to enter.

"You wished to speak to me, milord?"

The Viscount turned from the window. "Yes, I did. I believe you know why."

Jeannie's knees trembled. He looked terribly wroth, worse than she had ever seen him. His eyebrows were one fierce line. His lips were tight, and his dark eyes glared at her.

"I—I do not understand," Jeannie replied, fighting for time.

"You do not understand," repeated Trenton with heavy sarcasm.

Jeannie shook her head. "I know that you are angry with me, but I do not know why."

The Viscount laughed, the harshest laugh she had ever heard. "Do you *now* remember the name of the jeweler who fixed your clasp?" he asked.

"I—I think it was Carters."

"No, my love, let me enlighten you. It was not Carters. Nor was it Kerstons. Nor was it any other jeweler in the city."

Jeannie's knees threatened to buckle, but she forced herself to face him. "I—I am sorry."

"Sorry!" thundered the Viscount. "There were to be no lies between us. Do you remember?"

Jeannie nodded. "Y-yes."

"And did I not several times offer you the opportunity to change your mind?"

"Y-yes." She made herself remain standing. "But I did not want to."

"Of course not." Trenton glared at her. "Why should you want to return to the country when you can live in London with a titled husband—and open accounts at all the shops?"

Anger gave strength to Jeannie's legs. "That is unfair. Our marriage was your idea—"

"And an extremely ill-founded one at that," he snarled.

"I have said I am sorry," Jeannie cried. "Was it such a terrible thing that I did? Surely many London ladies would have done the same."

"Ah yes," roared the Viscount, "surely many London ladies would have turned to their husband's friends. But you, you were the innocent, the green girl from the country, who promised to speak her mind to me, who promised she would never lie."

She would never get him to forgive her, Jeannie

244

saw that now. He hated her and he was using this incident as an excuse to get rid of her.

"I have said I'm sorry," she repeated tearfully, striving for dignity. "I don't know any more to say."

The Viscount advanced until he stood only inches away from her, his hard, dark eyes burning into hers. The anger there was so strong that she could barely stand before it. "Being sorry has never mended anything. You have betrayed my trust. You have turned against me."

Jeannie quailed before that rage. She summoned all her strength. "You—you are unfair. This—this need not come between us."

"Need not come between us!" Suddenly his hands shot out and fastened on her upper arms, and he shook her until her teeth chattered. "Some things cannot be forgiven," he raged. "Never. Do not speak of such inanities to me. Do you understand?"

Her heart was pounding in her throat. Never had she seen anyone in such a rage. He terrified her. Suddenly his hands dropped away. Jeannie fought to keep her feet as the room threatened to tilt and whirl.

"Go to your room," his lordship said curtly. "I will deal with you when I am calmer."

Jeannie turned and fled toward her room, but she did not seek the sanctuary of the green bed. She flew instead to the wardrobe and began pushing dresses aside. Yes, there it was. Her gray gown and pelisse. So long ago it seemed, that trip to London.

Frantically she ripped at her gown. She was going back to Shropshire. She was tired of being treated like a stupid child. Aunt Dizzy would understand if she said she could not bear him. Once she was out of sight, no longer annoying him, he could return to his old way of life. A sob escaped Jeannie. He would go to Lady Frances or Harriette or both!

She tied her bonnet, pulled on her gloves, and tucked the few coins she had left into her reticule. There would be no wedding, no future with Trenton. The sooner she realized that the better, she thought with a last sob as she left the jewels on the bed for him to find.

Softly Jeannie crept down the backstairs and out through the kitchen to the stables. If she had a horse, it would be much easier, but she would not touch another thing that belonged to Viscount Trenton. She slipped quietly out into the back alley.

London's streets were crowded as usual and Jeannie hurried along, trying not to be blinded by the tears that kept rising to her eyes. Tears were a luxury now. She must put as much distance as possible between herself and his lordship. She had to get to the stage-coach yard.

"Miss Burnstead! Jeannie! Is that you?"

In surprise Jeannie looked up to find Verdon staring down at her from his carriage.

"What are you doing here?" he asked.

"I—I am going home. To Shropshire."

"Home? But why?"

"Verdon, please. Will you take me part way—to the stagecoach yard?"

The Marquess extended his hand. "Come up here and explain this to me."

"Only if you take me where I asked. I cannot go back there to him."

"Yes, yes." He was plainly impatient. "Only come up."

As Jeannie settled herself beside the Marquess, he passed her a fresh handkerchief. "No doubt you have use for this."

Jeannie did not smile. "Thank you."

"Now tell me what has happened."

Jeannie wiped at her eyes. "Last night everything was fine. I wore the jewels and he seemed happy." She sniffed. "But this morning he summoned me to the library. He said he knew the truth. He absolutely raged at me, saying I had betrayed his trust. And—and—" The tears were threatening again now as she scrubbed at her face. "And when I said that this need not be between us, he said—he said that some things could never be forgiven." She turned to the Marquess. "Why couldn't he forgive me?"

"Did you tell him that you love him?" asked Verdon.

Jeannie raised shocked eyes to his face. "Of course not. He hates me now. Should I have him pity me, too?" She swallowed. "I made a mistake, Verdon. I should never have consented to such a match. I must go back to Shropshire. I have cost him a great deal of money. You, too." She pressed the Marquess's hand. "And there is no way I can repay it."

She sighed. "But I can at least get out of his life. I need not burden him forever with a woman he hates."

"Verdon! You are going the wrong way. I will not return there. I will not." She tried to stand up in the moving carriage.

"Easy now, Jeannie." The Marquess covered her hand with his. "I will not force you back there. But in good conscience I cannot allow you to set off on such a journey alone and unattended. I am taking you to my place and I will get my steward to engage a place on the mail coach for you and send a maid along to accompany you."

"I cannot put you to any more expense," cried Jeannie. "You have done so much."

The Marquess frowned. "I am your friend. If you like, you may get your uncle to reimburse me, but I simply cannot allow you to go off alone."

Jeannie had very little fight left. "All right, but I must leave as soon as possible. I cannot face him again."

"I understand," said the Marquess. "Be assured I will get you away as speedily as I can."

Verdon was a good man, thought Jeannie. It was too bad that she had not fallen in love with *him*.

For the rest of the trip to Verdon's house Jeannie was silent. The failure of all her dreams had left her numb. Tomorrow perhaps, or the next day, she would feel the pain more intently, but for now there was only a dull ache.

As the carriage pulled up in front of his house, the Marquess alighted and extended his hand. "Let me help you down, Jeannie. You look exhausted."

"I am, milord."

Jeannie leaned heavily on Verdon's arm as they went up the walk. It would be good just to sleep, to forget for a little while the heavy ache of her heart.

The Marquess turned to his butler. "I am not in. And you have seen no one."

"Yes, milord."

Verdon began to help Jeannie across the room, but before they had reached the stairs there was a sudden pounding of the door knocker. Jeannie's heart flew up into her throat. Could it be Trenton? But he couldn't know she was here.

Verdon gestured her to one side, out of sight of the door. Then he nodded to his servant.

The butler moved to the door. "I'm sorry, sir. His lordship is not in."

"Then I shall wait."

It was the Viscount!

"Please, milord!" The butler's tone was pained, and then the door flew open and Trenton forced his way inside.

"I am sorry to bother you," cried the Viscount angrily as his eyes lit on Verdon. "Especially as you are quite obviously busy."

As his eyes swept over her, Jeannie began to tremble violently. Why must he hate her so?

"Calm yourself, Trenton. This is a time for reason."

"Reason!" The Viscount laughed savagely. *"You* can talk of reason? Was it not beyond reason that my best friend should steal my intended?"

"You did not want her," said the Marquess calmly. "You told her she could never be forgiven."

Jeannie stared at him. Why didn't he explain? He hadn't stolen her. He didn't even want her. He had a partiality for Lady Helena.

"She betrayed me, lied to me," snarled Trenton.

"She asked for your forgiveness," Verdon reminded him calmly. "She is young and innocent. She loves her brother."

"Her brother! I paid his debt. He has nothing to do with this." Trenton's mouth closed in a bitter line.

"Nothing?" asked the Marquess, motioning to Jeannie to remain silent.

"Nothing," repeated the Viscount crisply. "He has the gaming fever. He will never change. I did not expect gratitude from him. But from you—"

"You do not love her," said the Marquess. "She told me of your bargain. It is your pride that is hurt, that's all. Come, man, there will be other women. You can go back to Lady Frances, or Little Harry."

The Viscount glared at him. "Do not speak such nonsense to me. Those women are nothing to me. I love Jeannie. Love her? My God, I love her past all understanding."

Jeannie's knees buckled under her, and she slid slowly to the floor, but the men were so engrossed in each other that they did not notice. She could not be hearing such things, she thought; this could only be a dream.

"Have you told her that?" inquired the Marquess.

The Viscount glared at his friend. "Of course not. She's a green girl. Or at least, I thought she was. I did not want to frighten her. And I did not know myself—at first."

He laughed again savagely. "But that matters little now. She has made her choice. She did that when she gave you the jewels. You were fortunate to be able to regain them. I could hardly believe Atwood's story. He saw you leave the moneylender. But when the moneylender himself confirmed it—" His voice broke.

Suddenly Jeannie was on her feet, running to him. "But you don't understand," she cried. "I did not choose Verdon. I was running away. He stopped me."

She saw the disbelief on his face. "Oh please, Trenton, listen. I did not give my jewels to Verdon. He redeemed them for me. I gave them to Jeremy."

"To Jeremy?" Incredulity was written on his face.

"Yes, he got into more debt. I had no money. And you had said—"

He grabbed her shoulders. "I know what I said. Verdon was only redeeming the jewels for you?"

Jeannie nodded, her eyes brimming with unshed tears. "So that you would not discover the awful thing I had done."

The Viscount looked down at her. "You have not betrayed me? You did not choose Verdon?"

"No, of course not." The tears rose again to Jeannie's eyes. "It was only to help Jeremy. And I shall never do it again. Jeremy has changed. He is not my twin anymore."

The Viscount took a deep breath. "You are still young and innocent," he said stiffly, though he did not release her shoulders. "And I—I have no enviable reputation to offer such a one as you. I will send you back to your aunt."

"No!" The cry escaped from Jeannie quite before she knew it. "You cannot. I—I am in love. I love you."

There was silence in the room as the Viscount stared at her. "It's true," she cried. "Dear God, I know I should not say it, but I love you to distraction."

"Come, man," said the Marquess. "Have you no ears? The girl loves you and you love her. What more can you ask?"

"Nothing, nothing," said Trenton in wondering tones. "But—but I find it so hard to believe."

"Kiss her," advised the Marquess. "If that doesn't convince you, nothing will."

Trenton spoke. "As usual, my friend, you are right." And then Jeannie found herself pulled close to a striped waistcoat, enfolded in a pair of strong arms. "Oh Jeannie, *my* Jeannie," he said as he bent and covered her lips with his own.

Jeannie, her senses running riot, had never imagined that such joy could exist. When he released her, she was forced by the melting of her bones to lean close to him.

"Are you now convinced?" inquired the Marquess solemnly.

Trenton, holding Jeannie close, chuckled. "Indeed, I am quite convinced, Verdon. I am also convinced that I am the biggest fool on the face of the earth."

"Sssssh," whispered Jeannie.

The Viscount looked at her in surprise.

"Ssssh," she repeated. "We must not let the news get abroad. I still intend to marry London's greatest—"

The Viscount laid a gentle finger on her lips. "London's greatest *reformed* rakeshame," he said.

"An admirable decision," agreed the Marquess. "And now, may I loan you my closed carriage so that you can get your intended home before dinner without adding any more to your reputations?"

"An excellent idea, my friend," replied Trenton. "Do not forget. We will expect you Thursday next to stand up with us."

"That will be my pleasure," said the Marquess, his eyes twinkling. "I suspect I shall ask you to return the favor quite soon." He departed to summon the carriage.

"What does he mean by that?" asked Trenton.

Jeannie raised her lips to those of the man who was to be her husband. "I shall tell you on the way home. But now listen. I love you, milord."

"And I love you," he replied. "My Jeannie, now and forever."

INTRODUCING...

The Romance Magazine For The 1980's

Each exciting issue contains a full-length romance novel — the kind of first-love story we all dream about...

PLUS

other wonderful features such as a travelogue to the world's most romantic spots, advice about your romantic problems, a quiz to find the ideal mate for you and much, much more.

ROMANTIQUE: A complete novel of romance, plus a whole world of romantic features.

ROMANTIQUE: Wherever magazines are sold. Or write Romantique Magazine, Dept. C-1, 41 East 42nd Street, New York, N.Y. 10017

Once you've tasted joy and passion, do you dare dream of

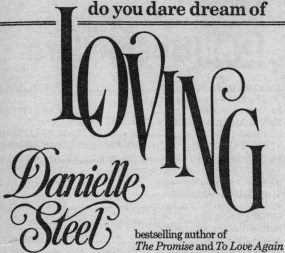

LOVING

Danielle Steel

bestselling author of
The Promise and *To Love Again*

Bettina Daniels lived in a gilded world—pampered, adored, adoring. She had youth, beauty and a glamorous life that circled the globe—everything her father's love, fame and money could buy. Suddenly, Justin Daniels was gone. Bettina stood alone before a mountain of debts and a world of strangers—men who promised her many things, who tempted her with words of love. But Bettina had to live her own life, seize her own dreams and take her own chances. But could she pay the bittersweet price?

A Dell Book ══════════════════ **$2.75 (14684-4)**

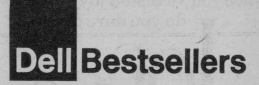

Dell Bestsellers